At the mercy of a gaming hell owner, four gentlemen must perform a shocking task. But claiming their inheritance might just lead them to the women who will steal their hearts!

Don't miss this wonderful new quartet by

Mills & Boon® Historical Romance author

Elizabeth Beacon

Already available

The Viscount's Frozen Heart

The Marquis's Awakening

Lord Laughraine's Summer Promise

AUTHOR NOTE

Welcome to *Lord Laughraine's Summer Promise*, the third part of *A Year of Scandal*, in which Lady Virginia Winterley has left a quest for each of my four heroes to solve, one season at a time. It all began with winter in *The Viscount's Frozen Heart*, and then there was spring with *The Marquis's Awakening*. Now my third hero and heroine are struggling with a passionate attraction under the English summer sun.

Sometimes a quiet man has the deepest secrets, and I knew Frederick Peters had plenty of those the moment he strolled into action in *The Scarred Earl*—part of a different series of books altogether—and made himself at home. Under his true identity, Sir Gideon Laughraine has the hardest task so far: to persuade the woman who once loved him so much that he really is still her hero and that they deserve a second chance.

I really hope you enjoy Gideon and Callie's story as much as I did writing it, and I thank you for coming with me through this vintage year for Lady Virginia's beloved band of heroes.

LORD LAUGHRAINE'S SUMMER PROMISE

Elizabeth Beacon

Published in Great Britain 2015
by Mills & Boon, an imprint of Harlequin (UK) Limited,
Eton House, 18-24 Paradise Road, Richmond, Surrey, TW9 1SR

© 2015 Elizabeth Beacon

ISBN: 978-0-263-24791-6

Printed and bound in Spain
by CPI, Barcelona

Elizabeth Beacon has a passion for history and storytelling and, with the English West Country on her doorstep, never lacks a glorious setting for her books. Elizabeth tried horticulture, higher education as a mature student, briefly taught English and worked in an office, before finally turning her daydreams about dashing piratical heroes and their stubborn and independent heroines into her dream job: writing Regency romances for Mills & Boon®.

Books by Elizabeth Beacon

Mills & Boon® Historical Romance

A Year of Scandal

The Viscount's Frozen Heart
The Marquis's Awakening
Lord Laughraine's Summer Promise

Linked by Character

The Duchess Hunt
The Scarred Earl
The Black Sheep's Return

Stand-Alone Novels

An Innocent Courtesan
Housemaid Heiress
A Less Than Perfect Lady
Captain Langthorne's Proposal
Rebellious Rake, Innocent Governess
The Rake of Hollowhurst Castle
Courtship & Candlelight
'One Final Season'
A Most Unladylike Adventure
Candlelit Christmas Kisses
'Governess Under the Mistletoe'

Visit the author profile page at millsandboon.co.uk

Chapter One

'So where is this Cataret House School you might recall if you weren't feeling "quite so mazed" by the heat?' Sir Gideon Laughraine, otherwise known as Mr Frederick Peters, asked the pretend idiot he'd hailed for directions.

The idler scratched his grizzled head and shrugged as Gideon bit back a curse and wondered if anyone else would be about on such a sweltering afternoon. Unless he found a field being worked close to the road, there was probably nobody who wasn't at work or staying inside out of the sun within hailing distance, so he dug in his waistcoat pocket for a small coin and held it up to encourage the man's memory.

'That's it over yonder,' the man finally admitted with a nod towards a farmhouse on the opposite side of the valley that looked as if it had delusions of grandeur. 'Likely you'll find the old girl in, but young miss went down the track to Manydown a half hour ago.'

Gideon bit back a curse and flipped the coin to the knowing rogue before turning his weary horse and following in young miss's footsteps.

'I wouldn't want to find the old besom in a hurry either, mister,' the knowing idiot told him before slouching off to spend his windfall in the local ale house.

'Needs must when the devil drives,' Gideon muttered grimly, not much looking forward to that encounter either, then he forgot the 'old girl' by wondering what the young one might be up to.

Would she blench at the very sight of him and look as if the devil was on her heels, or give him that delightful smile he still remembered with a gasp of the heart all these years on? Who knew? Lady Virginia Winterley was right though; he had to find out if his wife would ever smile at him again outside his favourite dreams.

Dear Boy, his late patroness and friend began the letter that heralded the third quest on her list, left in her will to chime with every new season of the year after her death. He'd had no inkling he was one of the unfortunates she'd decided to do good to until that demand

he do as he was bid for the next three months
was put in his hand by the new Lady Farenze.

*I am quite sure it will come as a great
surprise to you when dear Chloe tells you
that you have the next quest on my list.*

Well, yes, you're quite right there, my lady,
he thought with a shake of his dark head to
admit she'd outfoxed him once again.

It should not be, she continued, as if she
were standing at his shoulder and could see
the sceptical expression on his face when he finally realised why Luke Winterley's new wife
had sought him out to hand him the letter from
Lady Virginia.

*You are my beloved Virgil's secret
grandson, and it is only out of consider-
ation for your cousin, Lord Laughraine,
that we have not been able to claim you
openly. If we did so it would take away
the only legal heir he has left to carry
on his titles and estates and we both love
and respect Charlie Laughraine far too
much to do that to him or you. I know the
true facts of your birth have been a trial
to you ever since you were old enough to*

realise what the gossips had to say about your father's true parentage, but they are a great comfort to me.

I shall always be glad I had time to watch you grow from the haunted, unhappy boy I first encountered into the fine man you are today, even though I've had to do so without my darling Virgil at my side. It has been such a pleasure to see you make your own way in life, much as I know Virgil would have done if he wasn't born the heir to vast estates and the Farenze titles.

I don't have words to say how much I loved my husband, and finding a way to drag you into my life was a selfish act, since you resemble him so closely in ways that go beyond a purely physical likeness. You do have that, of course, although I think James favours him more in outward details than you do, dear Gideon. You also have a true heart and a kind nature to balance that sharp mind of yours and it has been a delight for me to come to know you so much better these last few years than Virgil ever could while he was alive, for all his pleading with your father to let him at least know his grandson.

*I think Esmond would have done any-
thing to hurt his true father and withhold-
ing you from him was a way to show he
had the power to hurt the man he blamed
for ruining his life.*

Gideon stopped and stared into the middle
distance. He refused to think about his vexed
relationship with his father and both Virgil and
Esmond were beyond his intervention now, so
he could worry about his wife instead. Callie
had gone a determined distance from her aunt's
house on this devilishly hot day. He managed a
rueful smile at the thought of what she would
have to say about his heart and even the faith
in his kindness Lady Virginia made so much
of in her letter, not much to his credit he suspected. Once again he wondered what was so
urgent Callie needed to walk out to find it on
such a sweltering afternoon. Was she meeting
a lover? A jag of hot jealousy made him gasp
and a shaft of pain clutched at his gut.

After her last arctic-cold letter telling him
never to contact her again, then nine years of
silence, she wasn't going to welcome him, but
Lady Virginia was quite right, drat her. He
checked the inner pocket of his coat where it lay
across his saddle brow and heard the reassuring

crackle of hot pressed paper against silk lining. An unconventional lawyer like him often needed a safe place to keep important letters, but this one was a very mixed blessing and its contents were already imprinted on his mind.

I know what I am going to ask of you is more than I demanded of dear Luke and my beloved godson, Tom Banburgh. I hope you have come to know them as a true kinsman and a stalwart friend these last six months, by the way, for you have lived without either for far too long.

So, your quest is to find your wife, my darling boy, and ask her for your heart's desire. I can't tell you if she will listen or be generous enough to give it to you, but you have to find out if there is any chance for your marriage, or between you make an end to it with dignity. If you go on as you are, you will be a haunted and lonely man for the rest of your life and I do so want you to be happy.

I was lucky enough to find the man I could love with everything I am, even luckier to live with him as long as I did, but you two children managed to love and lose one another before you should have been out of your schoolrooms.

Seek out that unlucky girl of yours with an open heart and discover if you can live together, Gideon. If you cannot, then agree on a separation and make some sort of life apart. I believe two such stubborn and contrary people were made for one another, but there's no need to prove me wrong for the sake of it.

What you choose to do about Raigne and the splendid inheritance you are legally entitled to, as the last official Laughraine heir, is up to you. My advice is to stop being a stiff-necked idiot and listen to your cousin. Charles Laughraine has never been in the least bit like your supposed grandfather and his uncle, and I thought Sir Wendover Laughraine one of the most soulless and heartless men I ever came across, but his nephew is a very different man. As you have called him your Uncle Charles ever since you were old enough to talk I have to suppose you realise he is very happy to consider you part of his family, whatever the true facts of the case may be.

No doubt your wife will go her own

way, but as you and I both know her to be Lord Laughraine's natural granddaughter, she owes him a hearing even if she won't listen to you. The future of such a large estate and all the people who depend on it must be decided before many more years go by. I wish it could be otherwise and please believe Virgil would have been delighted to openly claim you as his grandson, even though your father hated any reference to his own irregular birth and would never hear of it.

Charlie Laughraine is nigh as old as I am now and time will outrun you three stiff-necked idiots if you are not careful. All I have to add is a warning never to take anything that aunt of hers says at face value and look deeper into why that young romance of yours went so badly awry.

Don't you shake your head at me again, Gideon Laughraine, I know you long for the love of your young life with everything you have in you a decade on from losing her. Admit it to yourself, then all you need do is find out if your wife suffers the same burden and do something about it.

Gideon almost wished he could forget the last letter from his friend and one-time mentor and ride back to London as fast as this unlucky beast would go. He could carry on with the nearly good enough life he'd made without his wife and the family they might have rejoiced in by now. What a fool he was to have agreed so readily to act as an extra pair of ears and eyes during Lady Virginia's year of discovery for her four victims, though.

How had he thought he could stay uninvolved, even without this latest bombshell? No, a strong sense of justice made him corrected himself; they weren't victims. The first two quests made Luke Winterley and Tom Banburgh the proud husbands of much-loved new wives. Two triumphs chalked up on the slate for the Lady then and, if he knew anything about himself and James Winterley, the score would be levelled by two lone wolves beyond redemption. Would Lady Virginia had wasted her energy on a more worthy cause and let him and Winterley go to the devil in their own way.

When she set out so determinedly this afternoon Callie intended to get to Manydown as fast as possible, so she could get back before anyone noticed she'd gone, but this clammy heat was defeating her. She slowed down but carried on, despite the nagging suspicion she should go back to Cataret House and give up on her dream for today. The sad truth was she couldn't face another afternoon of idle boredom now her pupils were with their family or friends for the summer. After a week of this heat and being at the beck and call of her aunt with no excuse to be busy elsewhere, she felt she must leave the house before they livened up a dull summer with an argument that ended in tears and days of stony silence.

It was quite wrong of her to feel like a virtual prisoner at Cataret House when the school wasn't keeping her too busy to notice. Aunt Seraphina had been quite right—they'd both needed to start their lives anew nine years ago. They were let down and betrayed by two very different husbands at the time, so why not pool their limited resources and hire a house big enough to start a school? It had seemed a wonderful idea back then; they could live modestly on the profits and she could help fifteen young girls of mixed ability and middling birth learn about the world, or as much of it as young ladies were permitted to know. Her life had felt blank and hopeless at the time and Aunt

Seraphina's idea was inspired, but now a little voice kept whispering *is this all*?

No, she wouldn't listen. She had experienced the storm and lightning of her great love affair and all it turned out to be was a mistake that hurt everyone she had ever cared for. The school made enough and their pupils were happy. If future wives and mothers were better informed people for having passed through their hands, maybe in time the world would change and ladies would be more highly valued by a society that regarded them as the legal chattels of their husbands, fathers or brothers. Here she was busy and useful and known as spinsterish Miss Sommers, and that was enough, most of the time. Nine years ago it had been impossible to drag the failure of her marriage about like a badge of stupidity so she reminded herself why she had wanted to leave youthful folly behind and shivered even in this heat.

Living in genteel poverty as her true self somewhere out of her husband's orbit would have been worse than waiting on her aunt when the girls were away and feeling shut into this narrow life. Most of the time she enjoyed helping other people's daughters learn about the world; and they employed a visiting dancing teacher and music mistress to add to Callie's more academic teaching. Knowing her niece had absorbed the late Reverend Sommers's scholarship far more eagerly than his daughters had, Aunt Seraphina let Callie teach the girls some of the lessons their brothers could expect to learn as a matter of course and where else could she do that? She reminded herself she was always a stranger to herself during the summer when there was little to distract her from the life she'd chosen. At this time of year she must fend off memories of passion and grief that were best forgotten; the secret was to occupy herself and this was as good a way as any.

Her mind was racing about like a mad March hare this afternoon, so even tramping the hills on a blazing hot day obviously wasn't distraction enough. Perhaps it was time to escape into daydreams then. They gave her a way to ignore all but the worst of Aunt Seraphina's scolds even as a small child and now they took her to places she hadn't even thought of back then. The hope of living a different life firmed her resolution to find out if her writing could lead to more than she dared hope when she first put pen to paper.

It was probably best not to speculate on the reply she might find waiting for Mrs Muse at the receiving office in answer to her latest correspondence with a maybe publisher. She had to distract herself from this wild seesaw of hope and dread. So she gave up looking for wildlife to identify on a day when it was asleep and wondered idly how ladies lived in more exotic countries where it was like this much of the time. She was sure high-born women rested during the burning heat of the day and did not walk alone when barely a breath stirred grass grown lifeless as straw against her bare ankles. Right now she could be lying on a silk-cushioned divan, saving her strength for the cooler night to come and dreaming of her lover. The contrast between such an idle and slumberous afternoon and this one snatched her back into the present. She sighed and wished she could ignore questions about where she was going on such a sultry day, so she could order the gig and drive herself to Manydown.

At least her ancient straw bonnet kept the full force of the sun off and Aunt Seraphina couldn't accuse her of ruining her complexion, but she dreamt wistfully of airy silks, made to whisper against her limbs as she strolled about her fantasy palace. It would feel sensual and pleasantly wicked to go barefoot on a satin-smooth marble floor and for a moment she felt as if silky stone was under her feet and wriggled her toes in sensual appreciation, which made her jolt back to reality again to hot, sweaty and gritty English feet tramping through a baking landscape.

It was nearly nine years now since Grandfather Sommers had caught the fever that killed him from Aunt Seraphina's late and unlamented husband. When Reverend Sommers followed his unworthy son-in-law to the grave there was nothing to keep either of them in King's Raigne, and leaving the village where she grew up meant Callie could be herself again. It was a common enough name and nobody was going to look for her, so she went back to being Miss Sommers, spinster, and Aunt Seraphina became Mrs Grisham with an imaginary husband to mourn when their new neighbours came to gossip. They were less than twenty miles away from Raigne and it felt a world away from that famously grand house and the tightly knit Raigne villages.

Better not to think about her old life, she decided, dreading the hurt and sorrow those memories threatened even after nine years away. Where was she? Ah, yes—going without stockings, partly for economy and partly because it was too hot to endure them. Perhaps the old, impulsive Callie was alive under the schoolmistress, after all, so she concentrated on walking and her quest, but it was too hot and familiar a walk to distract her for long.

Anyway, it was impossible to feel bold and sensuous and longing to be shameless with a handsome lover when you were weighed down by chemises and corsets, petticoats and a sternly respectable cambric gown. Somehow she couldn't force the fantasy of that longed-for lover back into the dark corner where she kept her deepest secrets today, but nine years on he wasn't the man she had fallen in love with, anyway. If her husband stood in front of her now she probably wouldn't recognise him, and the thought of the painful arguments and angry silences before they parted made her happy to dive back into the life of a fantasy Callie, who longed for a very different lover from her one-time one, so where had she got to with that?

Ah, yes, she was languorous with longing to see him again after spending mere hours apart. There would be cooling fans waved by unseen hands to stir the heavy air and cleverly devised cross-draughts in that marble palace under a merciless sun. She drifted away from the court ladies idling away the scorching afternoon with gossip as they waited for the world to stir again. When it did the scent of exotic flowers and rare spices, the flare of bright colours and wild beat of music and dancing would light up the night with an urgent promise of excitement and passion and longing fully sated at long last. It was too exciting to allow her to worry about who was in and who was out at court. Of course, they would all be weary again the next day and doze through the hot afternoon, so they could dance when night fell, but it would be worth sore feet and all day waiting for the thrill of being totally alive again in her lover's arms when darkness fell.

Something told the real Callie if she had to live such a life she'd rage against rules that forbade a lady contact with the world beyond the palace walls, but flights of fancy weren't meant to be realistic. She sighed and knew she was hot and sticky and unpleasantly dirty once again, so what would the eager Callie Sommers of seventeen make of her older and wiser self? Not much, she decided, wishing she could go back and warn the headlong idiot not to dream so hard or passionately so that her today could be different.

Shrugging off memories that wouldn't change for all the wishing in the world, she resisted the urge to throw her bonnet into the nearest hedge and be less suffocated by the life of a confirmed spinster. She untied the shabby ribbons instead and felt the faintest trace of a breeze on her damp skin. It was the gritty unpleasantness of grey dust changing to mud between her sweaty toes that made her escape into a dream of walking naked into a wide pool full of rose-petal-scented water this time. Imaginary Callie felt coolness and luxury surround her and knew she was loved and valued above riches by the prince of this splendour.

Now that was the most dangerous fantasy of all. She shook her head to refuse it and felt a brief thunder of blood in her ears. Aunt Seraphina's dire warnings about females who recklessly strode about the countryside with no regard for the conventions might come true if she was overtaken by dragging heat on a public highway. Wondering if her aunt ever looked at her, Callie tried to be amused by the idea plain Miss Sommers could excite ungovernable passion in any male who found her sprawled on the road.

She needed to keep her wits about her if she was going to walk to the receiving office and be home before she was missed, so no more daydreams until she was back in her bedchamber, where she could work on her next book in peace. Today even her aunt had succumbed to the heat and left Callie free to do as she pleased for once. So she couldn't let another day go by without finding out if the novel she had laboured over so hard in secret might be published. So, yes, it was worth being hot and sticky to get word Mr Redell might agree to publish it at last.

Despite the heat she managed an excited hop and skip at his opinion her work showed promise. He had suggested changes and refinements, of course, but it wasn't a flat refusal. Perhaps she could earn enough to rent a little cottage one day and mix with friends she chose, get ink on her fingers whenever the fancy took her, then dig her garden and cook whatever she wanted to eat out of it. It was such a heady daydream she didn't hear a hot and weary horse coming up behind her until the animal was close enough to shy at her modest bonnet.

His rider cursed him for a jingle-brained donkey and consigned him to the devil even as Callie's thoughts span back with a sickening jolt. Shocked to her toes by the sound of that particular male voice, she froze as if an enchanter had put a spell on her. No, she wouldn't look round, but he was taking in her unfashionable bonnet and faded gown as he fought to control the skittish beast, because he realised he was blaspheming in front of a lady. Callie was far too busy coping with absolute shock to take note of his apology. She was wrong; she must be. Gideon was miles away, probably in London, and this was a stranger. Turning to reassure herself she was imagining a nightmare, Callie found out exactly how wrong she could be.

'Oh, the devil,' she said flatly.

All the blood in her body seemed to have drained from her head into her hot, dusty feet and taken her panic-stricken heart with it. Black spots danced in front of her eyes and now her fickle heart was thundering a tattoo so loudly her head was full of the relentless beat. Panic raced over her skin in shudders of cold on the hottest day of summer so far.

'How missish of me,' she managed in a fading murmur, but neither willpower nor vanity could stop her reeling —the truth of him beating against her hastily shut eyelids, as if he was stamped on them like a brand. This *was* Gideon.

After all the years of wanting him night after night—so much useless longing—then wishing they had never met, he was back and there was only so much abuse a woman's body could take. Callie let the darkness suck her in so he didn't matter any more.

Chapter Two

Gideon fought to hold his much-tried horse back from bolting. The woman Lady Virginia ordered him to seek out and come to terms with had wilted like a faded lily at the sight of him and made the wretched beast panic even more as she fell to the ground. As he tried to soothe the beast his heart thudded to the beat of iron-shod hooves too close to her contrary head.

'To think I was afraid I wouldn't find you here,' he murmured between curses as he finally fought the animal to a weary standstill.

Nobody could accuse the Calliope Sommers he knew of being vapourish and his heart ached. Sir Gideon Laughraine must be a worse rogue than he thought if his wife fainted at her first sight of him in nine years, so what hope was there for his sooty soul?

'And a very good afternoon to you, too, Lady

Laughraine,' he muttered, wondering what his noble clients would think of 'Mr Frederick Peters' under his real identity.

He almost laughed at the idea; this name was hardly a true one, but it *was* the one he had to call himself when all aliases were stripped away. Too late to gallop back to town and save her from confronting her worst nightmare now, so he quietened his hack and avoided looking at his wife until his breathing calmed as much as it was going to today. The bitter knowledge that she once told him not to bother her again as long as he lived made him gasp as if she had written it a moment ago. She hadn't replied to a single letter he sent since so she still thought their woes were his fault. Still, he'd be damned if he'd ride off and leave his wife sprawled in the road for any fool to trip over, so he couldn't leave again yet.

Gideon jumped from the saddle of his weary horse to crouch over his wife with a fast beating heart and a gut-deep fear for her safety that told him he still cared. He frowned at the shadows under her eyes, then his gaze lingered on the dusky curve of her eyelashes as he recalled how they felt blinking sleepily against his own skin. No, that wasn't a road he could travel and stay sane. Compared to the skinny girl she was her face was softer and yet more defined; his coltish Callie had grown up and he hadn't been here to watch it happen.

Of course, the old Callie was vital and lovely, her glossy dark hair always tumbling out of whatever style she tried to tame it with. Her dark brown eyes were full of life and often brilliant with mischief, or passion, as she urged him recklessly to match her, as if he needed urging. Of course, the young man he was must be flattered, but he'd truly loved her. No other woman could rival her even now. He'd met accredited beauties and numbered one or two as true friends, but they didn't hold a candle to the Callie he first fell in love with. His young love was as lively and adventurous as she was lovely and it tore at his heart to see so little of her in the contained and outwardly staid woman lying in his path.

He watched her slavishly for signs of returning consciousness, or was that a story he told himself so he could gaze at her? Her lush curves were accentuated by the tiny waist he used to span when he lifted her off her grandfather's steady grey horse when they met secretly. He could only see it because gravity defeated her high-waisted gown and was it foolish or wise of fashion to conceal such a figure from the gaze of hungry male predators like him? he wondered. Considering the allowance he'd struggled to make her in his days as a clerk, then an unconventional lawyer, and the increases he'd made since, he wondered what she spent his blunt on, though, because it sure as Hades hadn't gone on clothes.

Her gown had been washed so many times the white of the base cotton was yellowed and a simple print of gold rosebuds faded. It was hard to pick out pattern from background and he doubted it was in the first kick of fashion when it made its debut far too long ago for her to be wearing it now. Shock at the sight of her dropping to the ground in a dead faint might be making his attention swerve to unimportant things, but it was a puzzle he intended to solve as soon as she felt well enough. It *was* infernally hot, though, so maybe she didn't want to mire a good gown on a tramp through a sweltering countryside.

'What the devil are you up to, Callie?' he murmured as he settled his hack by a nearby tree and frowned as if he might read answers on her pallid face.

She looked heartbreakingly vulnerable lying in the dust as he strode back to her. The rise and fall of her bosom told him she was breathing steadily, but she had been unconscious far too long. He wanted to pluck her up off the dusty road and guard her from any threat life could throw at her, even if he was the worst one she could think of. For a breath-stealing moment he wondered if she had a terrible illness. No, he could see no sign of prolonged ill health in her smooth skin and unwrinkled brow, so she hated him so much she lost her senses rather than meet him face to face.

He checked her breathing, then stood over her so his shadow would shield her from the sun. He watched her achingly familiar heart-shaped face for a long moment, then averted his gaze. He was too much of a coward to watch her wake up and see revulsion tighten her features when she realised he wasn't a bad dream. His wife lay unconscious at his feet and now he was lusting after her like a green boy as well and it shamed him. He also felt fully alive for the first time since he left her, despair biting harder with every step he took. She was smiling faintly in her sleep next time he looked, as if drifting happily in a world that didn't have him in it. He suppressed the urge to howl like a dog at her latest rejection and went back to brooding over a past that couldn't be altered.

* * *

Callie was drifting on a thick cloud of feathers while angels whispered benedictions in her ear. For a moment she really believed Gideon had come back for her, so it was perfectly rational to hear angels, but why did this one sound so angry? And did they really carry tall ebony canes and have masses of snow-white hair and piercing dark-brown eyes? Her grumpy angel frowned and remarked it was little wonder she was bad-tempered with two idiots like her and Gideon to worry about when she had better things to do.

Acting like a die-away miss never solved anything, young lady. A fortnight of Gideon's three months has already been used up with his shilly-shallying. Best to let sleeping dogs lie indeed—whatever is the boy thinking of? It doesn't make sense to do anything of the sort when they're only sleeping their lives away as if that's all there is for them to worry about. Just you wake up this minute, my girl, and stop being such a ninnyhammer. You haven't been happy without him since you sent him away, so get up and face him and a few facts at the same time, the spectre ordered her with a stern look and Callie frowned as waking up suddenly seemed a good idea.

Her airy cloud deflated and she felt far less comfortable avoiding Gideon than she had when she welcomed unconsciousness with a sigh of relief. She wrinkled her nose as a bit more reality crept in; this was a hard resting place with too many stones for a lady to lie about on as if she had nothing better to do.

'Go away,' she croaked, hoping to reclaim her quiet cushion of feathery peace instinct warned her not to relinquish as the dragon-angel ordered. She might be lying on a dusty road dreaming impossible things, but she didn't want to face real ones right now.

'Would that I could,' Gideon's voice replied and a heavy thump of her heart reminded her why she'd welcomed an attack of the vapours in the first place.

At last she gave in and blinked her eyes open, because she didn't want to dwell on the regret in Gideon's voice. He sounded absolutely here and far away all at the same time and wasn't that trick typical of him?

'What *are* you doing here?' she murmured with an unwary shake of her head. Dark spots wavered in front of her eyes and warned her some shocks weren't to be got over lightly and she lay down again until they went away.

'Straight to the nub of the issue, as usual,' her husband said wearily.

She glanced up at him looming over her and saw worry and frustration in his grey-green eyes, but still couldn't stand up and face him. Maybe in a moment or two she'd find the right blend of courage and calmness, *and maybe never*, a sceptical voice whispered and she wasn't sure if it was hers or belonged to the forceful spectre she dreamt up just now.

'If you can endure me carrying you, you'll recover far better in the shade.'

'Be quick then,' she ordered, waving her dusty hand imperiously as a defeated queen.

'Your wish is my command, Highness,' he joked as he lifted her up as if she were made of fairy dust.

Callie knew perfectly well that wasn't so and felt the power of him when he plucked her from the ground without a hitch in his breathing. Was it right to be insulted by his rock-like composure? The Gideon she remembered was slender as a lath and she could read him as easily as a child's primer, yet this man was a closed book to her. Her body responded to his as if it recognised him and that would never do. Callie the lover—the wife, came alive again in a hot flash of fiery need. Horrified to feel so aware of him, she squirmed and he told her testily to keep still lest he drop her.

Once upon a time he was the sun to her moon; the reason she got up in the morning and slept at night, if they could spare time for sleeping. Surely she had more sense than to fall under his spell twice? Of course she had. The moment she could set one foot in front of the other without falling over, she'd march away and prove he meant nothing to her.

'Put me down, Gideon,' she demanded in a breathy voice she hardly recognised.

'You'll fall over if I do.'

'Nonsense, I'm perfectly well.'

'Of course you aren't.'

'I wish you'd let me walk, I'm not a child,' she complained, even though she sounded like a pettish one to her own ears right now.

'Stop behaving like one then,' he said in a preoccupied tone, as if he had more important things to do than tidy his inconvenient wife off the King's Highway.

'I'm not. I feel sick,' she said querulously, wondering what had come over her. Gideon had, of course, and he was as calm as a rock while she felt as if her whole world had been turned upside down.

'Then I'm definitely not putting you down.'

'It's a lie,' she confessed with a blush she hoped he couldn't see under the liberal coating of dust miring her cheeks. 'I thought such a neat gentleman as you wouldn't want that fine silk waistcoat spoilt and you'd put me down.'

'You really can't wait to get out of my arms, can you, Wife?' he said with a quirk of his mouth that might pass for a smile in a dark room.

'No more than you can to ride off and forget me for another nine years,' she retaliated childishly, unable to stop her tongue saying things she'd rather it kept quiet about.

'You do me an injustice, Calliope. How could I ever forget you?'

She distrusted his words, took them as mockery. Tears stung her eyes for a perilous second, but the thought of tear tracks in the dirt made her wince. She blinked hard and stared into the little wood he was carrying her towards until they dispersed. She should dismiss him from her life as lightly as an old gown, but perhaps she could lie about a lover to disgrace him with and persuade him to go away. Except she'd never met a man who made her feel the way he did. If she wasn't careful she'd become the sort of female who lay about on sofas half the day and wafted about like a low-lying cloud for the rest of it. Or hoped for impossible things, and wouldn't that be a waste of time?

'I *can* still walk, you know,' she said crossly.

'Of course you can,' he replied, a hint of laughter in grey eyes that had an inner ray of green round the pupil only a lover would know about.

The thought of long-ago intimacy with this man caught at her heart. Now he looked and sounded almost familiar it made her recall times when they looked and looked at each other for what felt like hours, or simply lay close marvelling at one another until desire was too hot for peace and they peaked into the sort of earth-shattering climax that made her shiver even over such a chasm of time. That wasn't the way to be cool and armoured while they agreed terms. It was good for him to hide his true self now; it would make life easier while she waited for him to go again.

'And I wish to do so right now,' she told him emphatically.

'I may not be much of a husband, but I'm not going to watch my wife stagger about the countryside half faint in this heat like a drunkard.'

'Nonsense, I can cope with the sun perfectly well.'

'Of course you can,' he said indulgently.

How come she could hear him smile as he soothed her like a fractious infant again? 'The shock of seeing you made me faint, but I would be perfectly well if you hadn't taken me by surprise,' she claimed with a frown that was clearly wasted on the barbarian.

'You were so overcome with delight at the sight of me you lost your senses then?'

'That wasn't delight,' she snapped.

'I know.'

'And what the devil are you doing here, Gideon?'

'Now *that* sounds more like the outspoken Callie Sommers I know. I thought I'd mistaken you for someone else for a moment back there.'

'I *am* someone else,' she told him gruffly, doing her best to believe that was good.

'Not from here you're not,' he teased as he shifted her slightly in his arms and they finally reached the little wood that ran alongside the road. 'You feel exactly like her to me.'

'Well, I'm not,' she said crossly. She hadn't been since Gideon put his ring on her finger and the blacksmith at Gretna pronounced them man and wife.

'No, you're Callie Laughraine,' he said blankly and she told herself that was a good thing. One of them should have their feelings under control and hers were anything but.

'I spent a long time forgetting her and manage perfectly well without a husband to tell me what to do and how to do it nowadays,' she insisted.

'As if I ever could awe, persuade or bully you into doing a thing you didn't want to. You were always your own person and even as a silly stripling I never wanted you any other way, Calliope.'

'I have no idea why my mother gave me that ridiculous name,' she said to divert them from the memory of how much he'd loved her when they eloped to Gretna Green. It hurt to linger on the past and wonder if they could have built a wonderful marriage together, if life was a little less cruel. 'She might as well have put a millstone round my neck as named me for one of the Muses.'

'Lucky you have a beautiful voice and a love of poetry like your namesake then, isn't it? Perhaps she simply liked it. I always did.'

'Yet how you used to taunt me with it when you were a repellent boy. If I had the gift of epic poetry, would you stop carrying me about like an infant?'

'Because you're named after a goddess?'

'No, because I asked you to, although I should like to be a bard, if we lived in better times and women were taken seriously as such, but I never wanted to be a goddess with so many unpronounceable sisters to quarrel with.'

He wasn't to know how serious she was, so she supposed it was unfair to stiffen in his arms when he chuckled. At least now she felt icy and remote again and he'd almost done it—he'd nearly disarmed her with flattery and wasn't that another warning to be wary? Best to remember he was a professional advocate now, a pleader for apparently lost causes, and that they could never be friends. At least then she would hurt less when he walked away again.

'You can put me down over there,' she ordered, pointing at a convenient tree stump.

'I'll drop you in the stream if you're not careful, Your Majesty,' he muttered darkly.

She shot him a glare as he set her down as if she was made of bone china, then stepped back with a mocking bow. 'Now go away,' she said sternly.

'I wouldn't leave your aunt stranded in the middle of nowhere ill and prey to any rogue who happened along and I never liked her, so how can you imagine I'd leave you, Callie?'

'I'm not my aunt,' she defended herself absently.

'Something I thank God for on a daily basis, my dear.'

'Don't call me your dear and don't blaspheme.'

'But I'd hate to be wed to your narrow-minded and joyless relative, my dear.'

'She stood by me when nobody else would and I told you I'm not your dear,' she told him shortly and wondered if it was worth standing so she could stamp her foot and show him she hated that false endearment on his lips. Deciding it wasn't a good idea to stand up and wilt, then sit down again before she proved anything, she tried to look serenely indifferent instead. Clearly it didn't work; he was having a job to conceal a grin at her expense.

'Perhaps you'll allow me the one freedom a married man can safely claim, which is the privacy of his own thoughts?' he said with a pantomime of the henpecked husband that made her heart ache for all they'd lost.

'And perhaps I won't,' she snapped.

'Afraid you won't like them, Calliope?'

Terrified if he did but know it. She sniffed and tossed her head to let him know she was completely indifferent, then regretted it imme-

diately as the wild thundering in her ears told
her she hadn't recovered enough to flounce off
and leave him standing like a forlorn knight
spurned by the damsel he'd got off his horse
to rescue.

'If I was I'd have no wish to know, would I?'

'As well if you don't, perhaps,' he told her
gruffly as he turned from rummaging in the
pack of his weary horse and removing a flask.

'Please don't try and force brandy down my
throat, Gideon,' she protested.

'I don't indulge in alcohol now,' he said as
he handed her a flask of clear water lukewarm
from its journey.

He drank too much wine during the latter days of their marriage and the memory of
him drunk and bitter as gall made her shudder.
Not that he'd laid violent hands on her, but the
thought of all that darkness and despair chilled
her to the bone.

'Never?' she was startled into asking as his
words sank in.

'Only when a cook puts it in a sauce or some
fanciful dessert when I dine away from home,
but not otherwise. I drank too much and made
things much worse between us. So you see, I've
managed to put one of my baser impulses be-

hind me,' he said with a rueful smile that did unfair things to her insides.

'Abstain from alcohol for your own good, but don't pretend it's got anything to do with me. If you set any store by what I wanted, you wouldn't have come here and cut up my peace like this,' she told him disagreeably to disguise it.

'I can't leave yet, but the drunken, headlong boy I was back then was repellent and I promise you I've done my best to kill him off. I doubt anyone mourned him.'

I did, argued an inner Callie who refused to be silenced. *I wept myself to sleep for the lack of him by my side every night for far too long. Until I realised he was never coming back and I was the one who told him to go, in fact.*

'Devil take it, but I'm a rogue to plague you when you're as unwell as a person can be without being carted about on a hurdle,' Gideon exclaimed and she couldn't stop a wobbly smile at the sight and sound of him as familiar to her as her own face in the mirror at last.

There—he was her Gideon again; a quick-tempered and passionate young man who could turn her knees to water at the very flicker of that self-deprecating smile or a sudden urge to wild action that made living with him such a clash of surprise, dread and delight. 'Come, Wife, let's get you home before you drop unconscious at my feet for the second time today,' he added masterfully and she frowned at him again, wondering if she could ever bring herself to live with a gentleman who was so used to getting his own way, then shocking herself with the idea she might like to try, if things were different.

'If you arrive on her doorstep, Aunt Seraphina will have the vapours even if I don't,' she warned him, and he actually paled at the thought of her aunt, who hadn't liked him even before he ran off to Gretna with her niece.

'She has plenty of experience,' he said darkly and turned towards his hitched horse.

'You could simply ride away again, nobody would know,' Callie suggested desperately. Being lonely and a little unhappy was a state she knew so well that the idea of changing it in any way looked strange and frightening from here.

'We would, wouldn't we?' he said as if that decided the issue.

'Yes,' she admitted with a sigh, 'so we would.'

Chapter Three

Simply getting Callie to ride his horse while he led it caused an argument. Gideon wondered if they could stop carping long enough to put the fragments of their marriage together and called up all the patience he'd learnt during his years without her. He should have remembered that aspect of marriage better and the magical glee of loving her less, he supposed grimly. Still, they were talking, even if it was in snaps of irritation. The odd moment of rediscovery made this all seem heartbreakingly familiar then strange by turns and he almost wished he'd slung his unconscious wife across his saddle brow and ridden off with her like a pirate with a princess.

'Comfortable?' he asked after the silence had stretched so thin he couldn't endure it any longer.

'What do you think?' she challenged. 'You should have let me ride astride as I asked instead of perching me up here like a doll.'

'And have half the yokels in Wiltshire looking at your legs? I think not,' he managed to say as even the idea of it made him rampantly jealous.

'I doubt they would bother when they saw the rest of me,' she said with a sweep of her hand at her dusty person that set his steed dancing and set Gideon's overstretched nerves on edge. He tried hard to rein himself in at the same time as he clamped a firm grip on the bit and forced the idiot horse to stop wasting its energy, as well.

'They would. You look magnificent,' he told her tersely and surely that wasn't a pleased little smile she was doing her best to hide behind that hideous bonnet? 'As a girl you were lovely, now you're beautiful, Callie,' he added and heard her snort of disbelief with mixed feelings.

If she thought herself an antidote, would it make his task as her jealous and fiercely protective husband easier? If he ever managed to win her back, of course. Yet if she was blind to her own attractions she would draw in wolves the moment she set foot in a ballroom at his side. So, on second thoughts, his life would be hell if she had no idea how potently her lovely face and fine figure and that firm disbelief in her own charms could affect a man. He groaned aloud at the idea of following her about like a possessive stallion for the rest of his life in order to make it very clear she was his mate and he didn't share. No, that really was putting the cart before the horses and he had to hold back all this hope in case it crashed to the ground around him again.

'Are you hurting in some way, Gideon?' she asked innocently, and what was he to do with such an odd mix of *naïveté* and sophistication as his estranged wife?

'It's been a long day,' he said with a shrug.

'It's probably about to get a lot worse,' she warned as Cataret House came into view again and she was quite right, just not in the sense she thought.

'Aye, your aunt never could abide me, could she?' he replied as if that was all that troubled him right now when even the thought of her as his true wife again was rendering him unfit for any company at all, let alone hers.

'No, she's deeply distrustful of all men and, considering the one she was wed to for so long, I'm not at all surprised.'

'So why *did* she marry Bonhomie Bartle,

Callie? They never had children, so I doubt they were forced to wed for the sake of a child as my parents were. It always puzzled me what those two saw in one another as they seemed to hate each other every bit as much as my mother and father did.'

'Grandfather told me she insisted on marrying him, although he begged her not to go through with it, so I suppose she must have loved him once upon a time. Nobody forced her to wed the man and I never knew what she saw in him, but why do any two people wed each other when they don't have to?'

'Because they want to spend the rest of their lives together, I suppose,' he said and cursed his clumsy tongue when she refused to meet his eyes. Finally they had reached the sloping drive and he and his weary mount slowed in deference to the day and the incline and at least despair was having a dampening effect on his foolish manhood.

'Mr Bartle was heir to a wealthy baronetcy, before his great-uncle took a young wife and began producing heirs in his old age.'

'So they ended up poor and disappointed?'

'Yes, but I don't think either of them ever thought the world well lost for love.'

'Perhaps not,' he agreed and refused to make

the challenge her averted gaze and tight fists on the reins told him she expected. *But we did once,* his inner idiot argued all the same and he told it to be quiet before it drove the rest of him mad.

'Nobody will answer the front door, you might as well lead this unlucky animal to the stable.'

'Where are your outdoor staff?' he said with a frown at the sheep-cropped turf and the faintly down-at-heel air of the whole place.

'Aunt Seraphina says the war has made everything so expensive it's impossible to keep a handyman and a groom. We have maids and a good cook she insists we employ to keep our young ladies healthy.'

'And her liking for fine dining has nothing to do with that, I suppose? What have you been doing with the allowance I make you, Callie? You certainly haven't spent it on yourself, so I hope you haven't been learning your aunt's nip-farthing ways.'

'As senior schoolmistress I take a small stipend out of the fees, but it's not enough to turn myself out in the sort of style you seem to expect, Gideon,' she said as if he was being deliberately obtuse and the notion of who gained most from their estrangement took firm root in his mind as Virginia's warning about Callie's aunt rang true yet again.

'At first I could only send enough to clothe you decently and live in modest comfort, but now the money I pay into an account in your name every month could easily run a house twice this size and still allow you to dress in style without penny pinching.'

'It would? Why don't I seem to be receiving any of it then?'

'An interesting question, don't you think?'

Callie looked thoughtful as they rounded the corner into a modest stableyard and he saw two good carriage horses and a trio of fat ponies looking curiously back at them from a nearby paddock.

'You keep a pair of carriage horses, yet I see no riding horse? How do you endure it, Callie?' he asked as the memory of her riding like the wind at his side slipped into his mind and made him wonder what other privations she suffered while he had been coward enough to take her at her word and stop away all these years.

'I'm not a wild young girl now, I grew up.'

'Did you? Have you ever taken a good look at what you prefer to a life with me, Callie? By heavens, you have a very effective way of making me humble for all the sacrifices here seem to be yours and the luxuries your aunt's.'

'She stood by me. She made a home for us both and at least we had each other—there was precious little else to be glad about at the time.'

'A far more comfortable home than she could afford without you.'

'No, Gideon, you don't understand. The school produces a reasonable income, but I have no desire to cut a figure in local society. My aunt likes to pay calls and it keeps our school in the minds of potential clients. She sees to the business side of our enterprise while I tend to the girls in our care. We do well enough without you.'

'So you must always believe her before me?'

'No, of course not,' she argued half-heartedly.

Gideon had to bite his lip as he helped her out of the saddle, then steadied her, because she had endured a great shock today and, if his suspicions were right, there were plenty more of those to come.

'The household has been at sixes and sevens since we found you gone,' Aunt Seraphina scolded benignly as she bustled towards them as soon as she and Gideon walked out of the baking stableyard and into the cool of the stone-flagged hall of Cataret House by the garden door. 'How could you wander off on an afternoon like this, Calliope? You should be resting or keeping yourself occupied indoors during the heat of the day if you really must be busy.'

'I felt restless and miss the girls, Aunt, but you must see we have a visitor. I'm sure you don't mean to scold me in front of him,' Callie said.

Gideon was right here and Aunt Seraphina knew her niece had come home on a hired horse led by a stranger in shirt sleeves, because the maids were on pins at the sight of any man in this out-of-the-way place. One as handsome as Gideon would set their hearts aflutter and their tongues wagging nineteen to the dozen, but Aunt Seraphina was stalling while she took stock of the situation. Callie knew her aunt a lot better than she had when Aunt Seraphina was a rather aloof figure during her childhood and she had seen that look before. The sight of Gideon had unnerved her and she was turning over ways to turn the situation to her advantage in her mind before she acknowledged his presence. A little while ago Callie would have blamed him for the unease between him and her aunt, but now she wasn't quite so sure all the faults lay on his side, after all, as she sensed a mighty fury kept under iron control in her apparently calm relative.

'I considered it best to pretend you are not here, young man. You have more cheek than I thought you possessed to walk in here and expect to be welcomed after what you did,' Aunt Seraphina said as if he was a naughty schoolboy.

'My husband has a right to be here, Aunt Seraphina,' Callie surprised all three of them by asserting.

One of the maids listening on the stairs let out a gasp and another nudged her to be silent so they could keep listening, but Callie knew they were shocked Miss Sommers was claiming a husband at all, let alone one like this.

'The man isn't fit to black your boots, let alone saunter in here as if he has a right.'

'Since I'm not one to wash my dirty linen in public, I suggest we adjourn to a less public space for the rest of this discussion, Mrs Bartle,' Gideon said smoothly, and it said much for his new air of authority that all three were inside the drawing room with the door shut before her aunt protested his use of her true name when she was known as Mrs Grisham here.

'Now, how do you explain yourself, young man? As if that's possible,' Aunt Seraphina said in a voice that made schoolgirls tremble, but didn't affect Gideon at all.

'Later. Now your niece needs peace and a cool bath after her exertions and if you had half the real concern for her welfare that you managed to fake all these years you would stop arguing with me and see she is cared for.'

For a moment there was such tension in the carefully gentrified parlour that Callie fancifully wondered if it might become visible as a lowering mist in the overheated air. She blamed this odd sense of detachment on her faint. Her aunt's gaze fell under the chilly challenge in Gideon's and she waved a long-fingered hand to concede a skirmish, but not an entire war.

'Calliope is very pale, but you insisted we come in here to argue over the matter whilst she could have been resting before her bath, so you can ring for the maids and see if you can get them to do anything sensible now your arrival has set them atwitter,' her aunt said as if recovering from the sight of Gideon walking in through her garden door as if he had every right to be here.

'You're giving me carte blanche to reorganise your household then, ma'am? Rather reckless of you, don't you think?'

'What does a man know of domestic economy?' Aunt Seraphina scoffed and Callie reminded herself they always brought out the worst in each other.

'Enough,' Gideon said wearily and surprised Callie into staring at him again.

Once upon a time he would no more have dreamed of running a household than he would of swimming to the Americas. Now he rang the bell, ordered tea and a bath for her and approved a light menu for dinner in an hour's time before Aunt Seraphina could regret her dare and take back the reins of her household. Callie had made him into this self-sufficient man by refusing to be any sort of wife to him, so why was she feeling nostalgic for days when he would look helpless and wait for her to correct his feckless bachelor ways?

'Well, I'm ready to admit you have changed in that aspect at least. It proves nothing about the rest of your life,' Aunt Seraphina told him severely.

'I have no need to prove anything to *you*, madam,' he replied shortly and they waited in stiff silence for news that Callie's very necessary bath and tea were ready for her.

'There we are, miss. No, I mean madam, don't I?' Kitty the upstairs maid told Callie as if she might not be able to see the bathtub and waiting tea tray herself.

'Thank you, Kitty. I can manage very well by myself now,' she said quietly and refused the silent invitation to confide her secrets. 'You may go,' she added as the inquisitive young woman stood as if expecting to outwit her mistress's unassuming niece by sheer persistence.

'Don't you want your back soaped, ma'am? Oh, no, of course you don't. You've a fine husband to do that for you, don't you?' the girl said impudently.

'If you don't want to be turned off without your wages, I suggest you think about that and do as you're bid, Kitty,' Callie said and met the girl's bold gaze serenely.

'I dare say the mistress would have something to say about that,' the brassy piece said as if she hadn't a worry in the world about being dismissed.

'I doubt it. She didn't want to take you on in the first place and I suggest you consider which of us is the teacher and Mrs Grisham's niece and which one the maid,' Callie said so quietly the pert creature looked away as if there was a lot she could say but she didn't choose to right now.

The girl managed an insultingly small curtsy

as she left to prove she wasn't cowed. Kitty had turned up here all but destitute and begging for work, then managed to go from maid of all work to head housemaid in a matter of months. Callie wondered if she had a hold over her aunt to manage such a rapid rise at the same time as it occurred to her she should have been more aware of what was going on around her. Lately a few of the schoolgirls had come to her with tearful claims that Kitty took their secrets to Mrs Grisham after she snooped to find them. Aunt Seraphina claimed Kitty was doing her duty and punished the girls, not the maid. Absorbed in writing her book at nights and teaching the girls all day, had she been making herself too busy to miss Gideon? And had she let her pupils down by being so preoccupied?

It had hurt to even breathe without him near her in the early days when she began to come alive again and had to live without him. As she undressed and slipped into the unheard-of luxury of a bath before dinner, Callie let her thoughts drift. How were Gideon and her aunt to coexist under the same roof even for one night? They had always loathed each other and it disturbed her that Aunt Seraphina made no effort to hide her dislike. She'd better hurry down before they came to blows. Of course, then her thoughts must veer back to Gideon and the power he seemed to exude now as she sighed blissfully at the kiss of cool clean water on her overheated skin.

Her cheeks flushed ridiculously as the idea he would once have insisted on climbing into this tub with her and done all sorts of sensuous things to persuade her it didn't matter if they slopped bath water on the floor. Had he been tortured by such wanton longings all this time, as well? No stern lectures from her sensible side could kill off the little sensualist who recalled how hot and passionate a bath with the man you loved could be, but he had all the skilled beauties of the *demi-monde* to choose from whenever he wanted to slake his lust, hadn't he? The idea of such a virile young man enduring nine years of tortured celibacy, because he'd wed in haste and repented at leisure, was laughable. That blush of hers went places he would have followed with hotly fascinated eyes in the old days as her whole body overheated with remembering what a passionate and driven lover he was.

She shook her head at the very idea he'd burned and cursed the lack of a wife in his bed all this time as she had the loss of her one and only lover in hers. No, it was simply impossible for him to have lived like a monk for the sake of a woman who'd told him to leave and now she shivered and told herself not to be a fool. He would keep his mistress in comfort and lavish all the fiercely focused passion he'd once saved for his wife on a beauty who couldn't demand a joint share in his life. Her hands clawed at the vengeful thought of how she'd like to use them on his mistress and it took more force of will than she liked to make them straighten again at the idea of another woman in thrall to her husband, her lover, and hadn't she needed him far more than some beauty who could take her pick of keepers and chose Gideon?

Yet if he made love to the confounded woman half as ardently as he had to her, the wretch must simply live for the next time he felt in need of a woman. Even when he must have hated her more than he loved her after their first flush of wild infatuation, he'd still wanted her very urgently indeed, she recalled with a feral shiver of heat that reminded her how much she had longed for him all these years all over again. And wasn't it ridiculous that here she was, lying in her bath, dreaming of her one and only lover, when she should be busy arming herself against his lies.

She couldn't pretend he'd ever forced her.

Most of the reason she made him go was her endless need of him and his passionate love-making. It was destroying her self-respect and making her hate her dependency on a physical act that no longer bonded them like twin souls. Instead, it made the chill between them when they were not making love more arctic. Squeezing her eyes tight shut, she forced herself to remember all the reasons why Callie Laughraine couldn't need her husband and let out a stuttering sigh. There, she was rational again now. It was folly never to dare risk carrying his child again, but it was what kept her tightly hemmed inside the closed world her aunt decreed since the day Gideon rode away, in return for pretending her niece never married him in the first place.

'I'm not a silly little girl in thrall to a lone wolf any more, Gideon Laughraine,' she muttered into the sultry air. 'Don't you dare dream of pulling the wool over my foolish eyes and enchanting me into thinking the sun rises and sets in your eyes ever again.

'Of course not, Callie, why would he think you a passion-led fool when you're sitting here dreaming of him, as if every moment he's not close to you is wasted as far as you're concerned?' she chided herself. 'And I refuse to be that girl again. She hurt too much to dare it twice.'

Galvanised into action by the dread of dreaming her evening away like a besotted girl, until someone came to find out why she was still sitting in her bath like a very odd exhibit in a museum, she washed the dust out of her hair, then soaped herself vigorously until even the memory of her sweat-streaked face and mired feet was gone. She stood up and used the rosemary-and-cider vinegar rinse she made to tame some of the wild curls her dark hair sprang into if she let it. It would soon dry in the heavy warmth of this July evening and she sat on her bed to comb it out, reluctant to put the practical petticoats of Miss Sommers on over her cool, clean skin.

The weight of her long hair as it began to dry against her bare back felt sensual and a little bit decadent now Gideon was in the house. Yesterday it would have been a damp nuisance against a workaday body she did her best to ignore; today Callie Laughraine was alive again and waking up after her long hibernation felt almost painful. A wary inner voice whispered it was better for her darkest secrets if she slept on, but her lover was nearby and she squirmed against the plain bedcover in a rush of hot an-

ticipation she hadn't let herself feel so power-
fully in years.

Even before she knew what love was she'd
felt that forbidden flash of excitement at the
very sight of Gideon Laughraine, she recalled
guiltily. She and Bella from the Grange and
Lottie from the Home Farm used to run wild
over the Raigne estate as girls. She recalled
with a wistful smile the chance of meeting
Gideon busy with some boyish mischief was
the highlight of her day back then. As a girl she
secretly adored that gangling half-wild boy and
when she began to grow to what she'd thought
a woman, her feelings ran much deeper. She
loved him; no point pretending it was a girlish
obsession she would have grown out of.

That girl thought she'd been put on earth to
love Gideon Laughraine and there didn't seem
much point pretending she had never done so.
It didn't matter—she didn't love him now
and hadn't done for years, had she? Idealistic,
dreamy Callie Sommers put an angry boy on a
pedestal. It was as much her fault as his that he
wasn't the hero she thought him. She stopped
combing her hair and stared at nothing in particular as if it might tell her why she committed
all she was to him at seventeen to his eighteen.

The truth was that lonely, uncertain girl was

ripe to fall headlong at the feet of an unsuitable young man. Perhaps that was why her grandfathers connived at the union they wanted and Gideon's father did everything he could to stop it. Of course, the legal heir and the last real heir's bastard child marrying each other would set the succession right and secure the future of Raigne once and for all, but she and Gideon were real people with hearts and souls who deserved to make such life-changing decisions for themselves.

Except they conveniently fell in love with one another and what would it have taken for them *not* to back then? More than they were capable of, she decided, as the huge power of that feeling threatened to remind her how little this life away from him was. The enormity of it, as if a pent-up dam of emotion was about to wash her along in a great flood, echoed down the years. Instead of wild passion it threatened huge sadness now, though, so she built the dam back up and pretended it wasn't there as best she could.

Even so she donned her lightest muslin gown and pinned her hair up loosely, because it was still damp and she couldn't bring herself to screw it into the tight knot her aunt thought proper tonight. She wasn't a spinster schoolteacher, she was Lady Laughraine, and what was the point pretending now Gideon was here? Feeling a little more like a baronet's lady, she went downstairs and could tell her husband approved of the small changes in her appearance from the glint of admiration and something more personal in his grey-green gaze as he rose to greet her.

Chapter Four

'Hmm, I'm not sure about that hairstyle, my dear, and white has never suited you, but I'm glad to see you look better than when you came in this afternoon,' Aunt Seraphina said as soon as Callie joined her and Gideon in the sitting room that evening. She caught a glimpse of Gideon's quick frown and it made her think about her aunt's words a little more deeply.

'I prefer my hair like this,' she said calmly. 'It feels cooler and all those pins were making my head ache.'

'And I hardly recognised you in that governess's bonnet and tightly bound hair this afternoon,' Gideon said, as if they had been parted only a few weeks and he was marking a few subtle changes in his wife's appearance.

'I suppose a married woman is permitted a few liberties that would be folly in a single lady of your advancing years, Callie, my dear,' Aunt Seraphina conceded doubtfully.

'I will never aspire to the extremes of fashion that lead fast young matrons to damp their muslins and crop their hair, Aunt, but Sir Gideon Laughraine's wife cannot dress like a schoolteacher.'

'You were content to dress modestly until he arrived.'

'I should have found the line between modest and frumpish sooner then,' Callie said, feeling rebellious when she thought of all those long nights inventing characters and living her life vicariously so she could pretend it was enough.

'You do seem to be longing tonight for the very life you begged me to take you away from the day he left you alone and bereft, don't you?' Aunt Seraphina asked, the thought of all her niece was risking by doing so clearly paining her.

'I'm not sure,' Callie said, but for a moment she thought her aunt's gaze was hard when it met hers this time. She was wrong, of course she was. They couldn't have lived and worked together all these years if her aunt secretly hated her, even though her aunt was so distant and disapproving when Callie was a child. 'I shall always be grateful to you for standing by me when I needed you to so badly, Aunt Seraphina, but I'm a relatively young woman and can be permitted a little vanity on occasions like this,' she teased, but Aunt Seraphina's lips tightened and her hands clenched before she managed a polite titter and an airy gesture to deny she was a killjoy.

'Of course, my dear, you will have to excuse an anxious old woman who wonders if you're playing with fire.'

'I'm hardly flaunting myself like a houri because I left a few hairpins out of my toilette tonight,' Callie protested because she couldn't imagine how anyone could see her plain gown and simple hairstyle as provocative.

'I'm glad to see you looking more like yourself, but Mrs Bartle obviously takes her duties as chaperon and mentor seriously, my dear,' Gideon said silkily.

Her lamentable wardrobe and lack of a riding horse might be behind his suspicion her aunt had not been acting in Callie's best interests all these years. She thought of his assertion that he had sent large sums of money to her over the years and noted a bead of sweat on her aunt's upper lip. It was very hot, perhaps even she couldn't stay cool and composed in such weather.

'Of course, Calliope is my niece,' the lady said stoutly. Once it would have been a huge concession to call Callie *niece*, as she was the by-blow of Mrs Bartle's younger sister. The fact she owned up to her now persuaded Callie this was all a misunderstanding.

'Thank you, Aunt,' she said sincerely.

'And therefore you must want her to be happy,' Gideon said so smoothly that Callie really didn't know why her aunt shifted under his steady gaze, 'must you not?'

'Of course, which is why I never encouraged Calliope to get in touch with you,' Aunt Seraphina countered as if it were war.

'Or to reply to any of my letters, perhaps?'

Callie had difficulty not gasping out loud at the implication he had written more than once. A single letter would have soothed some of the jagged places in her heart, but more than one? That would have been like a bridge between the old Callie and Gideon and the new world she had no map for after he left. She eyed them both warily and wondered who was lying now.

'I have no idea what you mean,' Aunt Seraphina said smoothly, but Callie saw a few giveaway signs under her front of unruffled confidence that her aunt was less sure of herself than she pretended.

'What a convenient memory you do have, ma'am,' Gideon countered.

'A very *inconvenient* one as far as you are concerned, young man. Time has not wiped out any of your past sins for me even if my niece seems to have lost her memory of them tonight. I might have kept one or two letters from Callie when we came here, but she was in no state to read your self-serving excuses for what you did at the time.'

Memory of exactly how painful that period of her life had been made Callie glare at her husband and wonder why she doubted the one person who stood by her. 'Thank you, Aunt Seraphina. I don't think there was any excuse for what you did either, do you, Gideon?'

He held her gaze as if he had nothing to be ashamed of and suddenly Callie felt weary half to death and wished he would simply state his business with her then go.

'Of course there isn't,' her aunt answered for him.

He was about to deny it, but Kitty came in to say dinner was ready before either of them could say another word and then they only exchanged small talk. The maids were in and out with this and that and Kitty's busy ears were always on the alert for gossip. Tonight they must be aching with the need to know more about the handsome husband Miss Sommers had brazenly owned up to as if she had never lied about him in the first place.

Somehow Callie got through the meal without blurting out something indiscreet through sheer tiredness. She felt horribly confused every time she glanced at Gideon and wondered if he was right to jolt her out of the settled life she had made without him. Maybe Aunt Seraphina had got carried away by a desire to protect Callie. If she had to walk the line between protecting a close relative or telling the strict truth, how would *she* cope with the dilemma her aunt faced?

The idea she would have preferred to make her own choice slipped into her mind. She had a right to know Gideon had tried to contact her or even win her back. At first she would not have listened, of course, but what about later? Maybe, she let herself know. She wasn't quite sure if she should despise herself for being weak or add another reason not to trust Aunt Seraphina as unquestioningly as she had for too long to the list.

'I believe we may have a thunderstorm tonight,' her aunt announced once it was clear

none of them could take another bite of whatever it was Cook had served them.

Callie had no idea what she ate while she
struggled with her confusion in silence. Grandfather would be appalled by her lack of manners tonight and she wondered if either of her
dining companions had noticed. The other two
were probably too busy eyeing each other suspiciously to note that conversation wasn't flowing merrily tonight.

'Your stableman assures me the weather
won't break for another day or two. I agree it
feels clammy enough to whip up a storm at any
moment, though,' Gideon said, as if trying to
pretend there wasn't an atmosphere of sticky
tension in the room that was nothing to do with
the summer heat. He shot a concerned look at
Callie and she realised he was doing his best to
stop more worries adding to her growing pile
of them tonight.

'I don't fear thunder and lightning as I used
to, Gideon,' she said calmly enough, for if
she had gone pale it was out of weariness and
not her old terror of storms. After their baby,
Grace, died at birth the weather was the least
of her worries and since then she'd comforted
so many terrified schoolgirls she could endure
the worst storms without flinching.

'I'm glad to hear it, but you do look weary, my dear. Perhaps we should all retire early to try and sleep as best we can, despite this ridiculous heat?' he suggested.

'Where will you sleep?' she asked unwarily, then blushed at the impossible notion a husband might expect to share his wife's bed.

'Apparently there are plenty of rooms that lie empty here over the summer,' he said as if the idea had never occurred to him.

'I will ask Kitty to have a bed made up for you then,' she said stiffly. She wouldn't have welcomed him if he'd made a move to share her bed, but it felt a little bit unforgivable that he hadn't bothered to try.

'No need, the kitchen maid found me bed linen and we sorted it out between us. I shall be sleeping in one of the pupil-teacher's beds tonight, since none of the younger ladies' accommodation is big enough for a full-grown male,' he said with a shrug that told her he understood her inner conflict about his sleeping arrangements and wondered why she thought he was so insensitive as to demand his marital rights when she was so pleased to see him she lost her senses this afternoon.

'Then can I be rude and retire betimes, Aunt? I am very tired.'

'Of course you must do so, my love. Little wonder you feel exhausted after such a shock as you suffered today, although I still have no idea what you were doing wandering about the countryside alone?'

It seemed a good idea to pretend she hadn't noticed it was a question, not a statement of exasperation. Callie placed a dutiful kiss on her aunt's expectantly raised cheek and gave Gideon a look that challenged him to demand the same. Surely he couldn't expect her to take up marriage where they left off, even if he was willing to sleep elsewhere tonight?

'I can't do right for being wrong, can I?' he whispered when he opened the door for her, then lit her a candle from the store in the hall, despite the fact it only ever seemed to get half-dark at midsummer.

'No,' she said as she went past him with as much dignity as she could manage. 'Goodnight, Gideon.'

'Goodnight, Wife,' he murmured and the shiver that softly spoken challenge sent down her spine sped her upstairs more swiftly than her weary feet wanted to go.

Gideon wished his reluctant hostess good-night and retired to the narrow room a girl who wasn't rich enough to continue her education without acting as an unpaid teacher to the littlest members of this school warranted in this household. He was sure Callie tried to prepare her for life as a governess or schoolteacher as best she could, but all her aunt would care about was that she cost next to nothing.

He shivered at the thought of any daughter of his enduring such a regime at this school without Callie here to soften its hard edges. He must be very weary, because the idea of his lost child made tears stand in his eyes. They lost so much when their little Grace died before she was born. His little girl wouldn't be so little now. Nine years old, he thought, as he stripped off the stifling correctness of summer coat, neckcloth and waistcoat. He could almost hear her furtive giggle as she peeked into her father's room to see if he was asleep yet and might not notice if she crept downstairs now the house was settled for the night.

Perhaps she would be leading the rest of her parents' brood astray by now, as well. Encouraging the little ones to join her illicit feast of whatever leftovers sat in the larder from dinner, or daring them to join her in the gardens by moonlight to pick strawberries and peer at a nest of kittens in the gardener's bothy. He missed her so much tonight. Now he and her mother were under the same roof for the first time in years he felt she should be here, too. Even the slight chance of being properly married again made their daughter seem so alive he could almost hear and touch her. The one ghost he desperately wanted to see was never quite there to be marvelled at; his little girl was always just outside his field of vision, hinted at in the odd little whisper and gleeful laugh his imagination allowed him to know of her.

'Ah, Callie, we would have loved our little angel-devil so much, wouldn't we?' he whispered to the still hot air and called himself a fool.

Hope was almost as bad as despair in the still silence of this sultry night. Yes, there was a slim chance he and Callie could try again, but it wouldn't work if she carried on relying on her aunt to tell her what to think. He *could* force himself on his wife; take her away from here and show her how skewed her aunt's view of him and the rest of the world was. Legally he could make her take him back into her life. It wouldn't feel much better than enduring life without her if she didn't want to be with him, though, and he sighed bitterly at the very idea of such a hostile and empty marriage.

Impatient with himself for wanting the whole loaf when half a one might be all he could have, he opened the window as softly as he could on to a listening sort of night. He'd learnt years ago there were far worse terrors lurking in the darkness than the suggestion of a breeze. Too on edge to undress fully, he heeled his evening shoes off and pulled back the covers on the pallet-like bed, so he could let his body rest while his mind went round in circles like a spit dog on a wheel.

'Good morning,' Callie greeted Gideon the next day.

She wasn't fully awake yet, after swearing to herself she wouldn't sleep a wink, then dropping straight into it as if she hadn't done so for a week. Still she felt her heart flutter at the sight of him so vital and handsome as he strode into the breakfast room. Part of her had missed him every hour of every day since they parted. That Callie saw the world in richer colours now the love of her life was back in it; the rest was deeply sceptical about his return and eyed him warily.

'Is it? I thought we might have slipped into afternoon while I was waiting for my lady to leave her chamber,' he teased and she made a face, then took a closer look under her lashes.

'Where on earth did you get that bruise?' she asked, suddenly more wide-awake and able to stare right at him.

'You might well ask.'

'I am doing so,' she said with a stern frown that told him she wasn't going to be fobbed off with a rueful shrug this time.

'I'm staying in a house I don't know,' he said as if that explained everything.

'And...?'

'And I walked into a door in the dark?' he offered, as if he didn't think it was a very likely story, either.

'A door with a fist?'

'It wasn't a fist, it was a ewer. I suppose I should be grateful your upstairs maid didn't have a chamber pot in her hand at the time.'

'What on earth were you doing chasing the maids round the house in the dark?'

'I'd as soon pursue the Gorgon with lustful intent as that sly minx, even if I was given to preying on servants,' he said quietly and stepped over the close the door, clearly aware Kitty would listen if given the slightest excuse.

'I heard someone creeping about the house

in the small hours of the morning,' he admitted as if he hadn't wanted her to know.

'Kitty might be sly and untrustworthy, but she has access to any room in the house by daylight, why would she steal about in the dark?'

'Apparently she heard whoever was tiptoeing about and decided a housebreaker was searching the attics. I admire her courage, even if I abhor her curiosity.'

'She left her room in the middle of the night to pursue a burglar with only a water jug? I'm not sure if that's brave or reckless.'

'Neither am I,' he said with a preoccupied frown. 'But she was a damned nuisance either way. Whoever was creeping about the house heard us and got away while Kitty was using her weapon on me.'

'Yet it was a bright moonlit night and almost too hot to sleep, surely someone would notice a felon running from the house into the countryside?'

'So you would think.'

'And if they didn't, the prowler you were both chasing must have come from inside the house,' she said it for him, so he couldn't pretend not to know.

'Possibly.'

'You have a suspect?'

'Maybe,' he answered even more cautiously.

She wondered if it was possible to box your husband's ear at the same time you were making it clear he meant nothing to you. Probably not, she decided, and plumped down in her accustomed seat at the breakfast table after gathering up her breakfast more or less at random. It was an occupation and she had to eat if she wasn't to risk another attack of the vapours.

Chapter Five

'How odd that nobody bothered with us before you came here,' Callie said once she had chewed a corner off a piece of toast and sipped a little of her tea to force it down.

'Hmm, or that my arrival caused it to happen,' he countered.

'Why are you really here, Gideon?' Callie asked, weary of dancing round such an urgent topic and eager to get back to real life. This whole situation felt far too dangerous to her peace of mind and she simply wanted him to go, didn't she? 'If you have met another woman and wish to marry her, I must disappoint you, I fear. I won't take a lover so you can sue him for criminal conversation, then divorce me.'

'Well, I certainly didn't come here for that,' he said fastidiously, as if the very idea was unthinkable and a bit offensive.

'Then why *are* you here? There's nothing to interest a man like you here.'

'Of course there is, there's you.'

'No, there isn't. I won't be used because you suddenly find yourself in need of a wife and I'm the one you have.'

'That's never how it was between us and you know it, Callie.'

'Oh, really?' she asked scornfully. 'So our silly little love story wasn't a plot to put the broken parts of our families back together, after all, then? I must have imagined those furious accusations you threw at me after we got back to Raigne from our hasty flight to the Border. Miss Calliope Sommers dreamt a fine young buck carried her off to Gretna so they could wed for love. His father forbade it and her grandfathers schemed to help them elope, oh, yes, it's obvious now—you must have been right all along, Gideon. That naive seventeen-year-old girl obviously planned every step of the journey with your furious father pursuing us to spur you on. What better way to be my Lady Laughraine one day and rule the place my illegitimate birth cut me off from? Wasn't that how your neat story to absolve you of guilt and pile it on me went? Such a shame I didn't know who I really was until you told me, don't you think? Or are you still convinced I'm lying about that and wed you because Lord Laughraine's son died without legitimate issue and he wanted his great-grandchildren to inherit everything I couldn't lay claim to without you?'

'No, although I don't doubt Lord Laughraine and your other grandfather schemed to marry us to each other and tidy up two mistakes at one go. I still can't believe they thought it a good idea,' he said with a bitter grimace. 'No need to remind you I'm the son of Virgil Winterley's bastard and have no right to Raigne, but I wonder your grandfathers didn't see what a poor bargain they were offering you.'

'And I was such a good one? The by-blow of a sixteen-year-old schoolgirl and the artful young rake who refused to marry her? Don't make me into someone I'm not, Gideon.'

'You bear no responsibility for them, Callie. You're a fine person in your own right and I was as deeply honoured you agreed to marry me back then as I am now,' he said as if he didn't regret their hasty marriage over the anvil, but how could he not?

'Thank you, but if that's true you should stop blaming yourself for your father's and grandfather's sins,' she said with a wry smile at his false view of her as some sort of paragon she shouldn't find flattering. 'I've been told your real grandfather was nothing like his son in temper, even if your father was his spit in looks, so you must follow him. I deplored your hasty temper and love of danger, but I was never afraid of you. Even when you were in your cups I knew you would never hurt me or our child.'

She saw him flinch at the mention of their lost baby and wished she'd minded her tongue. It was too soon to revisit that sore place again, so Callie remembered Esmond Laughraine raging how he'd kill Gideon before he let them wed instead and wondered how a good man was fathered by an angry bully. Had Esmond suspected who she really was and hated the idea a future grandson of his might truly inherit Raigne? Such a bitter man might do everything he could to prevent the marriage for that very reason.

She was as puzzled by his furious opposition as Gideon at the time, but she supposed selfish jealousy could explain it. At the time she knew she wasn't a brilliant match for the grandson of a baronet and a peer of the realm's great-grandson, but even she knew Gideon wasn't quite that. She recalled the love in Lady Virginia's eyes when she talked of her late husband and knew a lady of such character and spirit could never love a man who was anything like Esmond Laughraine at heart. Her Gideon must be like his grandfather in more than looks then and shouldn't that possessive worry a wife who expected him to leave as soon as he'd told her what he'd come for?

'I would cut my own arm off rather than hurt you, but I managed it, didn't I?' Gideon said at last. He watched her lower her eyes, then stare out of the window to avoid his gaze and sighed as if he had the weight of the world on his shoulders. 'Sooner or later we must talk about it, Callie. If either of us are ever to be father or mother we can only be so together with any honour, unless you'd rather stick the carving knife in me and risk the next assizes?'

'Don't joke about murder,' she snapped, shaken to her core by the very idea.

'I think I must, Wife, or sit and howl for what you don't want us to have.'

'Now you're being ridiculous and where were we with this sorry tale of loss and betrayal, and why you're bothering me with it now?'

He sighed and poured himself a cup of coffee to wash down the breakfast he seemed to enjoy about as much as she did. 'I admit when your maternal grandfather told me the true tale of your birth, I only saw concern for your future and the Raigne inheritance behind his plot with Lord Laughraine to set the succession straight again. I never stopped to see you had no idea who your father really was until I told you. Little wonder you didn't defend yourself against my wild accusations when you must have been shocked to your core by the news and never mind the interpretation I put on it. Hasty boy that I was then, I felt more like a stallion put out to stud than your proud husband and lover all of a sudden and I came home and accused you of ridiculous things in the heat of temper, then made things worse by refusing to back down after I'd cooled off, even though I knew I was wrong to suspect you of being in on their plans. I never really considered how you must have felt when you found out who your father really was from a furious young idiot. It was that crack in our marriage that finally opened up and ruined everything we had wasn't it? I ruined it all simply because I was too proud and arrogant to admit to being wrong,' he said bleakly.

'You were very young,' she heard herself excuse him.

At the time it seemed inexcusable, yet it

must have been agonising for the boy he had been to wonder if his wife married him to get the heir Raigne needed so badly. Sir Wendover Laughraine's three legitimate sons were dead from fever, accident and battle by then and the current Lord Laughraine's only child, her father, had died before she could even remember him. So why on earth had Sir Wendover still refused to admit his wife had imposed another man's bastard on him as his youngest son? Because that bitter old man was too proud to publically admit the truth, Gideon was heir to a huge fortune and vast old house he didn't want or believe he deserved and she was the last true Laughraine. Except she wasn't a true one at all, was she?

'You were even younger,' he replied, 'and already carrying my child so it was unforgivable to storm and rage at you like that, even if there was any truth in that tale I made up to make myself feel better. I was so afraid you didn't love me at all, you see?'

'Why wouldn't I?' she said with a reminiscent smile for the handsome, brooding boy he was at eighteen she hoped didn't look as tender as if felt.

'Because I'm not a lovable man. All my life my father cursed me as the reason he had to marry my mother. He'd call her a sanctimonious prig one moment and whore the next because she let him seduce her. Heaven knows he could be charming when he wanted to and she had a reputation for being far too proper for her own good, but she was a naive and sheltered young woman who believed him when he said he loved her. She said a lot less than him about how much she hated being trapped in a marriage neither of them wanted because I was on the way, but I doubt she could put her hand on her heart and swear she loves me even today. We meet once or twice a year now my grandfather has taken her back into the fold, but so far we haven't managed to like each other very much.'

That confession of how bleak his childhood really was almost broke her heart. How could they not have blamed themselves when he was the innocent party? That disgusting bet Esmond Laughraine had made to seduce a bishop's daughter no other man would dream of even trying to get into bed without a very public ceremony and a wedding ring was appalling, but the bishop's daughter had succumbed of her own free will and Gideon had no choice about the matter at all. He wouldn't quite believe her if she championed him now, because she had turned away his love, as well. Despite all the good reasons she thought she had at the time for doing so, how much damage she had done by taking the easy option? Yes, it was simpler to cut out the despair and hurt from her life and go on without him, rather than patch up some sort of marriage between them. But none of that would put things right between them now and make him believe he was a deeply lovable and honourable man, despite his shocking betrayal of her when she was at her most vulnerable.

'You make me sound so meek and mild, Gideon—as if I sat and softly wept all the time you were accusing me of luring you in with my witchy wiles,' she chided lightly, because it was better than weeping and letting him see she pitied the boy who grew up with parents who didn't deserve him.

'You gave as good as you got, didn't you, spitfire?' he said with a wry smile, as if he remembered those furious rows and their making up afterwards with affection.

'And will again if you're not careful,' she said, chin raised to warn him she was no doormat nowadays, despite her nun-like existence since they parted.

'Good, because I wouldn't have you any

other way,' he said with a boyish grin that did something unfair to her insides.

'It's just as well I have no intention of changing then,' she said.

Was she secretly conceding that, for the right incentive, she might be tempted to try again? No, she didn't want to be a convenient wife, primped and perfumed and ready to oblige her lord in the marriage bed as part of a cynical bargain. If they resumed their stormy marriage it must be as equal partners. Yet he was so self-sufficient he looked as if he didn't need anyone nowadays, let alone a wife who would demand a place in every aspect of his life she could get a toehold into.

'What will happen to Raigne if we remain apart?' she asked abruptly, the thought of being with him for the sake of a huge inheritance sour in her mouth as she tried to swallow it down with cold tea. 'I dare say you would be accepted as the heir without me.'

'I might be the legal heir, but you're the true one.'

'Yet you love Raigne and nobody else will keep the place as you will.'

'You could if you wanted to.'

'I'd be laughed out of court. I'm your wife, so everything I own is yours.'

'And what if Prinny decided to challenge me on the strength of some old gossip and the wrong family resemblance? You can see why they were so keen for us to wed, can't you? Still, at least when we eloped we simply wanted to be wed and never mind anything else.'

'We should have known better,' she said sadly.

Her husband stared out of the window at another cloudless morning as if he was unable to feel the warmth and she tried not to care. 'Indeed we should,' he said at last in that clipped, carefully controlled voice she was learning to hate.

'I'm sure Grandfather Sommers wanted us to be happy,' she said as if that made the gulf between those young lovers and now a little less.

'I wish you'd believe Lord Laughraine does, as well, Callie. It's not his fault we looked for reasons to hate each other when our baby died. I wish you could find it in your heart to forgive me for that, even if everything else I did and didn't do is beyond it.'

He looked as if memory of the quarrels and furious silences that marred their marriage had been a hair shirt to him ever since. Memories of long, hot nights of driven passion after they found out what her grandfathers were up to slipped into her mind and whispered they couldn't have felt such endless need for each other if all they had was lust. Then she thought of their baby and shivered. Nothing had mattered to her but the terrible space their little girl left behind her in the dark days after that terrible journey from London to King's Raigne to bury their child in Grandfather Sommers's recently dug grave.

She simply hadn't any emotion left over for Gideon or anyone else after that. Even the irony of hearing her real mother invite Gideon, Callie and Mrs Willoughby's sister, Aunt Seraphina, to stay with her whilst they considered what to do next, since they had nowhere else to go at the time, was wasted on her. For the first time her true mother opened her life to her secret child and they might as well have been on the moon for all the difference it made to Callie. Her withdrawal from the world was a way out of heartbreak and she'd dived into that grey nothing as if not feeling anything was all that mattered. No doubt Gideon felt desperate for comfort, painfully young and bereft as he was, as well. It wasn't an excuse for what he did, but she wasn't as blameless as she liked to believe at the time.

'First I'd have to forgive myself,' she said

with a sigh, and half-heartedly pushed a slice of cold bacon round her plate so she wouldn't have to meet his intent gaze.

'You must, Callie, there won't be a pinch of happiness for either of us until you do.'

'I'd have to look past a lot more than petty quarrels and grief for there to be an "us" again, wouldn't I?' she challenged him.

'Ah, and there's the rub. You don't want to see past that farce, do you?'

'No,' she admitted bleakly. 'There's no excuse for what you did that day.'

'Yet even in a court of law a person is innocent until proven guilty. You didn't bother to wait for niceties like that before you condemned me, did you?'

'I expect that's why you like them. I prefer to believe my own eyes,' she said bitterly.

'You still want to think I was unfaithful, don't you? Whatever I said fell on deaf ears because you had already given up on us. It was a good excuse to finally push me out of your life and you've certainly done your best to forget I exist ever since.'

'How could I? We had a child,' she said with the sadness of losing her daughter still raw in her throat after all these years, and her absence seemed all the more savage now they were in the same room and she wasn't here.

'Yes,' he said bleakly, '*we* did.'

'Ah, there you both are,' Aunt Seraphina said as if she had been looking everywhere for them before she breezed into the room.

Anyone else would feel the tension and leave them in peace. Callie caught herself out being disloyal and managed to smile a half-hearted welcome.

'I thought you two had broken your fast and gone out long ago,' Aunt Seraphina remarked blandly, although the door would hardly have been shut in that case, so why lie?

'I had a disturbed night,' Gideon said, reverting to unreadable again.

Callie felt as if some golden opportunity to understand all they'd lost and gained had been brushed out of the room like house dust.

'Poor Kitty is mortified she mistook you for a burglar in the dark last night, Sir Gideon,' her aunt went blithely on. 'We can't sleep safe in our own beds of a night any more. I really don't know what the world is coming to,' she added, shaking her head as she poured herself coffee and refused anything more substantial as if it might choke her.

Her aunt did look careworn this morning, as if she hardly slept last night. So why didn't she admit hearing noises in the night if she was sleepless for most of it?

'Whoever it was knows there is a man in the house and a very alert housemaid now, so I doubt they will ever come back,' Gideon said, as if he'd never discussed the likelihood of the disturber of the peace coming from inside the house with Callie.

'Well, I admit now that I should have listened to you, Calliope, and found another handyman when we found out the last one was more often drunk than sober, instead of trying to manage without as best we could,' Aunt Seraphina said, and why did Callie feel as if every word she said had a ring of falseness this morning?

'We could get a dog,' Callie suggested with a half-hearted smile to admit they had had this conversation many times and her aunt still couldn't abide dogs.

'I think another man of all work would be less trouble,' Aunt Seraphina replied with the polite titter even her niece was beginning to find irritating.

'There are plenty of dogs at Raigne. Lord Laughraine has a pack of assorted ones that follow him about the place,' Gideon reminded his wife as if it might be a carrot to get Callie there, if his own desire to have her home wasn't enough.

She felt little and petty for making him feel he had to tempt her, but couldn't he see what a huge undertaking it was for her to go there with him? It would mean trusting all she was to him and, without the headlong, driven love between them ten years ago, how could she do that when even mutual obsession hadn't kept them together before? Her heart raced at the very idea and she searched her morning for an excuse to avoid him and work out what she really wanted to do.

'I dare say the servants hate the work such hairy animals cause,' Aunt Seraphina said sourly and Callie felt guiltily irritated by her naysaying ways.

'They are as happy to see them as he is every morning,' Gideon said with a fond smile for the man he had no right to call uncle, but Callie never doubted the affection between two men who had every reason to dislike and distrust one another, yet did not. She wriggled in her seat against a pang of guilt because she had cut herself off from her grandfather as well as her husband and that too seemed petty and rather little this morning.

'I'm glad to hear the creatures don't sleep in his lordship's room,' her aunt went on with her subject like a bulldog worrying at a bone.

'Only two or three at a time,' Gideon said, as if enjoying Aunt Seraphina's reluctance to call a peer of the realm's habits distasteful. 'But I doubt anyone could get into the house without them raising the roof.'

'Oh, but I couldn't endure all that mess to keep a chance felon away,' she said with a shudder. 'I shall trust employing an extra man will put the housebreakers off trying again.'

'I should like to have a dog about the place,' Callie said wistfully.

'His lordship would be very happy to find you one,' Gideon said.

'There you are, you see, my dear? Your husband has found the perfect way to lure his wife back to Raigne and keep her happy, has he not?' her aunt said with false brightness, as if he was offering Callie a childish bribe to resume their marriage and she might not be clever enough to spot it.

'If you will excuse us, Aunt, Gideon and I have a great deal more to talk about than our pets or lack of them,' Callie said and rose from her seat before the lady could argue.

'You mistake my concern, Calliope. I know

you are a woman now and not a silly girl taken in by bribes and promises,' her aunt said with such dignity Callie knew she was offended.

'Then why make such belittling comments in the first place, Aunt?'

'Because he always set us against each other and now he's doing it again,' Aunt Seraphina said with an accusing gesture at Gideon, who looked impassive and made Seraphina seem shrill and begrudging by contrast. 'It's my duty to point out you always were a fool for this man and don't show many signs of learning from past mistakes.'

'I have run the academic side of this enterprise and proved myself a woman of ability and character. You cannot trust me with all that, then accuse me of being an empty-headed idiot the first time I show any sign of questioning your wisdom, Aunt.'

Aunt Seraphina looked unconvinced for a tense moment, then sighed heavily and nodded as if to affirm Callie was a different creature from the heartbroken girl of nine years ago. 'Very well, my dear, I must trust you have learnt judgement, I suppose. You will remember what happened last time, though, won't you?' she said with what looked like such genuine anxiety for Callie's well-being that Callie branded herself an ingrate and reassured her aunt she could hardly forget.

The insidious thought slipped into her mind that, if Aunt Seraphina was truly as devious as she must be to have hidden hers and Gideon's letters for so long, she would know arguing against her niece and Gideon having time alone would make them more suspicious. No, that had to be unjust and unkind of her, she really didn't think her aunt could have kept so much of her essential self hidden for so long when they lived in the same house.

'I don't know why I'm letting you drag me out here when I need to get ready for the new term,' Callie protested half-heartedly ten minutes later. 'But why did you refuse my aunt's offer of the gig so we could take a drive before it gets too hot to move, Husband? Are you ashamed to be seen with me in such a drab getup?' she added.

Gideon saw self-doubt was tripping her up again and how could she not know she was one of the most beautiful creatures he'd ever laid eyes on?

'Don't put words into my mouth, Wife,' he teased and got a half-hearted smile out of her. He resolved to make sure she never had to worry about being less than perfectly turned out ever again and promised himself yesterday's gown would go into the ragbag as soon as she had even one new gown to eke out her meagre supply.

'Then why don't you want to leave the house or gardens?' she asked suspiciously.

Did she think he was lying to disguise his distaste for her plain round gown and old-maid-like cap? In fairness his first impulse was to rip that monstrosity from her head so her glossy dark curls framed her enchanting face again, but he had to tread on eggshells around his love if the hope he couldn't quite keep bricked up in his mind wasn't to crash and die, and he would never do that to her, anyway. She had endured enough slights and humiliations at the hands of her sly aunt over the years. So he would go on treading carefully round the snags that had been put in her self-confidence for as long as it took him to reassure her she was his lady and his love and beautiful to him whatever she wore. Best if he didn't think about what she might not wear and look even more superb and delicious if they ever got close enough to be man and wife again right now.

Meanwhile they had set out on a sedate stroll towards the orchard. Callie must have noticed how closely he was watching the house and was looking suspicious about his motives for staying within sight of it until he was proved right or wrong about her aunt's motives for keeping her so close all these years and him so far away.

'You were ill yesterday and today you need to rest. Anyway, perhaps I'm curious about this house and the people you have lived with all these years?'

'Why? We are a simple people living a quiet life.'

'I doubt there's any such thing as simple people with straightforward lives.'

Gideon had half an eye open for the signal the little downstairs maid agreed to make if the Missus or Kitty-Cat, as she called Mrs Bartle and Kitty, went up to the attics. The rest of his attention was caught by his wife flushing as if he'd smoked out her darkest mystery and he almost forgot to watch for a duster being shaken out of the window three times, after all.

'What guilty secrets are you keeping, Callie? Besides me, of course, and I think we can say that cat is already well and truly out of the bag.'

'I am a simple schoolmistress, I don't have time for secrets,' she said, but didn't quite manage to meet his eyes. Gideon felt a terrible, heart-plunging fear she might have a furtive admirer or even a lover, after all.

'Am I going to have to kill some besotted country swain, Wife?' he managed coolly.

'What's sauce for the goose, Gideon dear...' she said and let her voice tail off so sweetly he felt his old wild fury stir under the goad of hot jealousy.

'Don't play with fire,' he warned her austerely.

'I told you yesterday that I have no lover.'

'So you did. What's this mysterious secret you feel so guilty about then, Wife?'

'I don't feel guilty exactly,' she prevaricated, clearly wondering if she trusted him enough to let him know what it was and that didn't hurt him, of course it didn't. It wasn't as if he needed to know the inner secrets of her very soul. Such intimacy was for true lovers and she didn't have one of those any more—not even him.

'Then what do you feel?'

'Disloyal, I suppose,' she admitted at last.

'To me?'

'Of course not.'

'Oh, no, of course not,' he echoed rather hollowly and told himself not to be a fool. He hadn't expected to be welcomed back into her life with open arms, so he couldn't complain she didn't think he deserved her loyalty.

'You weren't here to be disloyal to,' she explained as if that covered everything.

'So I wasn't. What is this dark secret you don't feel guilty about then?' he asked grumpily, wondering if he was wrong about her aunt, after all. Maybe Mrs Bartle didn't have a secret cache of his and Callie's letters hidden somewhere. Perhaps she received his and found them so distasteful and embarrassing it was easier to pretend she did not.

'I write books,' she confessed as if it were a sin on a par with poisoning ambassadors or defending guilty criminals against the might of the law.

'You do?' he asked, startled to hear it, but instantly proud of her all the same. 'Should I have heard of you?'

'Not yet, I am trying to correspond with a gentleman who says my work is nearly ready for publication, but my aunt and my husband seem determined to get in the way.'

'So *that* was what you were up to yesterday?'

'Yes, I use another name to exchange letters with him, since Aunt Seraphina disapproves of lady novelists. I have a dream of living on my own and teaching only one or two days a week and Aunt Seraphina certainly won't approve if I succeed. So I pick up his letters and send mine off to him without my aunt's knowledge.'

'What a dark horse you are, my Callie,' he said, thinking that at least those letters stood a better chance of reaching their destination than any she entrusted to her aunt ever had.

He had always known where she was, of course—what sort of an investigator would he be if he hadn't?—but she made no secret of her identity when she reverted to her maiden name. He should have sent his letters by courier and insisted he put them into her hands only, but he had been as taken in by Mrs Bartle's air of refined integrity as everyone else. After that letter setting out Callie's hatred of him and fervent wish never to set eyes on him again, he lost heart and his letters were desperate pleas for a hearing and protests of innocence she didn't want to believe in.

Except Callie hadn't written it, had she? It occurred to him Reverend Sommers had made a far better job of raising his granddaughter than either of his daughters. Was that why he taught Callie as if she were a boy rather than a girl? Maybe that good and clever man saw the mistakes in his daughters' upbringing and devoted himself to teaching Callie his moral code and fine principles instead of leaving it to a governess to instil a set of ladylike accomplishments that had little practical value or interest to a girl with a fine mind like hers.

'You really don't mind?' she asked as if she had been expecting doubt or fury.

'No, why on earth would I? And after you informed me I have no right to be offended about anything you do, I'm surprised my feelings matter so much to you, anyway.'

'Of course they do, but you know perfectly well that if I had admitted to a secret admirer you would have torn him limb from limb and locked me up in the highest turret of your castle,' she teased back, and didn't that feel wonderful?

Gideon stamped down hard on a fierce need to kiss his wife senseless. It was best not to run before they learnt to walk again as man and wife and he didn't want to let his raging need of her stampede through the fragile relationship they seemed to be building brick by careful brick. He wondered how he could convince her he was perfectly happy for his wife to write, as long as she did it while she was living with him instead of alone or with her aunt.

'Why is Biddy waving her duster so wildly

from the landing window, Gideon? It really looks most peculiar.'

'She is?' he exclaimed and turned to see the tail-end of the signal he and Biddy had agreed on. 'The devil, that's even sooner than I expected. Excuse me, I must hurry or I'll be too late,' he said absently, then loped off, hoping she understood he'd far rather stay and talk to her, but time was a-wasting.

Chapter Six

For a startled moment Callie watched her husband dash back towards the house as if it were on fire. She could stay out here and wait for him to come back and tell her what he was up to, she supposed, but he had a poor record for sharing secrets, so she hurried after him. It wasn't because she couldn't stand being parted from him now they were within touching distance of each other once again—it was curiosity, plain and simple. Her heartbeat quickened, anyway, but she was running to catch up now and that was perfectly understandable.

'Stay here,' he ordered when they reached the hall and he realised she was on his tail, then stopped so abruptly she cannoned into him.

'No,' she murmured and gave him a push towards the stairs to let him know there was no point arguing.

'Exasperating woman,' he mumbled under his breath. She glared when he half turned to glower at her and bade him watch his step. 'Keep quiet then and don't give us away,' he told her softly and they went up the stairs while she was trying to think up something pithy enough to demolish his arrogant certainty he was in command.

Tight lipped, she did her best to tread as stealthily as he did, but that was impossible. She managed to avoid the stair that creaked after he did the same without seeming to think about it. He must have explored the house with this sort of stealthy pursuit in mind. It looked as if the dangerous adventures Lady Virginia hinted at when she visited were very real and not a cunning scheme to soften her heart as she thought at the time. She was glad she hadn't known what he was really up to at the time and terrified he knew too much about the darker side of life to be her idealistic and loving Gideon again. Now where had that come from? She didn't want this man to be anything of the sort to her again, did she?

Never mind that now, they were on the half-landing and heading for the attic stairs. That seemed so absurd she stopped wondering how she felt and kept as close as she could to him. Her world felt right and safe when she was near him and that should worry her. The door opened without a sound and why were the hinges so well-oiled when these rooms were full of lumber? The maids slept on the other side of the house and the stableman lived over the stables, so what had once been the male farm-servants' quarters were now empty.

Why was Gideon creeping towards a lot of dusty rubbish as if on the track of lost state secrets? Callie noted footprints in the dust on the twisting staircase and held her breath for a moment, then shook her head in disbelief. There was nothing much up here and it was already uncomfortably hot. His tension still made her listen for the slightest noise and she recalled a few Gothic touches in her own novel then wished she hadn't. It was absurd to let her imagination run riot, but she felt a flutter of superstitious fear before she told herself sternly this was no time for spectral visitations. They were a few steps up the twisting stairway when Gideon waved his hand to stop and she forgot imagined horrors for real life.

Frozen in her tracks, she was cross with herself for obeying orders like a soldier on parade. From the soft murmurs ahead it sounded as if there were two people in the little storeroom furthest from the stairs. Impatient at him for being a step closer to danger than he was prepared to let her go, she pushed the small of his back to urge him on. He resisted, as if he had to stand between her and hurt like a wall. He must have felt her impatience with such overprotective nonsense, because he reluctantly went up a step so she could hear, as well. First there was her aunt's voice saying something impatient and a lighter voice in reply. Why was Kitty arguing with her aunt here when they could do it downstairs in comfort? It didn't sound as if they were discussing using the rolls of dimity and calico stored here to make new gowns and aprons for the maids. Her aunt economised on them until threadbare, but surely that wasn't an important enough to linger over in a stuffy attic on a day like today.

'You are impudent,' her aunt raised her voice to say regally, as if trying to overawe Kitty with her importance as head of a school and Kitty's employer. 'Nobody will believe a vagrant maid over a lady of means and standing in the neighbourhood.'

'They won't have to. I'll have my money *and* keep my place till it suits me to leave. You won't want me to tell the constables what I know, will you, Mrs Bartle?'

'I changed my name to avoid being known as the widow of a depraved fool. That will earn me more sympathy than censure.'

'You can say you're the queen of the fairies if you want to. It's what you did to him that'll make them prick up their ears. I can read, you see? I wonder you never bothered to find out I was hired to keep an old woman out of mischief in my last place. She taught me to use my talents, then I learnt how stupid it was to trust anyone when she turned on me.'

'I expect she saw you for the cunning little ferret you really are.'

'I'd be careful what you say, Mrs Bartle. When the world knows what you did to keep your niece here and her husband's money flowing into your pockets, nobody will believe you. Such a sweet story for the scandal sheets, I dare say I'll make a fortune if you're too stupid to pay up.'

Now Callie knew why Gideon warned her to stay silent. Kitty's words seemed to echo like a clap of thunder and fell into her mind so surely she knew they were true. She managed to stifle a gasp of horror, but her senses were intent as Gideon's as she realised everything she and her aunt had built here was a sham. With him here—the real Gideon next to her—the truth of him somehow cancelled out her aunt's lies.

How had she believed every word Aunt Seraphina said against him until yesterday? Was he right; did part of her want to believe him guilty? Maybe it had been easier to blame their ills on her husband, but didn't that make her a coward as well as a fool? She had hardened her heart against him and believed her aunt must love her because she was there after everyone else fell away. Every artlessly accidental comment about her appearance, Aunt Seraphina's clever slights and well-placed reminders of all Callie had lost at the hands of a careless husband kept her locked down and hurting, but she hadn't seen the truth because it was easier not to.

'No one will believe *you*,' Aunt Seraphina was sneering and how hadn't Callie seen through her until today?

'The stableman is coming to take this lumber down so the boxes are empty for my niece's luggage and he certainly can't read, so it will all be ashes in a few minutes.'

'No, they stay here and I keep the keys.'

'You couldn't stop a fly doing what it wanted, let alone me, now could you? A fall down those awkward stairs will remind you who is mistress here and who is the servant.'

If Kitty didn't have the sense to shiver at the casual malice behind that question Callie did it for her. 'If aught happens to me, the landlord of the Crown in Manydown has a letter saying who to look for. Do you want him and half the county on to you for attempted murder?' the girl said boldly and she was evidently a more subtle opponent than Aunt Seraphina thought.

'So that's where you've been sneaking off to. I should never have let my niece persuade me to give a trollop like you a chance when your last employer turned you off for chasing her sons. She never mentioned blackmail, though, curse her for a soft fool when you should clearly be in the local bridewell.'

'We're both bad, but you could've been better if you wanted. As for that milksop I worked for, I knew far too much about her spindle-shanked sons for her to risk it and they weren't worth it, anyway. Miss Sommers is a better woman than either of us and took me in despite that woman's spiteful tales, but you betrayed her long before I got here, didn't you? So who will the world judge the worst rogue of us two, Madam Bartle?'

'You spied on her for me, despite owing her a

roof over your head, and blackmail is a serious crime. If you survive the little accident you're about to have, you will regret relying on that weak sot from the Crown for aught but a roll in the hay, you know that, don't you?'

'He has me to put steel in him, Mrs Bartle, and I have this,' the little maid said triumphantly and Callie heard her aunt gasp. 'An account written by your husband of times he was ill after he ate with you and accidents he had on his way *out* to get drunk and not coming back as you claimed. He even knew a man you paid to murder him. They had a fine spree with the money, then you decided to do the job yourself and he went in fear of his life. He should have run instead of staying, but what a fool you were to keep his evidence.'

'How did you get your grubby hands on such drunken nonsense?' Aunt Seraphina whispered as if she dared not admit it existed out loud. Through the heavy stillness of the hot attic Callie could hear fear in her voice and knew this was true, as well.

'I found the secret panel in your desk drawer I bet you wish was big enough for all the letters you stole over the years. Being bedridden herself, the old lady I was meant to keep quiet in my last position thought it a fine joke to teach me the tricks of such places and find things her son-in-law hid from his wife so she could make him do as she said.'

'That's where you learnt your disgraceful trade?'

'Of course, and a cunning old besom she is, too,' Kitty said admiringly. 'Why else would he pay a maid to keep her happy when he hates her like poison?'

'He still managed to dismiss you.'

'That's when I learnt never to trust sly witches like you and make sure I know more than they do. The old woman moved her treasures, then told her daughter I was warming her precious sons' beds.'

'You were lucky not to be whipped at the cart-tail,' Aunt Seraphina scorned.

'I knew too much, but then the old lady gossiped and I couldn't get work. Don't you look down your long nose at me, Mrs Bartle, I was born with nothing and make my way as best I can. You were born a lady and only took me on because I'm cheap and you thought I'd be so grateful I'd do whatever you bade me.'

'And you would be on the parish now if not for me.'

'Not I,' Kitty said confidently and somehow Callie believed her. 'I wouldn't be set up for life neither, though, so I'm happy to tell your niece what you did if you don't pay up. If this paper gets to the magistrates, stealing from your family and keeping a man and his wife apart all these years will be small beer next to wilful murder.'

It went so quiet in the chamber under the roof Callie could hear the crackle of paper as the girl held that damning account out of the Aunt Seraphina's way as she did her best to grab it from her.

'Enough,' she whispered to Gideon, convinced the two people in that room were so absorbed in their struggle they wouldn't notice if a town crier was standing on the stairs.

'Indeed,' he agreed, and somehow managed to launch himself up the last few stairs and past the partition wall as swiftly and silently as a hunting wolf.

He easily topped Kitty and Aunt Seraphina and snatched the letter from Kitty before she even took in the fact he was behind her, throwing it back to Callie. Catching by instinct, she laid it on the stair and got ready to join in if he was too gentlemanly to ward off two biting, spitting furies.

Gideon must have learnt the folly of being a gentleman with she-cats since they parted. He grabbed Kitty by the waist and lifted her off her feet so he could aim her at Aunt Seraphina like a weapon. Her wildly kicking feet landed a good few blows on Aunt Seraphina's substantial person as the girl tried to turn in his arms to scratch and bite him. Luckily both women were soon winded and Gideon stepped back.

'How enlightening,' he said casually. 'See if Biddy's friend the groom has returned with the magistrate yet, will you, love?' he asked Callie without turning round.

'Of course,' she said, carrying Bonhomie Bartle's statement at arm's length as if it were as noxious as the man who wrote it.

She ran downstairs, unsure Gideon's gentlemanly instincts would let him hold those two at bay much longer. The memory of the deadly pistols he pulled out of his pocket as if he used them to hold felons up every day reassured her. For all she knew he ran such risks on a daily basis. She could see him doing exactly that when she turned her back on him. Occupied with her own thoughts, she watched Squire Evans ride up to the house as fast as his fat old cob would carry him and remembered the evidence in her hand. She darted into her term-time office and locked it in the box where she kept the girls' pocket money. If Gideon chose to show it to the authorities she would hand him the key, but somehow she didn't want her aunt's downfall to be caused by a man she had despised and feared herself.

'I still can't take it in,' the magistrate said after a spitting and furious Kitty was escorted off the premises with her bundle of belongings and Mrs Bartle locked in her room. 'Mrs Grisham seems such an upstanding woman.'

'I suspected nothing, Mr Evans,' Callie said with a rueful shrug.

'So why were you suspicious, Sir Gideon?' the squire asked.

'I just knew something was amiss,' he said with that closed expression Callie hated. 'I would rather our gullibility went no further, if you take my meaning, sir?'

'Ah, yes, well I don't see how that can be, Sir Gideon. If we prosecute the woman, we'll need a good case and yours is by far the strongest.'

'I intend to keep all the evidence pertinent to it in a safe place and if you return the letters Mrs Bartle used to blackmail her neighbours anonymously she will have nothing left to live on but her wits.'

'No doubt she'd thrive, since "the wicked flourish like the green bay tree" as it says in our prayer books. Inconvenient to have all that linen washed in public, is it?' The squire tapped his red nose with a beefy forefinger and reached for the glass of excellent brandy Aunt Seraphina kept for wealthier visitors.

'Lady Laughraine and I will be living not fifteen miles away and I don't want the whole world to know what fools we've been,' Gideon agreed confidentially.

Apparently her husband had become a fine actor over the years they were apart. Callie suspected he didn't care a straw what their neighbours thought, given the gossip it had been enjoying at his expense since before he was born. He was doing it for her. She shook her head to show him she could weather being thought a fool to tell the world her aunt was a thief and a liar. He pretended not to see, so she gave up and made an excuse about needing to steady the household and left the room. They would have to stay here another night at least now and, although Cataret House had been her home for nine years and she'd thought herself content here, she couldn't wait to be quit of the place.

'My aunt will spread all sorts of wicked gossip about us if you let her go, Gideon,' Callie warned as they went upstairs later to assess what to take with them and what she was happy to leave behind.

'If she tries it, I'll find her and stop her,' he said so coolly she shivered and believed him. 'Never mind her, how many of your belongings do you want to take with us, Callie? I'd prefer to travel as light as we can.'

'Exactly when did I agree to go to Raigne, Gideon?' she challenged half-heartedly. Somehow the thought of going home was very tempting, even if she would be going to the 'Big House' rather than comfortable King's Raigne Vicarage.

'Would you rather we went to London, or somewhere else altogether then? I don't much care where we go as long as you come with me.'

'Raigne is your home.'

'One you have a great deal more right to call so than I have.'

Callie shook her head, because that huge old barn of a house would never seem like home to her, but nine years of loneliness and longing told her pride would make a very poor bedfellow if she insisted on staying apart and aloof from her husband and refused to admit they might manage to remake their marriage if they both tried hard enough.

'If I come with you, it can only be a maybe

to resuming our marriage, not a fait accompli, Gideon,' she warned, but both of them knew it was a huge concession. Callie wondered if he felt as if he hardly dared even breathe deeply lest this hope for the future shattered in their faces all over again, as well.

'It's far more than I dared hope when I came here, so that will do me for now. In the meantime, how much of this do you really want to take now, and what can be sent on later, my not-quite wife?' he said with a smile that invited her to find their not-quite anything status almost comfortable.

'I don't have many possessions that really matter,' she said, gazing round the shabby room as if through a stranger's eyes. 'One or two books are from Grandfather Sommers's library and then there's my grandmother's pearl necklet and a miniature of them when they were young. Apart from my writing box, I can leave the rest without a qualm.'

'Then pack those and any essentials and we'll leave as soon as you're awake in the morning. I'd like to get to Raigne before my honorary uncle is out on the estate and it will be cooler and less trying to travel early in the day.'

'How can I stay at Raigne, Gideon? I hardly

ever set foot in the place when I lived at King's Raigne Vicarage,' she protested, the thought of bowling up to the Tudor mansion as if she had a right suddenly felt impossible again.

'It's your home and heaven knows you've more right to call it so than I have.'

'No, you love the place and belong there as I never will.'

'That's nonsense and I know Lord Laughraine wants you home nearly as much as I do. You're his only grandchild, Callie, and he's a good man who truly only wants the best for you. He might have seemed remote and uncaring when you were a child, but apparently your other grandfather begged him to let you grow up without the stigma of your birth shadowing your childhood. No, don't grimace like that, love, Reverend Sommers was quite right. I might have been born within wedlock by the skin of my teeth, but it's bad enough for a boy to be mocked and derided for what the gossips say his parents did. I would never wish it on a girl who might end up being tarred with her mother's supposed sins before she was old enough to know what they even meant.'

'We can't know now, can we?' she managed to say past the torn feelings that were threatening to clog up her throat and make her weep, not for herself but for him and all the slights and sly whispers he'd been left to cope with as best he could since he was old enough to take notice.

'I can, but it's quite safe to love him, Callie. Don't turn him into a conniving monster because your aunt was one and you don't trust your family now. It was wrong of me to drag you to London when we got back from Scotland. I should have left you at Raigne to learn to know Lord Laughraine. You were carrying our child. He and his household could have fussed over you while I was in town learning my trade. I was selfish to insist on having you near all the time. I can't tell you how much I wish you'd known him as the fine man he is before you went through hell, Callie. You might have turned to him for love and support when I failed you then, instead of your stony-hearted aunt.'

'If wishes were horse, beggars would ride,' she replied tightly as she began opening drawers and pulling out books so she wouldn't have to look him in the eye. 'And I wouldn't have stayed behind, anyway. I loved you far too much to be parted from you while we waited for our child to be born,' she finally admitted gruffly.

'You would have put up with it for her sake,' he said and bent to pull a little trunk out of the cupboard she was staring into without seeing the old clothes and winter boots that just wouldn't do for Sir Gideon Laughraine's lady.

'We don't know that it would have made any difference if I was anywhere else. Don't second-guess fate, Gideon. It does no good and will drive you insane if you let it,' she said, her own struggles with that particular demon haunting her.

'No dear,' he said with mock humility she knew was meant to lighten her thoughts. He went out to retrieve some of the boxes the stableman had emptied ready for her departure, those that really were full of worn-out clothes and ancient account books. 'Do you need anything else?' he asked, seeming to accept it was best to deal with details right now.

'I think not. Where do you intend to sleep tonight, Gideon?'

'I could insist on sharing this room, but I'm not a fool,' he said with a sceptical glance at the narrow bed and ancient furniture, as if he wasn't sure it was up to the weight of a fully adult male if he stayed.

'No, and it's best if I do this alone,' she said

mildly, refusing to hint at her feelings about sharing a bed with him again, mainly because she wasn't sure what they were herself.

'Don't forget I'm here now,' he told her mildly, even if there was an intensity in his complex grey eyes that made her long for things she wasn't even ready to admit to herself she wanted yet.

'I learnt to walk my own paths while you were away,' she warned.

'Part of being married is learning to walk together without stamping too hard on one another's toes, isn't it? I've been without you for a very long time, Wife,' he reminded her so softly it felt more significant than if he were to shout his frustration from the rooftops.

'I still lived a very different life from you and it will take a while to accustom myself to yours if we find a way past the pitfalls. My aunt isn't the sole reason we were apart these last nine years,' she reminded him with a severe look to remind him that war wasn't won.

And I need to work out if I can endure living with a husband who only wants to share my bed because he has no alternative without making our marriage vows a lie, she added an unspoken aside. He sighed and seemed to resign himself to her mistrust for a little longer. Then he smiled wryly to say he was tame again and there was no need to worry he was going to beg.

Chapter Seven

'What has it been like, Callie, this life you made without me? Not being a girl, I don't know what they're taught or how they are before they appear in society as if sprung fully formed from the egg.'

How could she refuse to try to breach the gaps between them? It was a start if they understood each other better, she supposed, but some of the old rebellious Callie whispered, when was he going to tell her the adventures he'd had without her?

'Much depends on the family she comes from and the one she might make one day. Grandfather Sommers's classical education didn't prepare me to instruct young women about the niceties of life and I left that to my aunt. I do know aristocratic young ladies have very different ambitions to genteel ones, though, and our teaching was always aimed at the latter.'

'So what does a genteel young lady need to know?'

He surprised her by meekly handing her any items she nodded at and putting ones she rejected in neat piles as they worked in an easy harmony she would have found incredible only yesterday. It felt oddly intimate having him share the room that was her sanctuary for so long, yet he made it seem normal to silently debate over her most intimate garments and possessions in front of the man who should have shared her life, so how could she tell him to leave her alone and go back to being the outsider in this otherwise all-female household?

'How to manage a household and control a budget, the details of her kitchen and how it is supplied. how to contrive and make do and be sure her family are in credit with the world in every way possible,' she said as she tested that question in her head and tried it out on what she had done her best to teach her young ladies. 'She needs to know enough of the world to keep certain parts of it out of her house and encourage other ones in with the right degree of hospitality. To record and examine accounts, visit her neighbours and be a useful part of her local community, and value truth over show, as well. I don't know if I can really describe an ideal wife since I doubt such a paragon exists. The closest I can get is to say she should be well informed and able to care for her family, ready to love her children and support her husband's endeavours as best she can, yet still be a woman of character in her own right.'

'And for all that they need algebra and natural philosophy and a smattering of Greek and Latin?' he asked, looking at the pile of books she was thumbing through to find which ones she could leave behind and which must go with her.

'I only teach those if a girl shows an aptitude for learning and a lively curiosity about the world. Their potential husbands are taught them as a matter of course, so I see no reason to rob a girl of a chance to explore them before she has to be busy with a family.'

'It's a wonder you restrict yourself to a few extra lessons with your brighter pupils. Your late grandfather seems to have treated you like a student at Balliol.'

'All that learning didn't do me much good, did it?' she asked, avoiding his gaze as she tried not to look back on the idealistic, impulsive girl she was when she fell in love with him.

'I was so full of wondrous myths and legends and tales of wild adventure I couldn't see real things as they were.'

'What were they then?' he asked quietly.

'Impossible,' she said bleakly, the gaps and betrayals of her young life piling up to remind her what a fiction her dream of perfect contentment with her hero-lover was.

'No, it was possible. We only needed time to grow up and cope with such hot passions in the everyday world. Left to ourselves we would have found a way, Callie. You have to believe that or we might as well set up a nice little school for you in Bath and hire a law office for me on the moon.'

'Perhaps we should,' she said with a half-smile at the thought of him negotiating with the ancient gods of Olympus for the rights of a celestial body.

'Don't. It's unthinkable to turn our backs on a last chance at love,' he said hoarsely and there he was again, the true Gideon under all that gentlemanly self-control.

'If we can't laugh together, we'll never be anything but strangers at heart,' she warned him. 'Half of what went wrong between us was because the intensity of our love felt so fierce.

If we're going to try again, our marriage must be rooted in real life.'

'I expect you're right, but could we agree not to laugh about parting again, if you want me to stay sane while we work our way round the thorns?'

'I'll agree to that, Gideon, but I refuse to be rushed into anything else.'

'What do I have to do then, Callie? I warn you I'll go down on my knees and beg if I have to sooner or later and you'll find it embarrassing and ridiculous. Just agreeing to come to Raigne with me is hope enough for now, though, so I'll excuse you that ordeal for as long as I can endure the temptation of you so close and not abase myself,' he said, and how much of what he said was serious and how much a joke? She eyed his careful smile and unreadable gaze and decided it would take longer than a day to read the true Gideon under all that armour nowadays.

'The world will still believe we're together again,' she said flatly and wondered if she had been stupid to agree to go to Raigne with him, after all. 'You only came back yesterday, Gideon, we haven't had time to get used to each other as we are now, let alone as man and wife.'

'At least at Raigne we can be the people we really were all along.'

'Without my aunt trying to wreck us all the time.'

'Yes, a new start, Callie, that's all. At least this time I won't have to spend hours at my law books and you won't be living in a strange city with people you have little chance to know.'

'I see the logic of it, but what if we fail publicly this time?'

'Would that be so much worse than not trying at all?' He strode over to the window and back again, looking as if this cramped little room was closing in on him. It felt too small to her now; a cell built with Aunt Seraphina's lies, and she bit back a reckless urge to go tonight, dark and dangerous thought it might be to risk travelling at night. 'Tell me truly you only want to find another school to teach in. That you can forget the chance of a family and I will smother my hopes and promise not to trouble you again,' he finally said as if it hurt.

He stood still and met her eyes, let the guard he kept round himself drop. Did she really want this man she once loved to beg? No, it couldn't have been love in the first place if she did. So here she was up against words she didn't want to say.

'Yes…' she breathed at last, then saw pain and bleak loneliness in his gaze before he blanked it and realised he thought she meant yes to him going away. 'I mean yes to Raigne and us, you idiot,' she told him brusquely. 'But that's all for now,' she reasserted even if she had seen the truth of his longing behind his wary eyes.

'It's enough,' he said shortly and she could see from the way his shoulders relaxed that the hard control he'd kept his mouth and those dear, familiar green-shot grey eyes under was lifted.

Feeling a little ashamed of herself for making him reveal more than he wanted to in order to combat her attack of the dithers, she still felt as if she were walking the edge of a precipice.

'Well, that's finally settled then,' she said briskly and began packing as few boxes as she could to take away tomorrow.

'Good, I'd hate to have come after you if you change your mind, because I warn you, Callie, I won't go away quietly this time. I'll follow you and make a nuisance of myself even if you travel the length of the land to avoid me. You have given me hope, Lady Laughraine, and I can't give up on it now.'

'I won't go back on my word now. I admit when I thought about it again the whole idea of being at Raigne together frightened me, but I'm steady now and only want to be quit of this place, so you'd best let me finish packing before I go to sleep on my feet.'

'Very well, concentrate then and stop trying to distract me, Wife,' he said with a cocky grin that reminded her again of her young love. Who would have thought she'd be so glad to see that young scapegrace under all the frost the years had put into Gideon's gaze?

It was done, her life for the past nine years packed and ready to go. The small pile of luggage by her bedroom door seemed a poor showing for twenty-seven years of life. Callie concluded travelling light taught her people matter more than things, but had she been weak to agree to go to Raigne with Gideon? Instinct said no, here was a chance for a bigger life than the one she had here, yet her imagination reeled at the very idea of being a wife again. Torn between hope and fear, she knew any chance for their marriage must be grasped, but it felt so huge to let go of the past and seize it.

She tossed and turned on the narrow bed that had seemed perfectly adequate for so long, but now felt restrictive and hard. The real trouble was she couldn't put all the wild hope

Gideon's arrival had rekindled in her heart back in its box and lock it away again. There had been such passion, such love, under their youthful infatuation with each other, that her most hopeful self whispered those huge forces couldn't simply be dead between them now. Yet their dreams of mutual love and need and a future together were smashed all those years ago. What if Gideon didn't share her fantasy? She squirmed against the sheets and told herself it was so humid tonight it was no wonder she couldn't drop off to sleep as if nothing much had happened.

Her whole world had changed, so what was the point of lying here fooling herself she was about to drop off as contentedly as if it was just another day? Unable to endure even the added heat of a thin and patched sheet over her as the heat seemed relentless and sticky all around her, she knew she must face the biggest fear of all about her new life some time. What if she still loved Gideon under all the bitterness and pain and loneliness? And what if he didn't love her? Impossible, she would never have been able to go on with her restricted and very single life for the past few years if she was secretly panting with passion for a lover who it turned out had not really existed.

Except maybe she had been secretly, deep down where she didn't let herself think too much but just feel, maybe there she had been waiting for him to ride up and carry her off. Despite all the pain and bitterness and tears and wild arguments of that brief year of marriage when they were both so young, looking back that was the part that felt like her real life and this one some sort of wicked enchantment that kept them apart and only almost alive. An image of her aunt as the wicked sorceress with legendary power to keep two lovers lost in a dream world and obedient to her commands almost made her laugh for a moment, until she reminded herself how serious Aunt Seraphina's sins were.

Unable to stay still and contain the fury that wanted to howl and weep at all the chances she and Gideon lost to live and love together because of Seraphina Bartle, she got out of bed to pull the curtains wide and very gently inch up the sash to let more air into this stuffy room. Never mind the dangerous night air Aunt Seraphina insisted on keeping out of the house like demons from hell, or the bright moonlight that shone in and might even keep a less wakeful person from their slumbers. It felt good to connect with the greater world, to feel the air and see the moonlight she shared with the rest of this vast racing world of theirs and Gideon in particular. Maybe he was doing just as she was, sitting in the uncushioned seat of his window and breathing in air still heavy with heat as he stared at the miracle of a night almost bright as day? Close on the heels of that thought came the idea of one day sitting with him dreamy, well loved and content as they shared everything she now had to sense alone.

No, that was going too far. If she was to stay sane she must learn to be practical and a lot less idealistic. For now she would learn to be as happy as she could be with what seemed graspable instead of aiming for the moon. If it all went wrong for them at Raigne, at least she and Gideon knew they could live by their own efforts now and perhaps be happier doing it. There, now she was thinking their reconciliation was inevitable and it couldn't be. How could she trust her inner self to a man who had betrayed her at least once already?

It was a dour thought to try and go to sleep on, so she pushed it aside as best she could for another day. It was time to stop looking back and go into the future as best they could, but she wished she was a wild girl again just for tonight, so she could be free to do as she pleased and walk into the hills one last time by the light of the July moon. She had come to love both the remoteness of this sturdy old house and the half-tamed emptiness of the wide hills all around it and she would miss that and the girls she had done her best to equip for lives that would not always be as easy as they might seem to anyone less fortunate.

So was Gideon struggling to sleep alone as well tonight, or already lost in weary slumber after his demanding wife-hunting trip and last night's excitements? No, thinking of him asleep without her was never going to lull her into dreamland; it felt too wrong for them to lie apart like enemies in different camps dreading the next battle. She sighed heavily, then went back to bed to try counting sheep. No, they looked too much like Aunt Seraphina, and wasn't that an uncomfortable thought? Sheep wearing unlikely flaxen wigs and a superior expression would put her off the silly creatures for life and there were far too many of them in this part of the world to risk that calamity.

In the distance she thought she heard a soft thud and a murmur, but it was over almost as soon as it began and she turned over when she heard a vixen bark a warning at cubs big enough to know better by now and blocked her ears to the normal noises of the night. It wasn't term time, so she didn't need to worry about nightmares or wakeful girls away from home for the first time and longing for their parents. She felt herself retreating from this little world that seemed so safe for so long, Miss Sommers's days were numbered, but could she really be Calliope Laughraine again? She had married Gideon ten years ago, but it would feel like living with a man she didn't know if they took up where they left off. Whatever happened between them, she was about to live in a house beyond most women's wildest dreams.

The very thought of trying to make some sort of life in the mansion she visited on sufferance as a child felt so alien she might lose an essential part of herself if she tried to see herself as wife of the next Lord Laughraine. Deciding she preferred a world she had some control over, she set about plotting the knottiest bits of her next book in her head. The intricacies of it soothed her and she was halfway to dreamland when she realised her latest hero looked exactly like Gideon. Already drifting, her mind was too wrapped up in a sleepy fantasy of finding a happy ending in her husband hero's arms to reject the notion he might still be her hero, after all, and she fell asleep with a welcoming smile on her face.

'So where *did* you end up sleeping last night, Gideon?' Callie asked the next morning when they were on their way from Cataret House so early this might be a dream, as well.

'On a chair in your office, lest your aunt can pick locks as well as escape from upstairs windows,' he replied gruffly.

'I knew I should have woken up properly and investigated the noise I heard in the night,' she said with a grimace for the empty room and improvised rope of bedsheets they had discovered this morning. 'At least Kitty wasn't here to give you a matching pair of black eyes, but I'm surprised you didn't hear my aunt escape as you seem to have the senses of a cat.'

'I knew she would go, why else do you think I was dozing in that uncomfortable chair? I had to make sure she took nothing of ours with her this time,' he said and shifted his shoulders as if they were still stiff from holding such an unnatural position for so long.

'You have had a difficult time since you arrived, haven't you?' she said with a wry smile for his poor bruised face and the shadows even under his good eye from lack of proper sleep.

'Poor Gideon,' she added and surely it wasn't quite right to feel such a rush of joy at the mere sight of the boyish smile she remembered from the old days in response?

'Lucky Gideon,' he corrected softly and the look he slanted her made it clear she was the reason he thought it was worth it.

She smiled back and let herself enjoy this odd journey through a luminous dawn. They were sitting on the box of what she still thought of as her aunt's carriage. As he was driving the sturdy pair she refused to be shut inside a stuffy, swaying box on wheels on such a perfect morning. So the little kitchen maid was inside the coach in her stead, dressed in her Sunday best and feeling like a Queen of England, she assured Callie, and shook her head at an offer to sit in the fresh air, as well.

'I've never rode in a real coach before, miss, I mean, my lady, and the missus would scold me something wicked if she caught me getting that wrong again, wouldn't she?' the girl said with a happy grin.

Callie smiled back in silent glee neither of them need tiptoe round her aunt's notions of propriety ever again. Now she let herself feel the thrill of a new start life in the shape of Sir Gideon Laughraine as well as the fears she struggled with last night. His stray lady was about to be reborn as a potential aristocrat and apparently Biddy was going to scale the dizzy heights of lady's maid without going through any of the stages in between.

'She's never going to fit anyone's idea of a proper lady's maid,' Gideon warned softly as they moved on to the main road to Manydown and Biddy waved regally at a startled farm labourer about to go off to the fields for the day.

'That's why I engaged her,' Callie admitted, the thought of a silently critical dresser who would sniff and disapprove of her new mistress making Biddy's pleas not to leave her behind a good excuse not to engage one. 'I couldn't let her be turned into the world with nothing, now could I?'

'Perhaps not, but we could still find her a place more fitted to her skills when we get to Raigne. Your personal maid will have to cope with a large collection of gowns and can the girl sew? She won't know how to clean a riding habit or wash the ostrich plume fashionable females festoon their bonnets with. If all Biddy can do is wash pots and pare vegetables, she'll be in the suds the first time she's called on to do something less than straightforward to my lady's wardrobe.'

'No, she won't, suds are what she's escaping from. For one thing, I'm not a fashionable female. For another, she can sew perfectly well, because my aunt insisted all the maids she employed could do so to save a sewing woman's wages. I'm sure someone at Raigne will be glad to show her how to keep my habits clean and what to do about anything I manage to spill on my favourite gown and she might as well learn to be a lady's maid at the same time I find out how to be a lady.'

'You are already a lady. Let's not have that old argument again.'

'Very well, we'll leave it for another day,' Callie conceded with a look about her at the early morning sunshine and another fine day. 'Where do you think my aunt has gone?' she asked after they had driven through Manydown to startled faces as the early risers saw Mrs Grisham's niece on the box and Biddy waving regally at them from inside the carriage as if practising for her coronation.

'How would I know?' Gideon said as he got the feel of the pair and set them bowling along the better road to the main highway that would lead them to the other side of the county and Raigne, hopefully before the sun could climb too high and make the journey wearisome.

'You seem to find out what makes a person tick a little too easily nowadays,' she replied, feeling the tug of intimacy as she adapted to the movements of his strong body brushing hers as he expertly flicked his whip or softly reassured the more skittish of the two glossy chestnut horses he was driving to an inch.

'I don't much care where she is or want to understand her,' he said shortly.

She sensed something held back and turned to give him a very wifely look. 'Now I'm wondering why I don't believe you,' she said as he tried to be inscrutable again.

'So am I.'

'Maybe I know you too well?' She paused and took another look at the blank expression he was trying to fix as he concentrated on his horses as if they were far more restless than they appeared on a fine morning with a smooth road ahead. 'You let her go, didn't you?' she said as the unlikelihood of such a daring escape dawned at last.

'Oh, yes,' he said with a smile that would have looked just right on a fox picking hens' feathers out of his strong white teeth of a morning. 'First we had a little talk and then I suggested she leave before I called the Runners.'

'I hope you're not going to tell me my aunt has taken to highway robbery?'

'No, but your unlikely maid is probably resting her feet on an extra box I slipped into the carriage before we set out.'

'She had my parents' letters as well as ours, didn't she?' she said, and it was as much a statement as a question. He'd seen the echo of their own tale in her parents' ill-fated love affair and known exactly what to look for. Apparently the wild young man she married had grown up to be a clever and subtle man.

'Yes. It's all about power, Callie, a need to control those around her without them realising she's doing it,' he said wearily and she felt cold even on this sunny July morning at the idea she'd been dancing to Seraphina Bartle's tune all her life without realising it.

'Why extort money from anyone else, though? She already had what I earned for her with our pupils as well as what you sent me to live well on while you struggled.'

'Only at first, I do very well now.'

'Stop trying to divert me with your tale of rags to riches, Husband, and kindly answer my questions, you're not in a courtroom now.'

'I feel as if I might be,' he teased her, then sobered. 'Last night she confessed Bartle ran through any money they had and left her a mountain of debts. Whatever the details of his death might be, she didn't deserve that.'

'Now who's making excuses for her?'

'I'm trying to understand. She always knew right from wrong, your grandfather would see to that, so why lie and cheat and take such pleasure in making her family unhappy?'

'Because she married Mr Bartle, perhaps? Maybe a cow looked at my grandmother the wrong way when she was carrying her and that did it? Who knows? She lied and stole and did her best to ruin our marriage and nearly wrecked my mother's life beforehand.'

'She didn't need to do much to part us, did she? I did most of it for her before you even got back to King's Raigne and fell into her clutches again,' he argued bleakly.

'Don't, Gideon,' she protested, fighting tears at the desolation in his voice.

'Very well then, let's talk of the weather, shall we?' he said bitterly. 'I'm heartily sick of your aunt as a subject of conversation and we might as well find something neutral to while away the tedium of our journey.'

'Of course, it seems set fair to last out the week, don't you think?' she said stiffly; she could hardly complain that he'd lapsed into brittle social chit-chat when she was the one who didn't want to talk about her aunt.

'The harvest will be ready long before its time if it continues thus, don't you think?' he went on relentlessly. 'Lord Laughraine must be fretting about the chances of sudden downpours and thunderous tempests ruining the crops as we speak.'

'If he happens to be awake so early in the morning, of course.'

'There is that,' he agreed as they reached the next village and he was so preoccupied holding back his pair to let a herd of sheep cross the road there was no need to talk at all.

Callie fixed her gaze on the horizon, but saw little of it. He was right to shut himself off from her in a way. Towards the end of their marriage he did all he could to keep them together, although they were so young they scarcely knew how to go about the daily business of life as man and wife, until that last day when she must have decided it wasn't worth it. She couldn't think about that right now, but wasn't she the one who never quite believed she deserved to find true love? Miles slipped by and they pretended interest in the passing scene and she tried to let the subject slip out of her mind, because they were too shocked and weary to talk of the past without making things worse right now.

She managed her usual escape from too much reality by considering how this scene or that chance encounter with a group of travellers, a market day, or a drove of cattle might change or bend the plot of her next book. Nothing more noteworthy happened until she was holding the horses while Gideon went to buy the next set of tickets from the toll keeper.

'You don't look like any coachman I ever encountered,' a deep and amused male voice drawled from behind her.

A gentleman she'd never seen before in her life halted his dancing mount beside the carriage very much against that fine animal's wishes. He bowed from his saddle with such elegance she felt dowdy and windswept and fervently wished he'd go away. 'Good day, sir,' she said with distant politeness.

'It is now,' he said with a rogue's grin. 'And a good day to you, as well, Miss Whoever-You-Are,' he said, with a wary glance at her gloveless left hand that made her blush and wish she hadn't thrown Gideon's rings back at him when they parted all those years ago.

'Sommers,' she said impatiently, more out of habit than a wish to deny her husband and then it seemed foolish to correct herself to a stranger she would never see again.

'I can see that,' he murmured with a grin that made her realise what was meant by wolfish and she wished Gideon would hurry back.

'I am called Sommers,' she explained shortly, doing her best to ignore Biddy's cough of disagreement and her fine imitation of a disapproving chaperon.

'And every bit as lovely as a summer's day you are, too, Miss Sommers. What a fortuitous coincidence that I happened on you today whilst we're in the midst of that fine season, as well,' the wolf told her with such admiration in his oddly familiar green-and-grey eyes she might have been all of a flutter, if Gideon hadn't already dazzled her for good.

'Nonsense, I'm not lovely and neither is being too hot for comfort day after day,' she snapped with a glare at the heat haze on the horizon. 'I do wish people would stop comparing me to a summer's day, it really is most unoriginal.'

'Shakespeare? I feel I ought to know, but I never did mind my books at school.'

'It is from one of the sonnets and I was flattered to have it quoted at me once,' she said, recalling the heart-racing sound of it on

Gideon's lips, but then, if he'd recited a list of linens when they were young and in love it would have taken her breath away. 'It grates sadly upon repetition.'

'I shall obtain a book of sonnets and learn them off by heart for future use,' the stranger said with what looked like real admiration in his eyes and Callie wished she hadn't forgotten her married status in a moment of absent-minded annoyance.

'I'm not interested in an idle flirtation, or any other sort of idleness for that matter. I wish you good day, sir,' she said firmly.

'It might not be so idle as you think,' the man said and made her wonder if all the gentlemen in so-called polite society required eye-glasses and were too vain to admit it.

'It had better be,' Gideon's darker voice said from behind them.

Chapter Eight

'Peters, what the devil are you doing here?' The stranger greeted him as if they knew each other. Plainly they didn't, or the rake would know her husband's real name.

'Winterley,' Gideon replied coldly and it made her think again about his other life and how many secrets it held. Apparently he had another name altogether and what else had he failed to tell her about his existence since they parted?

'You know each other then, gentlemen?' she asked as brightly as she could when they looked about to challenge each other to a bout of fisti-cuffs, if she was lucky.

'Not as well as we think,' Gideon said tightly and wasn't that the truth, Callie thought cyni-cally, wondering if anyone knew Sir Gideon Laughraine but Gideon himself.

'But perhaps better than you would like us to?' the man challenged him. If they were friends at all, it was clearly a prickly sort of friendship.

'Perhaps,' Gideon said, and addled Callie's brain by climbing back into his seat and holding her hand as they faced his dashing acquaintance together. 'We certainly don't know each other well enough for you to have met my wife, Winterley, and that makes me wonder why you felt free to accost her on a public highway.'

'Now here's a dilemma,' Mr Winterley drawled with a hard glance in Callie's direction to tell her what he thought of her lapse of memory. 'To give the lie to a lady, or admit you and I know each other not at all?'

'Well, my dear?' Gideon said with a frown as he dared her to deny him again.

'I am indeed Lady Laughraine, but tend to forget it now and again. I beg your pardon, Husband, Mr Winterley,' she said with a nod of curt apology towards each of them.

'Lady Laughraine?' Mr Winterley asked blankly. He shot another shocked glare at Gideon that said there was indeed more to her husband's other life than she knew. 'What a truly dark horse you are, Mr Frederick Peters.'

'My husband's full name is Gideon Frederick Peter Dante Laughraine, sir, but I shouldn't take it as a slight you didn't know him as such until today because he only lets the world see as much, or as little, of his true self as he thinks it needs to know,' Callie told him with that alias of Gideon's going round and round in her thoughts as she wondered what he had been up to in order to need it.

The tall stranger seemed to pause on the edge of giving at least one of them a blistering set down before he took in Gideon's ponderous string of names, then a look of unholy glee lit his face instead and he sent Gideon a mocking grin, as if he now knew far more about him than such a private man could want him to.

'You appear to be an even darker horse than I thought you, Laughraine,' he said slowly. 'Oh, well met, Sir Gideon, and how d'you do?' he added mockingly.

'Well enough, but I'll never understand you if I live to be a hundred, Winterley,' Gideon said with a manly shrug. 'Ours has never been a conventional marriage,' he added casually, as if he and Callie kept it to themselves out of a perverse delight in secrets. Since she was the one to demand it came to an end nine years ago, she could hardly complain if he was making weak excuses for that deception now.

'Then perhaps you should consult with your wife and match up your stories better in future. I wish you both a good morning and hope to see you at dinner. If you dine together as man and wife and not under your chosen aliases in different counties, of course?'

'Then you are staying at Raigne?' Gideon asked as if it confirmed his worst fears.

'Lord Laughraine will invite me, d'you see? This time I rashly agreed to stay for a week or two to escape the husband hunters, since the little darlings will go to Brighton on Prinny's coattails to carry on their craft out of season. Like a gullible innocent up from the country I agreed to his latest invitation to enjoy some bucolic tranquillity at his expense and quite forgot he was a great friend of Virgil and Virginia's. Although given what has happened so far this year, I should feel less of a fool now I'm looking at the very good reason he wants me there, shouldn't I?' Mr Winterley said mysteriously.

Callie supposed Gideon knew what the man meant, since she felt him flinch and heard a bitten-back curse. The only Virgil and Virginia she knew of were the last Lord and Lady Farenze; Gideon's late grandfather and his wife. Still with that look of unholy amusement in his eyes, Mr Winterley blithely gave them both a seated bow before wishing them a genial farewell. Then he rode off as if he'd happened on an amusing sideshow at precisely the right moment to enliven a tedious moment.

'Who on earth is that?' she asked.

'A friend, although you wouldn't think so at times,' Gideon replied tersely.

'A friend you were about to call to account for simply exchanging greetings with me?' she reminded him recklessly.

'I have no patience with Winterley's sort of politeness. You should be wary of him, too, Callie. He's slippery as an eel and about as trustworthy as a fox.'

'Maybe it takes a rogue to know one.'

She tied the trailing strings of her bonnet into a militant bow she regretted as soon as the close-woven straw closed the heat in and threatened to make her head ache. Refusing to undo it after making such a grand gesture, she silently dared him to comment.

'There's no maybe about it,' he said with an unrepentant grin and they resumed their journey in what she hoped was a dignified silence.

'I have no wish to know what you have been doing while my back was turned,' she managed to lie after they had continued for half a mile with her staring everywhere but at his face. An internal picture of a parade of his lovers kept plaguing her, as if a grey mist had settled on her shoulders in the most unlikely cloud and was blighting a glorious morning.

He sighed as if she were proving to be the most exasperating of travelling companions and answered the question she had been trying so hard not to ask ever since he came back into her life. 'No, Callie, I don't have a mistress, nor a discreet married lover bored with her husband after filling his nursery with heirs. I've been celibate as a monk for lack of you, but you'd be sensible to wish I was busy chasing every strumpet in town right now. You're right to watch me as if I'm a starving wolf about to swallow you down in one hungry bite, so maybe you'd best avoid provoking me with the likes of James Winterlcy again. I want you so badly every inch of me is on fire and at least now you can't say you haven't had fair warning.'

'No man who loves as passionately as you could go nigh on a decade without a woman,' she said sceptically, the image coming into her head of him in the arms of some sensual charmer purring with pleasure at his splendid body and skilful lovemaking.

'I am a married man, in case you had forgotten,' he said shortly.

She tried to shrug off the doubts that made her want to smack the smile off that smug imaginary siren's face, but he was a fully adult man and she couldn't seem to get reason to overcome jealousy now they were side by side and she had felt the flex and steel of his body next to hers for mile after mile. Perhaps she should have agreed to travel in the stuffy carriage away from him, after all.

'You revelled in being my lover, then my wife, before you decided I was a villain and you hated me. Don't pretend you don't want me nigh as much as I want you.'

'You taught me not to trust my one and only lover, Gideon,' she said as images of them locked in the wilder excesses of passion threatened to leave her certainty she never wanted to risk loving him again in the dust.

'This isn't the time or place for picking at old wounds,' he warned with a significant nod back at the carriage where Biddy was fanning herself in the growing heat and beginning to look as if she regretted choosing that seat over this one. 'I won't admit to something I didn't do, though,' he added in a low, driven voice.

'I don't want to love you again, Gideon,' she

warned. She was breathless and on the edge of something dangerous and had to protect herself from being so vulnerable again.

'Maybe I won't ask you to,' he replied flatly, before halting the carriage and insisting Biddy squeeze into the space atop the graceful little vehicle between them.

They were close to the end of their journey at last and Callie spotted familiar landmarks and the outlying parts of her grandfather's former parish. She distracted herself from her galling and petty jealousy of Biddy for her place next to Gideon on the narrow coachman's seat by wondering who still lived where they were when she left and who had moved on. Inevitably some of the parishioners would have joined her grandfather in the peaceful churchyard of King's Raigne Church. She winced at the very thought of that grave and knew she had to visit it before very many days had gone by in her temporary home to make peace with the past.

It seemed best to tell herself this was temporary. The very idea of being mistress of such a huge and venerable house one day might terrify her half to death if she dwelt on it. She glanced at her husband over the top of Biddy's head and knew she would be more open to his persuasion if he wasn't Lord Laughraine's heir. Then they could simply return to London when the heat of midsummer died down and live a humdrum life. A sense of justice her grandfather instilled in her argued she must put her dread of the Laughraine inheritance aside and see Gideon as he was, rather than one day lord and master of Raigne.

There, now they were almost through Great Raigne and a particularly strait-laced widow she recognised as an incurable gossip was waiting to cross the road. The lady took a second look at the modest carriage and exactly who was driving it and her mouth fell open like a cod fish.

'Oh, dear,' she muttered to Gideon, then summoned up a cheery smile as they swept past as if a Laughraine always drove his own carriage with his wife at his side and a maid-servant for company. 'Our eccentric method of travel will be all round the Raigne villages by the time she's walked the length of the high street.'

'I have no intention of keeping our arrival quiet so they might as well get used to us,' he said, a challenge in his voice she hoped Biddy wouldn't notice.

'If your uncle really wants you to stay here

and begin to learn the management of the estate we must live here for at least part of the year, though, and Mrs Prosser never did like me,' Callie said with a sigh.

'She doesn't like anybody much, but she does love a title. We should do well on that front.'

Callie stayed silent in deference to Biddy's eager interest and watched for Raigne's elaborately carved and twisted Tudor chimney stacks. There they were, as familiar and strange as ever. The sight of the mellow nobleman's mansion in the distance made her think of her childhood. She had thought it a palace full of exotic things and fairy-tale people. Later she was allowed inside the side door of the giant's castle at Christmas, when the Sunday School children had tea in the housekeeper's room and were given a present to take home. Aprons for the girls and shirts for the boys, she recalled with a grimace. If she had any say here she'd make sure children received something more interesting in future.

She wasn't even through the gates and she was rearranging cherished traditions. It wouldn't go down well in the servants' halls if she seemed ready to take over before she had her feet through the door, and she must step carefully if she was to be accepted as a proper wife for an heir to Raigne. The real question being did she want such a role in the first place? Gideon was Lord Laughraine's acknowledged heir, so she supposed she had no choice as she was Gideon's wife. She sighed gloomily and wondered how many girls in the Mayfair ballrooms she suspected Gideon was familiar with would give their eye teeth for the position she had no desire for.

Yet King's Raigne was home in a way Manydown never had been and this was Gideon at her side, as familiar and strange as the world she had left behind when she married him. It felt right to be back in some ways and so wrong in others she could hardly endure to think about it. Under the reproaches he hadn't made and the sore places in her heart, could they come to love each other in a less overheated and dangerous way than when they were so ridiculously young? They would be fools not to try, so she really had to stop being a fool and step into the future with a little resolution and more hope they would somehow find each other again.

Trying not to dwell on the challenges ahead, lest she jump down from the carriage and run away before they even got to Raigne, she eyed the shady groups of ancient oaks and elms in the parkland they were passing through instead.

The sun was high in the sky and cattle were sheltering from it under the wide-spreading trees, lowing to their calves and lazily swishing flies away with their tails. They looked timeless and indifferent to the comings and goings of men and that made her feel better somehow.

'Welcome to Raigne House, Biddy,' Gideon said as he drew the horses to a halt on the neatly raked carriage sweep and jumped down to help them down to solid ground.

'Coo, it's big, ain't it, Mr Gideon?' she said as she stood looking at the place as if it might develop a voice of its own and tell her to go away immediately.

'True, but it's also a home.'

'Not for the likes of me, though, is it?' she replied, and Callie wondered if it had been fair to bring the girl with her, after all.

'Come now, Biddy,' she said bracingly, 'would you rather have stayed at Cataret House and waited for the next tenant to take over?'

'Oh, no, miss. I want to stay with you, but people who live in a place like this will know I'm no lady's maid. You'd better send me round to the kitchens.'

'No, you took the job I offered and I need you,' Callie said. 'You will soon grow into your new tasks, as I must into mine.'

'If you say so, miss, I mean, my lady,' Biddy said with a harassed look at the boxes strapped to the back of the coach and another at the great front door as it opened and a very solemn butler came out. 'Shall I have to unpack for you, my lady?' she asked before he was close enough to hear.

'If you please, I don't want some smart housemaid looking down her nose at my humble wardrobe.'

'No, of course you don't, my lady. I suppose there's books and things about looking after a proper lady's clothes and whatnots, ain't there? Someone in this great place will be able to help me with the long words, won't they? You'll be far too busy to help me now, but I'm that glad you taught me to read, Miss Sommers because there's a book about most things, ain't there?'

'Of course and that's a very good notion of yours. I shall send for an appropriate one as soon as I can,' Callie said soothingly and turned to meet the butler's stern gaze with nearly as much trepidation as Biddy.

'I'd love to know what a lady's whatnots are,' Gideon whispered, and Callie laughed, then relaxed a little. 'You were quite right to insist on bringing your protégée with us,' he added, then turned to meet the ancient retainer as a long-lost friend.

They were conducted upstairs to a vast suite of rooms Callie concluded was the finest guest accommodation in the house. His lordship must have known they were coming because there wasn't a holland cover to be seen, or a speck of dust on the highly polished furniture and gleaming treasures in this glorious old state room. Gideon seemed to have taken a lot for granted in sending word they were coming before she agreed and she must point that out to him when they were alone again if she wasn't to develop into a mouse-like woman. Now she had to hide an impulse to follow Gideon into his splendid bedchamber instead of meekly heading for her own, because at least he was familiar in all this stateliness. The loss of him at her side brought back all her fears of losing herself in this vast old barn of a place in more ways than one.

'There's a bath being got ready for you in the dressing room yonder, Lady Laughraine,' Biddy informed her. 'You ain't half going to be clean, ain't you, miss?' she added, then realised she'd forgotten herself again. 'Blessed if I'll ever remember, my lady,'

'Blessed if I will either, Biddy, now please

shake out my best muslin and find a clean chemise and petticoat for me.'

'Yes, miss. I mean, my lady.'

'Don't leave me alone, will you, Gideon?' Callie asked an hour later as they met up in their vast sitting room ready to go downstairs and meet her grandfather in his own lair.

'What, never?'

'Idiot, I mean until I learn the way of the house, but on the other hand please don't leave me alone with his lordship, ever.'

'Difficult, he's been living for the moment you would agree to see him and make peace.'

'I can't see why. I'm a reminder of what should have been if I was born to his daughter-in-law instead of the Vicar's unwed daughter. He has to be ashamed of me.'

'No, but he is ashamed of what his son did to you and your mother.'

'How do you know?'

'Because I asked him about what happened back then and he told me. We have stayed in contact, since I saw no reason to cut myself off from him and he wanted to stay close to you by proxy. Not that I was close to you in any way or could tell him anything about you, since you told me I sickened you and you loathed me with every fibre of your being and never to contact you again.'

'I didn't, you know that now, but we must forget what my aunt did before it drives us mad.'

'I can't, Callie, any more than I can forgive what she's done, so please don't ask that of me next. Suffice it to say, Lord Laughraine and I thought you must be throwing his letters on the fire as well as mine and he's been too afraid of stirring up a past you found intolerable to ride over and demand you speak to him. He says he and his did enough damage to you and yours, but your aunt must bear a great deal of the blame for all of it, though, don't you think?'

'Yes, but does he truly think that?'

'Which bit are you wondering about being untrue this time?'

'I deeply regret not suspecting my aunt was destroying my letters and challenging her version of the truth, Gideon, but does his lordship really want to know me?'

'Of course he does, he's not the sort of man who judges a child for something they are completely innocent of. I'm a far greater obstacle to Christian forgiveness than you will ever be— he would have every excuse to hate me, given how the succession stands, but he can't even manage that, so just give him a chance, Callie. I promise you he's nothing like the ogre you seem to have made of him in your imagination.'

'I'm beginning to see that. For years I thought he was happy to leave me in ignorance of who I truly was so he didn't have to admit his son was a rake. I know we weren't going to talk about Aunt Seraphina, but she does intrude into our lives even now, doesn't she? Until we understand exactly what she did we can't forget her. She said my paternal grandfather is as proud as the devil and would never openly acknowledge me, but everything she told me was a lie. Yet the poor man's heart must sink at the prospect of me as the only source of Laughraine blood left, unless he's prepared to make an April-and-December marriage and that doesn't seem likely as he's been a widower for over twenty years, does it?'

'No, he was devoted to his wife and seems genuinely happy for us to inherit Raigne one day between us.'

'Who says there can be an us? I'm not sure I can do it again, Gideon,' she asked, panicked by the certainty if she was left alone with him too long she would make a fool of herself and beg to be his true wife again.

'Not yet, maybe, but one day I hope to

change your mind. Meanwhile I'm not made of stone, despite your obvious belief to the contrary.'

'You must be, if you really haven't had a mistress all the years we've been apart.'

'We're back to that again, are we? Very well, if it makes you feel better I'll swear on anything you ask me to that I'm telling the truth. I've been on the rack for you, Callie. In the early days I often couldn't sleep for the lack of you in my bed and at my side. I daydreamed about making love to you when I should have been slaving at my books and stayed working at my first and mostly hopeless cases late into the night because I hated going back to a place I couldn't call a home without you in it. I can't count the number of times I set out to find you because I couldn't stand being alone any longer. Then I'd remember the last weeks when you wouldn't even share a room with me and that infernal letter you say now that you never sent and it would strip me of any hopes or dreams and I'd go back to my law books and do my best to pretend living without you wasn't hell on earth. All I had left of you was those vows to be faithful only unto you and I kept them,' he ended defiantly and no doubt he had, after they parted, since he looked as if the emptiness of those years had been punishment enough for any man's sins.

'I'm sorry for all those wicked, wicked lies she told using my name,' Callie said lamely, reeling at a sight of her wild and passionate young lover fully alive under the cool facade he used to keep the world at bay. 'We were good friends, once upon a time, though, weren't we, Gideon? Perhaps we could be so again,' she added clumsily.

Chapter Nine

'Are you two coming down, or do you intend to camp out at the top of the stairs for the rest of the day?' Lord Laughraine asked from the great hall below them. Callie was touched to see he couldn't wait in some stately room for them to come to him and glad he had interrupted an awkward conversation with Gideon.

'My wife really needs a rest,' he told his honorary uncle, as if her welfare was far more important than protocol. It warmed a chilly corner of her heart to think she was his first concern, even now he was back with his family and clearly very welcome.

She tugged at Gideon's hand and led him towards the stairs to silently show him she had a mind of her own, even if she didn't want to challenge him for fussing over her in public right now. Who would have thought she'd ever be so anxious to meet her other grandfather again, after all her doubts and scruples about her origins? This tug of mixed emotions was pulling her first one way and then another and if she looked pale it was more an indication of her inner turmoil than some physical frailty Gideon had convinced himself she suffered from. She must find a way to prove otherwise soon, but now she was about to meet his lordship as her true self for the first time in her life and she needed all her energy for that.

Could Lord Laughraine really own her as his kin as well as Gideon's wife? She was unsure how she felt about that notion. A week ago she was convinced her aunt was the only member of her family she could rely on, and look how wrong she'd been about her. Now she was torn between wanting to love and trust her paternal grandfather and distrusting his motive for wanting her and Gideon here. Grandfather Sommers had brought her up to see the good in people and this wily old aristocrat was as lonely as she had been in his own way. If she locked up her heart and threw away the key because it was easier than trusting anyone, she would be no better than Seraphina Bartle. She raised her chin as she walked down the grand staircase at Gideon's side, doing her best to look serene and much calmer than she felt.

'If you have had as big a shock as I have today I'm not the least bit surprised you feel exhausted,' his lordship said genially when they were face-to-face. 'Welcome home, my dear. I'm so glad to see you back in King's Raigne with this young rogue again.'

Callie held out her hand, since she wasn't quite sure how to answer him, and Lord Laughraine surprised her by shaking it solemnly, then bowing to her like an old-fashioned gallant. He embraced Gideon as if he'd accomplished something wonderful by bringing her here and all her aunt's assertions a bastard grandchild would never be welcome at Raigne rang hollow. How much damage the wretched woman had done by playing on Callie's insecurities, a goodly few of them caused by her in the first place.

'Thank you for bringing her home, my boy,' he said gruffly as he stood back and seemed to recollect they were standing in a lofty hallway where anyone might chance on them. 'But you should have sent word you were coming sooner so we could receive you in a much more suitable style for my heir and his lovely lady.'

'I agree about Lady Laughraine's beauty, of

course, but bad pennies like me don't turn up every day, do they, my dear?' Gideon said with a sardonic smile that hinted it still hurt him that she had fainted at first sight of him after all those years.

'It is to be hoped not,' she replied tartly. 'One husband is quite enough for me.'

'You asked for that one, my boy,' his lordship interrupted.

'I did, and now we're keeping my lady standing in the hallway, Uncle Charles, whatever can we be thinking of?' Gideon joked with none of the defensive fury he would have shown after being wrong-footed in the old days.

'And here's Mrs Craddock with her bevy of chicks. It's a bit late to line up and make Lady Laughraine run the gauntlet now,' Lord Laughraine greeted his stately-looking housekeeper and a phalanx of maidservants. 'Where's Craddock with his cohort then?' he barked and made Callie feel better about the ritual of the heir's bride having to greet the household ten years after she and Gideon got back from their scandalous wedding.

'He's late as usual, my lord,' Mrs Craddock said repressively, but with a decided twinkle in her acute blue eyes that made Callie think she might be able to live with the formidable woman, after all.

'Here's my great-nephew's lady parched for some of that tea you all seem to set such store by nowadays and we're keeping her standing about in a draught.'

'Even if you were, I would be glad of any breeze on such a hot day, Craddock,' Callie told the now not-quite-so-stately butler as he puffed in at the head of his line of footmen and all the other male servants such a huge old house needed to keep it running smoothly.

'It's gracious of you to say so, Lady Laughraine,' he said with a harassed glance to where the smallest members of his troop were jostling each other as they got into line.

'What a splendid picture you all make,' Callie said in a louder voice and managed to place only her fingertips on Gideon's offered arm instead of hanging on to it with both hands as the enormity of the changes in her life sank in. 'Shall we begin at the beginning and work our way up, Sir Gideon?' she managed to suggest steadily enough as the ranks lined up in opposing lines from youngest up to Mr and Mrs Craddock.

'It's often the best way, Lady Laughraine,' he answered, as if rather amused by this peculiar situation and perhaps that was the only way to deal with being feted as the heir and his wife, considering they didn't really belong here at all.

Callie almost quailed when Mr and Mrs Craddock turned, ready to head down the serried ranks of servants and introduce them one by one. All those years ago when she used to come here with the Sunday School at Christmas she remembered being sure Craddock was more important than the owner of this vast, echoing house and Mrs Craddock must be on a par with the Queen. Now she knew they were slightly less important than that her knees were still wobbling and so much seemed to depend on making a good impression on this huge staff when she must look more like a governess than the possible lady of Raigne, but luckily Lord Laughraine waved them away.

'I hope I know everyone who works for me by now,' he told them and listed them with such accuracy Callie knew she had more to learn than she'd thought.

She was all too conscious of Gideon's presence as they made their way along the lines, feeling guilty about that interrupted conversation. He'd bared a young man's agony and in return she limply offered to be friends? She blushed for her own awkwardness as they reached the end of the line and solemnly shook hands with the butler and housekeeper.

'Perhaps now we could have that tea?' Gideon asked with a glance at her hot cheeks.

'Of course, Sir Gideon,' Mrs Craddock said as if she was worried Callie might not be up to the heat, as well, and the household hastily dispersed. 'Would you like it served in the Little Sitting Room or the Library, my lady?'

Callie tried not to look blank.

'As the Library is on the west side of the house it might be cooler at this time of day,' the woman suggested helpfully.

Callie meekly agreed, then had to rely on Gideon to guide her in the right direction. He belonged here as she never would, but if he had to live here then so must she, she decided stoutly. When he tried to tell her how much he'd missed her she'd panicked and fobbed him off with an offer of friendship. She almost wished she hadn't caught another woman leaving his bedchamber that awful day at Willoughby Manor. Her breath snatched at the remembered horror of seeing Cecily Willoughby all sleepy eyed and ruffled as she closed the door on him with a cat-like smile of satisfaction. Callie knew her mother's stepdaughter wanted her out of the house, but to seduce her husband in order to achieve that end seemed a little extreme now, didn't it? The very thought of them together made her feel sick even now and it was high time she got control of herself again. Gideon and his lordship were watching her as if they weren't quite sure how to cope with whatever ailed her.

'I'm a nodcock to let all that happen after our journey and everything else you have had to endure lately,' Gideon said. 'We will leave you to drink your tea in peace.'

'There's no need. You know I've never been given to wafting about like an invalid, Gideon,' she told him more impatiently than she meant to, because she was so confused by her new life and her feelings for him. 'I taught a bevy of girls their lessons day after day for nearly a decade, so I can assure you I'm more than capable of a journey of less than twenty miles, then meeting his lordship's staff. I shall contrive to stay on my feet for the rest of the day without too much difficulty, as well.'

'I'll leave you two to talk about whatever you have to talk about and find my pack then,' Lord Laughraine said. 'Do you object to dogs, m'dear?' he asked as if she had a right to say yay or nay to them.

'My aunt would never have one in the house, but I always wanted one, my lord.'

'Glad to hear it,' he said, and went off to resume his interrupted morning.

'I didn't mean to snap, Gideon,' she explained before he could use his lordship's exit as an excuse to make his own, 'and I'm not going to faint again, so there's no need to look at me as if I might explode at any moment, you know.'

'Was I doing that?' he asked, and relaxed when Craddock ushered in two footmen and a maid with the tea tray and enough little bits of nothing to feed a small army.

'You're right,' she said as soon as the butler shut the door behind him after a gesture from Gideon to signal they wanted to be left in peace.

'I am?'

'Yes, I wish you'd stop being so exasperating about it.'

'It happens so seldom,' he said with a grin that did those unfair things as she was trying to pour the tea.

'Now look what you've made me do.'

'See?'

'Oh, Gideon, now we're acting like an old married couple, aren't we?' she asked, and why on earth did her tongue insist on tying her in knots at the most inappropriate moments?

'It's what we are, or rather what we should be,' he said with a shake of his dark head as his smile faded and a brooding look took its place when he stared at the shabby boxes he had ordered carried in here.

In truth, she had very little experience of how old married couples were together. Her grandmothers were both dead by the time she was old enough to really remember them and nobody could call her aunt's marriage happy or harmonious. She felt a poignant sadness for the marriage she and Gideon should have learnt to live together these past ten years and for nine of them they had only been apart.

'We have to look at them some time, don't we?' she asked as she followed his gaze with a frown for the missed chances and lonely years the loss of those letters represented.

'Not now,' he said at last. 'I don't think either of us is quite ready yet.'

'We can't ignore them for ever or she will have won,' she cautioned.

'Leave it a day or two for us to settle into who we are now. It won't make much difference, Callie, and I'm not ready to be rational about the betrayal they represent yet.'

Here she was thinking he was almost too rational and yet there was fury and a terrible weariness in his eyes that made her heart thunder because she could see her beloved Gideon there, for all Mr Peters thought he had him so firmly under control. Surely it wouldn't be difficult to love that Gideon and the new one, as well? *No,* her inner wanton whispered, *it could even be delightfully easy. That one was a boy, this is a fully grown man.*

Gideon fought the need to crash his fist into the nearest wall and straightened his fingers before he did serious damage to the fine plasterwork and his wife's serenity. Such a hot blaze of fury roiled inside him that he paced over to glare out of the window until he could speak calmly again. No, calmness was too much to ask, he decided, as the magnitude of what that woman had done washed over him again and a red mist wanted to snuff out the self-control he'd learnt over the past, lonely years apart from his wife and what passed for his family, for a Laughraine who wasn't really a Laughraine at all.

'I should have come to find out why you didn't answer myself, but I was too much of a coward,' he said as his anger turned inward and mocked him for that oversight. 'There's no fool like a painfully young one, is there?'

'I don't know. I was being one myself at the time.'

'That's both of us blaming ourselves then, but going over the past isn't going to help you adjust to your true role in life now, is it, my lady?'

'I admit I don't feel I shall ever be a fit mistress for a great house like this. I'm not equal to your future peers and their aristocratic wives, either.'

'Neither am I, don't forget. I don't much care for all that pomp and social chatter, either,' he said truthfully. 'I want my wife back, Callie. If you decide you can be my lady all well and good and your grandfather will be delighted, but I never expected to inherit Raigne. We can live under any roof you like so long as we do it together.' His whole life hinged on her decision, he decided, with a sick feeling in his stomach she might still find the idea of being married to him again too awful to consider.

'I don't think we can refuse an inheritance like this, can we?' she asked, and at least she hadn't snapped an emphatic *no* back and him and flounced out of the room in disgust.

'I have no right to any of it except through

you. I almost wish I could prove my father was the late Viscount Farenze's son and not Sir Wendover Laughraine's, but if there was evidence Wendover would have used it years ago. All that talk about not lowering his pride to legally disown Virgil Winterley's bastard, once he realised who the boy really was, was made up to save face. He'd have done it in the blink of an eye if there was even a sniff of proof he was cuckolded so neatly he never suspected until it was too late.'

'I always thought your grandmother quite wicked to seduce a schoolboy like that. Lord Farenze was much too young to seek an affair with a woman old enough to be his mother,' Callie pointed out.

'True, but Sir Wendover was a harsh and sometimes violent man. I dare say he gave his wife every cause to stray, but no opportunity. Watching a young Adonis run tame about Raigne that summer must have tempted her to take a lover even her husband didn't suspect, don't you think? According to my uncle she was still a celebrated beauty well into middle age and I doubt my grandfather had the poise or maturity to resist her if she set out to seduce him.' The detail of his father's birth was something he did his best not to dwell on, but she was quite right. 'I don't know why I'm trying to defend her, though, because you're quite right. It was unforgivable to use a boy to take revenge on her husband, but how could she care so little for her son? She left my father to find out who he really was when he was not quite a man. Little wonder that he never recovered.'

The constant tension and bitterness of his childhood reminded him how far the shadows of that long-ago sin reached, but he wasn't the angry young man with parents who hated each other now. Being a churlish and rootless young cub lost him everything nine years ago and she had a right to know all he did about his father's birth. Not talking about such things had cost them too much last time. 'Lady Virginia believed in her husband, so I shall have to, as well. My grandfather told her of his first affair before they married since he was ashamed of it, but he swore he only realised my father was his get at the same moment everyone else did.'

'Did you know that she came to see me, your Lady Virginia? I don't think she had it in her to beg, but she did order me to relent and forgive your sins, both real and imaginary, and I refused to listen. Now I see that she must have been speaking from bitter experience, although I was so sure such a legendary beauty never had a real rival for her husband's affections. Lady Virginia would have had some very sharp questions for him to answer before she let him adore her again when they found out he had a son, though, wouldn't she? Especially considering they were not blessed with children of their own.'

'I didn't know anything about her finding you and giving one of her infernal lectures, Callie. She never said she'd met you face-to-face. I suppose even if you had written me a scorching rebuke for sending her, I wouldn't have received it, would I?' he managed to joke bleakly.

That chance his patron and step-grandparent tried to make for them felt like a new burden of grief. Lady Virginia loved him, despite all his attempts to cut himself off from any of the softer emotions by the time they got to know each other. She had regally ignored every barrier he put in the way of letting anyone love him after he lost Callie.

'People call me a clever lawyer behind my back, but I was an idiot not to suspect your aunt was stealing our letters until I arrived at Cataret House to find things so very different to how they should have been. I thought a stony silence was your reply to my pleas for any sort of reconciliation you cared to ask for, under any terms you wanted to name. It seemed like your way of making me understand you hadn't the slightest intention of listening to anything I had to say and, after that letter you sent to me through my then employer, Mr Poulson, telling him to make me understand I must never even try to contact you again, I was sure there was no hope for us.'

'I didn't send you any such letter, Gideon, I swear it. I felt raw and betrayed for a long time after we parted, but I would have read your letters anyway and certainly not have closed myself off from you so frigidly as that. I thought your refusal to send any sort of reply to *my* letters meant you were very happy living without me in London with some delighted young woman to make you very comfortable indeed when I had only made you sad and heartsick. I really should have listened to your Lady Virginia, shouldn't I?' Callie said, and it seemed so foolish of his young self to believe she had such cold hatred in her heart for her worst enemy as she had written to him. 'If I had received any of your letters I wouldn't have let you suffer unnecessarily, I would have answered you at the very least.'

'So if everything was as you thought it that

day and I really was unfaithful to you with your mother's stepdaughter, you'd have forgiven me for it in the end, would you?' he asked recklessly, tension twisting at his gut as he waited for her answer. Silence stretched. 'I'm a yahoo to even ask such a question,' he concluded when it went on too long for it to be a yes.

'I can try,' she finally managed and there was that half a loaf again. Why should she forgive him something so unforgivable? And why couldn't he settle for that half loaf and be grateful to have any bread at all after all that happened in the past?

'Drink your tea, Callie, and I'll go and see if your grandfather has found a puppy to chew up those deplorable shoes you were wearing the other day yet. We can talk of impossible things another time,' he managed to say as if his wildest hopes hadn't just fallen round his feet again.

'Gideon, no, you can't leave me sipping tea and wondering what happened,' she protested as he strode hastily away before he said something else he regretted.

'Yes, I can,' he said before he loped out of one of the full-length windows, then escaped from the terrace before she had time to put her cup aside and run after him. 'Oh, hell and the devil confound it, I have to, Callie,' he muttered as he strode towards the lake and launched into a pounding swim through the spring-fed water to wear his hurt and temper and sense of loss out against the indifferent elements. He wasn't a machine; he couldn't cut himself off from his feelings, at least he couldn't now she was here to tug them to life every time he laid eyes on her. 'You failed again, Gideon,' he murmured once he was finally exhausted, and still the hurt of wanting her, needing her in his life and never having her want and need him back pounded in his head like Odin's hammer.

A truly genteel lady left staring into space by her furious husband would take to her bed and remain elegantly exhausted until he grovelled for mercy. Callie dashed after hers, but soon got lost in the maze of ancient knot gardens and elegant parterres and realised she would never find him when he didn't want her to, at least until she knew this place better. Luckily the house was a landmark impossible to ignore, so she found her way back to the terrace and stumbled breathlessly towards the still-warm tea to slump in her chair with all the finesse of a half-empty flour sack. Now her previous soul searching was wasted she had it to do again. Why couldn't she settle for what she could have? Why chase the dream her passionate young lover was truly her perfect knight, faithful to her for life?

He was the man she longed for with every frustrated inch of touch-deprived skin. She wanted him so badly it hurt *not* to say all the yeses she'd had no chance to give him for years, but she couldn't get one past her lips at the right moment, despite longing for him with every fibre of her being. If only Lady Virginia was still here she would have the benefit of a female viewpoint on their situation, whether she wanted it or not. It would be skewed in Gideon's direction, of course, but Callie could see why the unpredictable old lady loved Gideon so much she couldn't admit he would even think about betraying a wife he loved as much as he had her back then. The fact she caught Cecily Willoughby leaving his bedroom in a state of dishabille was damning, though. What reason had the little cat got to lie that he was her lover?

Her gaze shifted to the battered boxes of papers from Cataret House he must have left here for safe keeping. His letters to her must be in there with hers to him. Why not read them and find out what excuse he had for wanting her stepsister when he couldn't get attention from his wife? Whatever they had to say on the subject they should have been in her hand years ago, hoarded under her pillow and carried about with her until they were illegible, even if she didn't act on them and go to London to seek him out as every instinct she had told her she would have done, if he could only persuade her that he still loved her.

She put down the teacup she had only picked up again for the sake of holding something a little bit warmer than she was. She felt cold to her fingertips, but surely that was impossible with the sun at its zenith and the heat unrelenting? Still, she shivered at the thought of that last day at Willoughby Manor and what felt like the end of everything that truly mattered. It would only take a few steps and a little more curiosity to find out what his letters had to say about it.

The leather covering and iron-edged corners of the boxes were battered and worn so the wood underneath showed through here and there. She suspected they once belonged to Grandfather or Grandmama Sommers before her aunt took them over. The Reverend Sommers had been a curate to her grandmother's governess when they met, so either of them could have owned such sturdy but unpretentious items as they moved from place to place until they could finally afford to marry. The fact their travelling boxes were so well used told her it was an agonising wait. No wonder Grandfather didn't want the same for her and Gideon. When they fell in love so young it must have reminded him of his beloved wife and the years they had had to wait to marry.

She was distracting herself from the rights and wrongs of doing this without Gideon. Callie recognised a scuff mark on the lid of the one from the attic where she finally found out what her aunt had been up to all these years. Was that really only yesterday? She flinched from what she was doing when she realised it was two days since she set out for Manydown with no idea Gideon was coming to change everything.

She stepped back from the little trunk that seemed too much like Pandora's box with all the sad secrets of the world inside it. This wasn't right. If they were ever to trust one another with all their secret hopes and passions, she and Gideon must read the letters together. If they never did trust enough for that, what was the point of looking at all? Inside a polite marriage of near strangers it didn't matter if his words had been a plea or a blame to her eighteen-year-old self. Wondering how she could hold back her very self if Gideon demanded his marital rights as a means to pass Raigne on to another generation, she shoved a clenched fist into her mouth to force back a sob.

Lady Laughraine did not sit and weep over tattered boxes full of old letters, or let the world know she was married to a man she couldn't stop loving and nothing would induce her to tell him so. Callie might, in private, but in company she would be my lady, as self-contained and miserly with her emotions as Sir Gideon Laughraine had learnt to be with his.

Chapter Ten

'Well, my boy?' Lord Laughraine greeted Gideon when he was finally fit for company and found the library occupied by its rightful owner again.

'Very well, thank you, Uncle Charles.'

'Hmm, well, you're here. I suppose that will do for now,' his lordship said with a shrewd glance at Gideon's damp dark hair and the bruise by his eye everyone else was pretending not to notice.

'The wonder is I'm not alone. I'm content with that small miracle.'

'Don't be a fool, of course you're not. You can pretend to the rest of the world you're as passionless as an iceberg if you like, but you won't take me in. Wouldn't think half as much of you if you were. The last thing this family needs is a cold fish like my Uncle Wendover,

just look at the mess he made of everything if
you don't believe me.'

'I try not to,' Gideon said with a genuine
smile.

How come he had always felt so close to
this particular Laughraine when they shared
not a single drop of blood? He supposed it was
kinship of the spirit—rather like the one Tom
Banburgh, Marquis of Mantaigne, had had with
Virgil and Virginia. Gideon had tried hard not
to envy his new friend that bond when he had
this adoptive uncle of his to thank for all the
lighter moments of his own early life. He wasn't
quite sure he had always succeeded. Virgil was
his true grandfather and part of him had been
jealous to begin with. In the end Tom's love
for Virgil had opened his eyes to the real man.
Gideon's father had reviled his true father so
often during his childhood that Gideon grew
up thinking he must be a monster. As he ma-
tured logic told him Esmond Laughraine wasn't
exactly a son to be proud of. Finding out what
a fine job Virgil Winterley had made of the
deprived and abused orphan boy Virginia res-
cued from his guardian as a ragged and barefoot orphan had fully opened Gideon's eyes to
his own grandfather's strength and kindness
and banished the spectre of a venal and neglect-

ful beast who had his fun with another man's wife then walked away whistling a merry little ditty. Esmond had built up that myth in his own head to obsess over in his drunken rages and it said a lot more about him that it did about Virgil Winterley.

'I wonder how different our lives would have been if my father took after his mother instead of his sire,' he mused now.

'I doubt Wendover would have noticed if it wasn't so obvious the boy and Virgil could have been struck from the same mould. Most of us Laughraines are dark haired like the Winterleys and Wendover never could see much beyond the end of his nose,' Lord Laughraine observed with a shake of the head for an uncle he clearly hadn't liked. 'He was a hard man, but you know that. I suppose he had good reason to be furious his late wife foisted her love child on him as if she had nothing to be ashamed of.'

'Yet my father didn't deserve to be hated for something that wasn't his doing.'

'Ay, it was a sad mess and Esmond always refused to have anything to do with Virgil, however he had tried to do his duty by the boy and your father did his best to keep you from your real grandfather, as well. Heaven forbid you should love one another and leave Esmond to his bitterness and the brandy bottle. Virginia kept a close eye on you after Virgil died, though. Dashed clever woman, Virginia, bit of a challenge as a wife, I imagine, but Virgil always loved one of those.'

'I must have inherited something from him then, but did Lady Virginia really open doors for me, then make sure they stayed open when I refused to use your family name to further my career? To think I believed I'd made my own way in life all these years.'

Gideon wasn't quite sure why it seemed so important to be independent of every part of his family when he left Raigne now. For that to work they would have to feel the same anyway and for some reason the man he had always called Uncle Charles, although he was officially his father's cousin, had always been ready to own him as the heir. Perhaps Esmond had worn out all the hatred between Laughraine and Winterley? Or maybe none of it mattered if his granddaughter ended up Lady of Raigne?

'All Virginia did was remove an obstacle or two, the rest was up to you.'

'And I'm not sure I want to know what they were.'

'Never mind that now, what matters is what you plan to do next. I'm past my three score years and ten, Gideon, and you two need to learn about the house and estate if Raigne is to flourish when you inherit.'

'I know very little about farming and less about estate management.'

'You do all that juggling with the truth and finding ways round an argument you lawyers use to get round the facts, don't you? A few surly farmers and the odd land dispute won't flummox a man who can hold his own with such slippery rogues as you're accustomed to. You won't be able to slip in and out of the dangerous places you frequent more or less unnoticed now, though, so perhaps it's as well if you put that part of your life behind you now you have a wife again. I need you to stay whole and hale and hearty if you're to keep my granddaughter happy for the next fifty years or so, my boy,' he added with a look that said his lordship kept a far closer eye on him than he had any idea of. 'Can you promise to stop getting yourself stabbed, shot or bludgeoned?'

'You make me sound so inept,' Gideon said lightly.

'Anyone would think you wanted to get yourself killed,' his lordship said with a challenging stare Gideon found hard to meet as he looked back on the hurt and angry boy he'd been nine years ago.

'At one time it seemed an acceptable hazard,' he admitted with a shrug.

'Not to me it wasn't and not to my granddaughter either, whatever the true reason you quarrelled, then sulked about it for so long. Don't you dare rake up all this business between you again and win her back, then go adventuring and risk yourself to some wild fool's bullet or knife. If she doesn't either shoot you or abandon you again for putting her through hell every time you're off on some mad start, I will do it for her.'

'After a threat like that one, I promise to leave Frederick Peters behind as soon as I can, as long as Callie doesn't throw me out of her life again. If I can't have her, I shall need an occupation desperate enough to stop me putting a bullet in myself.'

'Have you told her so?'

'Not yet. We only met again two days ago and she still doesn't trust me, although she may now trust her aunt even less.'

'So unless she trusts you and believes your side of whatever story that woman cooked up all those years ago, you won't admit you love my granddaughter every bit as madly as you did then?'

'I don't know yet, but please leave us be, Uncle Charles. Think what damage you and Sommers did between you with well-meaning interference last time and let us find our own path through the mess this time.'

'As long as you don't take too long about it and risk her thinking you don't care.'

'Untangling the misunderstandings of a decade takes time and I have learnt patience these last nine years since Callie and I parted, my lord. I suggest you do the same while we find out if we can endure being married again.'

'Oh, very well, but kindly remember I'm not getting younger and marriage is for more than the year you managed last time,' Lord Laughraine said with a resigned sigh. 'None of this matters tuppence ha'penny if you two can't happily run in harness together.'

'No, nothing matters then,' Gideon confessed.

'You weren't a slow-top ten years ago.'

'Ten years ago I thought she loved me.'

'Of course she did, the girl would never have taken such a risk on you if she didn't. You were a damned fool then and you're still one now, but for some reason she wanted you anyway so I dare say the rest of us can learn to put up with you.'

'Now I feel so much better about myself. Thank you, my lord.'

'Don't mention it, my boy. Now pass me another glass of that claret, then go and find out how that girl of mine is doing. I dare say she needs rescuing from one of Mrs Craddock's grand tours of every linen cupboard in the house by now.'

'Yes, my lord. Is there anything else I can do for you, my lord?'

'Can't think of it right now,' Lord Laughraine said as regally as the Prince of Wales. He raised the refilled glass to his lips to hide a smug smile and nodded in mock dismissal as Gideon went off to do as he was bid for once.

A soft knock on the door between one vast bedchamber and the next made Callie jump as if she'd just been prodded with a sharp stick. Surely Gideon wasn't going to demand his marital rights so soon after getting her to share this lovely, lofty and yet somehow intimate old suite of rooms with him? Her heart had done that familiar thump then race the moment Mrs Craddock told her there was no need to feel alone in such a vast space since her husband's room was just next door.

'Come in,' she managed to call as steadily as if she wasn't tempted to leave by the other door before he could open the one his side.

'Don't worry, I only want to know if you're feeling better,' he said softly as he entered on such silent feet she wondered again how he'd learnt to move so stealthily and, more importantly, why. 'Mrs Craddock suspects you have a headache.'

'I just wanted a little peace,' she admitted truthfully. 'Raigne is very beautiful and full of history and treasures beyond my wildest dreams, but I'm not in the frame of mind to appreciate it somehow.'

'I really have turned your world upside down, haven't I?'

'Well, of course you have, Gideon, isn't that what you intended?'

'Who knows?' he said, playing that infuriating trick of retreating into his thoughts. Since he was looking about as blank as a man could without actually being asleep, he must be fighting feelings he didn't want her to know about again. 'Nobody could say you were delighted to be my Lady Laughraine, could they?'

'No,' she confirmed shortly. 'Mr Winterley

called you Peters at the toll gate this morning, Gideon, so I must be Mrs Peters, as well, mustn't I? Has that been your alias all these years?'

'One of them,' he said cautiously, but he must have seen her mouth tighten at the thought of more secrets and he held up a hand to admit he was being defensive. 'Yes, then, but I use others to go places even Peters can't go. I have lived as Frederick Peters since we parted and Sir Gideon Laughraine would be torn apart in some parts of the underworld where Sir Wendover Laughraine made his name. My supposed grandfather was a ruthless, corruptible man, Callie. I should be glad that I stand very little chance of taking after him.'

'Is that why you stopped using his name?'

Gideon shrugged, then seemed to recall she had a right to know more than anyone else. 'I'm not entitled to it and I was tired of the lie. You didn't want me under any name, so it hardly mattered what I called myself.'

'Yet here you must endure the name you were born with, must you not?'

'Yes, since it's the one you took when you married me.'

'If I was born on the right side of the blanket it would have been mine by right,' she reminded him clumsily, but perhaps it was as well to get this tired old subject over and done with and hope they could move past it to something better.

'Well, I certainly didn't get it that way. Does that mean you resent me for bearing the name you ought to have had if your parents had married each other?'

'Of course I don't. Neither of us could help things that happened before we were born and I'm female, anyway. You would be the heir even if my parents had made me legitimate.'

'Not if they had had more children and one was a boy,' he pointed out with a mocking smile.

'Well, of course not, but they didn't and you are Lord Laughraine's heir whether you like it or not,' she told him, with a militant nod. 'My grandfathers went to great lengths to make sure the succession was wrapped up right and tight,' she reminded him, then wished she hadn't as that blank look came between them again.

'The estate could still end up in Chancery if the Prince chooses to challenge me,' he said, as if talking about an abstruse legal problem that had nothing to do with him.

'But you're the heir and I'm the last heir's

only child, even if I am a bastard, so he can't do anything.'

'Not if we are reunited,' he said, looking at the naked ring finger of her left hand.

'I gave my rings back to you. Produce them and I'll wear them again,' she challenged.

'When you're my wife again, I will,' he parried.

'We both know there's more to marriage than four legs in a bed, Gideon,' she reminded him even as hot colour bloomed in her cheeks and her most intimate memories reminded her how satisfying it was to share a bed with her lover.

'Don't be vulgar, Lady Laughraine,' he cautioned with a cynical smile that told her he'd spent too much time with the likes of Mr Winterley over the past few years.

'And don't pretend you're a prude, Sir Gideon,' she snapped back.

'This really is the most unlikely conversation, Callie,' he said with a real smile that threatened to leave her spellbound all over again. 'Two days ago I was a stuffy lawyer and you were a very proper schoolmistress, and now look at us.'

'I'm still dressed like a governess and you are a fine gentleman,' she pointed out.

'Tomorrow I will send a messenger to the

finest dressmaker in London with your measurements and a slavish description of your colouring and all the other perfections a besotted husband can boast about,' he promised, 'but you still don't look like any governess I ever came across,' he added huskily.

'Lady Laughraine is a married woman, so at least she can go about looking a little less buttoned up than Miss Sommers could in this heat,' she admitted as she fought a silly compulsion to do them up again, in case he didn't like what he could see of her.

'We're alone in Lady Laughraine's rather splendid bedchamber, Callie, you can go about it in nothing at all if you so desire,' he replied hoarsely.

'Would you desire me so?' she heard herself say, as if a siren had taken over her mouth and was determined to get her into trouble she wasn't ready for quite yet.

'I would desire you if you were dressed in armour from head to toe and fenced about with a hostile army, but you should be very wary of playing with fire, my lady.'

'I should,' she murmured so softly he bent his head to hear, or at least that was the story she told herself. 'I am,' she added even more quietly, and felt his breath on her lips as she slicked them nervously with her tongue and his gaze went molten.

'Quite right, too,' he affirmed so softly that they needed to be closer still. There, his mouth on hers. Firm and yet so gentle it almost brought tears to her eyes. She felt warm right into places that had been frozen ever since he left. Her breath gasped in and then stuttered out. This was her lover, her young love. Gideon was kissing her again and how had she lived without him for nine long years?

'You're right about the fire,' she managed to say as he raised his teasing mouth the sliver of an inch so they could breathe. Desire was simple enough, yet complex as the deepest labyrinth. This, though? This was far more than desire and she hardly dared find a name for it so she stopped trying as her senses searched for all that was her Gideon and unchanged and everything that was a new one and even more intriguing.

'How unexpected of me,' he joked, and this time she could feel the smile against her mouth before he took that kiss deep again and her very toes tingled. She could have sworn lightning flashed right through her and into him, or was it the other way round?

She gasped as another jag of heavy longing heated her beyond anything as simple as plain fire. Breathing in the scent of him, the sharp combination of shaving soap, clean linen and unique essence of pure Gideon she had deprived herself of for so long, she hummed with pleasure. So she forgot how it felt to say no to either of them, welcomed the heady thrust of his tongue with a moan to say it had been too long since they feasted on each other.

Now his fingers shook as he ran touch along her jaw, played with a stray curl of her raven-dark hair. Then he found the silken skin just behind her ear where he knew she was most seducible and used it to drive her even wilder. Her lover. Here was her lover and he knew every inch of her. Exhilaration coursed through her because he was back with her, kissing her, seducing her with all he was and all they could be on his lips and in her heart. The feel of his racing heartbeat under her hand said he was as caught up in the wonder of it as she was. Raising her hands to loop them round his neck and demand more and deeper, she heard bells ring and shook her head in puzzled denial. Thunder might crash through their veins, hot lightning was definitely trying to sheet through her as she shook with years of pent-up need and an-ticipation, but what had bells to do with their lovemaking?

'They tells me that's the dressing bell, miss, I mean m-my lady...' Biddy stuttered to a halt as she realised exactly what she was interrupting. Her face was a picture of such horror Callie had a hard time biting back a hysterical giggle. 'Oh, lawks, miss, that's just why I should be in the kitchen and not up here,' she said, and went to dash off and ask for something more like her old job back.

'Don't go, Biddy, your lady has need of you if we're to be ready in time for dinner,' Gideon said sharply.

After one huge gasp of protest he sounded as if he was used to being caught making love to his wife every day of the week and Callie jumped back as if she'd been stung instead of kissed within an inch of ecstasy.

'Indeed,' she managed, a little less smoothly, but if she refused to look at either of them she could push all that glory into the back of her mind, as well. 'Order some hot water brought up as soon as you can and lay out the good soap if you please, Biddy,' she said quite in the grand manner. Maybe she could be her ladyship, after all.

As Gideon stepped back with a shrug that

said goodness knew what, she wondered if she could be his lady, though. She didn't have it in her to cut off her emotions and parcel them up for the odd moment of sensuality before they set about the business of making heirs for Raigne House and its attendant acres. Still the inner heat and her heart racing and that rush of delirium in every part of her argued otherwise.

'After I have changed I will wait for you in our sitting room,' he said with that unreadable expression back on his face.

He refused to meet her eyes and let her see what he was thinking, so what else did she have to work with but the miserly part of himself he was granting her? 'No, please go down and join your uncle. I will be as quick as I can.'

'Very well, my dear,' he said, and gave her the sort of nod he might give any lady of his acquaintance, then he left before she could lose her own much less steady self-control and throw something heavy and breakable at the door as it closed after him.

'Oh, well done, Gideon,' he murmured to himself once he was safely through that devilish connecting door and safely on the other side. 'Your wife will feel so much better about being alone with you now,' he added and only had to picture her dishevelled and delicious and blushing like a schoolgirl to know he was a crass and lusty fool.

Idiot boy, she's a woman, not some Gothic heroine, he almost heard Lady Virginia's voice say, as if she might be sitting atop the cornucopia over the great canopied state bed when she was clearly busy enjoying her heavenly rest and being reunited with her adored husband at long last.

'Much you know,' he told a woman who wasn't there. If a mad doctor was about he might as well commit himself to his care and save himself weeks of torture while Callie decided whether or not she wanted a husband again or not.

Said you were an idiot, didn't I? Ought to know by now that her pride will keep her from admitting anything of the sort after you bungled that so badly.

'Oh, be quiet, woman, as if I need a ghost to tell me I'm a fool now when I know it perfectly well,' he told thin air as he strode about the room in a desperate effort to get his ridiculous body under control. The fact of his wife a room away and that reach halfway to heaven in her arms had him in such a state he was currently an embarrassment to both of them. He had a whole evening of frustration to get through without Winterley's knowing grin telling him what a lust-driven fool he was for Calliope, Lady Laughraine, all the time and a blush of embarrassed consciousness heating her cheeks every time she dared look his way.

If I didn't love your grandfather so much I might give up on you, Gideon Laughraine, that unreal echo of Lady Virginia informed him crossly. *With your share of Virgil's looks and a pinch of his charm it shouldn't be totally beyond you to win your wife back before it's too late.*

'What do you mean too late?' he gasped, a catch of fear in his gut for Callie's safety.

He glared about him as if he might still manage to surprise her late ladyship's shade perched on a window seat or lurking in a dark corner, but the room was serene and quiet and all he could hear now was his own quickened breathing. Any sense he wasn't completely alone had gone and he quartered the room like a dog chasing shadows before he chided himself for listening to a wild part of his own imagination. He breathed in deeply and made the effort to calm himself down all over again.

'Dratted contrary female,' he muttered darkly about a ghost he couldn't let himself believe in. 'Loving me didn't do Callie much good last time, so why on earth would she risk doing it again?' he said like a child whistling in the dark to convince himself.

A marriage of convenience was all he could expect now, he supposed. He was certainly done with chasing impossible dreams, and from her reaction to his arrival at Cataret House she wasn't exactly enamoured of him, but years of bitter regret made the dream he could have seem rosy enough, if it ever came true. A shaft of evening sunlight fell on the tapestry of a long-ago lady holding court and looking none too pleased with her adoring knights, 'Know how you feel,' he informed one dejected and lovelorn example and shook his head at his own folly. Then he went to his dressing room to wash and shave once more, then hurry into his evening attire so he could go and find some company to distract himself from his ills until his wife was free to disapprove of him again.

Chapter Eleven

'Lady Laughraine, what a pleasure it is to see you again,' Mr Winterley exclaimed the instant Callie stepped inside the small drawing room after a hasty wash and changing into yet another plain muslin gown Biddy had managed to iron creditably under Mrs Craddock's patient instruction.

'It would certainly be one for Lady Laughraine's husband if he could see past the prattling rogue standing between him and his lady right now,' Gideon said grumpily, and Callie's fickle heart raced again at the very sound of him. At least jealousy had jolted him out of his chilly lawyer's persona and made him sound like a husband again, so she smiled at the rogue graciously because that certainly felt like a favour.

'Good evening, my lord, Gideon and it is Mr Winterley, isn't it?'

'A very good evening to you, my dear, this old place seems brighter now you're back here with this scapegrace nephew of mine at last,' Lord Laughraine greeted her, and she was touched by his attempts to fit her into his household as his heir's wife, instead of a scandal waiting to happen. 'You appear to be blooming again after your rest, despite my staff and this restless nephew of mine doing their best to wear you to a frazzle. I told them to leave you to settle in at your own pace, but I might as well have saved my breath.'

'Thank you anyway, my lord, you are very kind,' she said with a smile for her secret grandfather she couldn't make stiff or chilly in the face of his genuine welcome.

He seemed happy to let her set the pace of their relationship, or maybe he didn't want to acknowledge her and rake up the past and who could blame him? Except without the facts of her birth coming out, Gideon's claim to Raigne was weak. She wished the whole business was pared down to a husband and wife finding out if they could live as that, but years of loneliness had taught her to take life as it was rather than longing for an elusive ideal.

'Lord Laughraine might be, but I'm not,' Mr Winterley interrupted her thoughts with an extravagant bow she suspected was meant to infuriate Gideon. 'You look more enchanting tonight than you did this morning, Lady Laughraine.'

'And I suspect you of being a flatterer, Mr Winterley,' she said coolly.

'Would that I was, my lady, but since you're wed to this unworthy and secretive fellow, I must learn to live with the sad fact he found you first,' he said with a wicked smile she ought to distrust.

'Are these what are commonly called town manners, Mr Winterley?' she asked with a wry smile, because it was heady to be lied to extravagantly by such a dashing gentleman.

'No, my lady, a sign I have good eyesight and the sense to know a diamond of the first water when I see one.'

'Speaking as the man who recognised my wife's unique qualities many years before you set eyes on her, Winterley, I'll thank you to stop flirting with my lady. I'd hate to have to break that arrogant nose of yours, although I really can't imagine why some public-spirited husband hasn't done so already.'

'From the look of you, Laughraine, you resort to pugilism more readily than I do as a matter of course, but perhaps you could persuade Lady Laughraine to own up to you a little more often so fellows like me might not be quite so awed by her beauty before they realise she has an attendant dragon?'

Seeing the underlying challenge between them was only half in jest, Callie moved to stand next to Gideon. 'I believe it's considered polite to overlook a fellow guest's eccentricities in the best circles, isn't it, Mr Winterley?'

'As I rarely move in them, Lady Laughraine, you're talking to the wrong black sheep.'

'Ah, d'you hear a noise outside? Expect that's Finch and his lady arriving for dinner,' Lord Laughraine intervened hastily. 'I trust you don't mind such company so soon after your arrival, m'dear?'

'Of course not, Gra…my lord,' Callie said and almost let the cat out of the bag in front of the far-too-acute Mr Winterley. 'I shall be delighted to see them again.'

Outside company at dinner suddenly seemed a wonderful idea, especially when it was her other grandfather's successor as vicar of King's Raigne and his gentle wife. The living was given to him as he was Grandfather Sommer's curate when Grandfather died. Callie suspected Lord Laughraine had persuaded the bishop to encourage them to stay in the Raigne villages to take some of the burden of a widespread parish off the Reverend Sommers's ageing shoulders when Mr Finch should have been going on to a parish of his own. Whatever the reason they stayed and, when Mr Finch got the living through circumstances he would never have wanted, it proved a popular promotion. It would be hard for even the most cantankerous villagers to dislike him, but it still felt odd for Callie to think of anyone but her grandfather as vicar of King's Raigne.

'My dear, I'm so glad to see you and Sir Gideon back at last. We all missed you sadly and his lordship has been longing to welcome you home again,' Mrs Finch said, and refused to shake hands politely as she gave Callie a motherly hug.

'Thank you, Mrs Finch. It's lovely to see you both and it feels so good to be back,' she replied, not quite ready to add 'where we belong' until she was sure of it herself. 'And, dear Mr Finch, how are you, sir?'

'All the better for seeing you, my dear, although I suppose we must learn to call you "my lady" now Sir Gideon is a baronet, must we not, my love?'

'I don't know about my husband, but I refuse to be called by a mere title when you mended my clothes and skinned knees when I was a child. You saved me many a beating from my aunt for getting into mischief when her back was turned, you must call me Callie and never mind such pomp between such old friends as we all are.'

'Only in private then, Callie,' Mrs Finch allowed with a look that said she considered Mr Winterley family for some odd reason.

'Aye, you're right as usual, my dear. We don't want to be encroaching,' her husband agreed, and Callie smiled and shook her head because she couldn't think of any two people less likely to step over the line.

The arrival of the now middle-aged couple broke the tension in the fine room full of mellow evening light and they chatted about hot weather and storms and the prospects for a good harvest. Even Mr Winterley forgot he was a sophisticated town beau and joined in the talk of a far smaller world than the one he was used to. Then Craddock came to tell them dinner was ready and they filed into the small dining room to an impromptu feast instead of the small family dinner they expected.

'I couldn't stop them, m'lord,' Craddock said dolefully as every luxury Raigne could command at short notice was brought in. 'You know how it is when a bevy of females get an idea in their heads.'

'Aye, well, I suppose our widows and pensioners will eat well tomorrow and for the rest of the week. Tell them they were quite right to make sure everyone can celebrate the return of my heir and his wife, but perhaps you might remind them Sir Gideon and Lady Laughraine are but two slender people when it comes to making preparations for feeding them in future,' Lord Laughraine said with a rueful look at the groaning board.

'I'm sure I can rein them in tomorrow, but they would insist on a feast to welcome Sir Gideon and his lady home.'

'Have you been dining on husks like the Prodigal Son for the last few years then, Laughraine?' Mr Winterley asked Gideon mockingly.

That trick he had of quirking one dark eyebrow made him look more cynical than usual, but who did it remind her of? Callie leapt to what should have been an obvious conclusion the moment she first set eyes on the man and almost gasped out loud. He was an inch or so taller than her husband and a year or two older, but standing side by side they could be brothers. Of course, the family name of Viscount Farenze was Winterley, wasn't it? This stranger

was Gideon's cousin on the wrong side of
the blanket, so what on earth was he doing
here?

Mr Winterley didn't seem like a man swayed
by family feeling, or altruism towards his fellow beings. Whatever his motives, why had it
taken so long for her to realise he was Gideon's
kinsman? Now she did she could see they were
as dark as one another. They shared a natural elegance and grey eyes set under strongly
marked dark brows. Their noses were Roman
enough to look haughty at times, but that was
where the likeness ended. Gideon's eyes were
kinder and he seemed less severe than his secret cousin.

Wasn't that an odd word to choose for a man
with the manner of a care-for-nobody? She
tested it against what little she knew of him
and, yes, it still seemed to fit. The real Mr Winterley was austere and a little fierce under that
careless charm, and a far more dangerous man
than he'd have you believe. That conclusion told
her two things—first to be wary; second that
Gideon was her touchstone and she judged the
inner life of other men by her husband. She met
Mr Winterley's bland gaze with a challenging
look and he smiled, as if acknowledging he

had his own reasons to be here when Gideon came home, but what they were was a mystery he intended to keep to himself.

'You know very well I haven't, Winterley, I'm surprised you need to ask,' Gideon answered his cousin's double-edged remark. He sounded careless, but the slight trace of a frown he smoothed away before anyone but Callie could see it said he was uneasy about Mr Winterley's unlikely visit to Raigne.

'You might have done before this January for all I know,' Mr Winterley said blandly.

'You may not have acknowledged my existence before then, but you know we lawyers rarely starve in garrets as poets and Jacobins are supposed to,' Gideon replied.

'I usually take care to avoid lawyers whenever possible, but at least they're not as annoying as brooding mountebanks and unwashed revolutionaries. I'm quite prepared to do the polite to either, if you have one concealed about the house of course, my lord, but please don't ask me to join the ladies at lionising either breed.'

'Do you really think us females so easily taken in by dramatic poses or a distracted manner, Mr Winterley?' Mrs Finch replied in her quiet way. 'I doubt Lady Laughraine or I will swoon with delight, even if we come across a real hero whilst in your company.'

'So a hero is like a prophet without honour in his own country, Sir Gideon. You appear not to be very good at crowing from your own dunghill,' Mr Winterley said, as if impatient with his cousin's secrets when he clearly had plenty of his own.

'I'm no hero,' Gideon replied as if it was close to an insult, but Callie saw a faint flush of colour tint his surprisingly tanned cheeks and wondered what he'd really been up to.

'Rich Seaborne and his Lady Freya would disagree with you, and Lord Forthin and his countess, oh, and most of the Seaborne interest, as well, don't you think? They would be a lot less happy today if not for Mr Frederick Peters,' Mr Winterley said as if he was a small boy dropping stones into a still pond simply for the love of making a disturbance.

Callie thought his reference to Gideon in association with the illustrious Seaborne clan and their web of aristocratic connections could be pure mischief, or a warning to her husband that he couldn't keep one side of his life away from the other any longer.

'None of that called for any great heroics on my part. Mine was mainly a supporting role and came about by chance,' Gideon said repressively, as if he didn't care to talk about it.

Callie made no attempt to set up a polite buzz of small talk with Mr and Mrs Finch to oblige him, because the slightest hint of what he'd been up to all this time felt precious.

'Come now, Winterley, you've told us enough of a tale to make us curious and now we're intrigued. First we'll dine, then I think we could eschew our brandy, gentlemen, or take it into the drawing room if the ladies permit? You can tell us the whole tale over our teacups,' Lord Laughraine said jovially and neatly spiked Mr Winterley's guns

Callie tried to do justice to Cook's feast, but her attention wasn't on her dinner. Her husband was good friends with the grandson of a duke and maybe the current Duke of Dettingham, as well, was he? Gideon belonged to a powerful family, was heir to another and had been hobnobbing with the great and the good. Now he encouraged a light flow of polite conversation, did his best to coax her into eating more than she wanted to and all she really wanted from him was a hint of who was really behind all those shifting personas of his and what that passionate kiss had meant to both of them.

'No more,' she said, shaking her head at the

peach he was about to slip on to her plate piece by piece. 'I couldn't eat another thing.'

'You're too pale,' he murmured as if he had been far more conscious of her every mood during this rather odd dinner than she had any idea of.

'Not from lack of food and it's just been that sort of a day somehow,' she told him clumsily, and his expression froze as if he thought that kiss part of the reason she had found it a little too much. 'You must admit it was eventful,' she added and somehow made bad worse.

He gave her a faint, polite nod, as if listening to a stranger he hadn't taken to and turned away to speak to Mrs Finch on his other side. Their tentative accord felt fragile as gossamer all of a sudden and why did she have to be so inept at expressing her feelings to the person they mattered to most? Wasn't a convenient arrangement a better future than the one she had woken up to every morning before he came? She flinched at the idea of going back to loneliness, then felt Mr Winterley's cool, assessing glance on her. Shocked by the perception in his hard green-grey eyes she tried to blank her own. If he wasn't such a detached and uncaring gentleman, she might almost believe he was challenging her not to hurt his secret cousin.

Could it be he cared about Gideon under that cynical detachment? It warmed her heart a little to think one member of his family was prepared to stand at his back if he needed it, but she took a second look and decided she wasn't quite sure she would want this dark knight behind her in any fight—in front where she could see him perhaps, but not with the most vulnerable part of her trustingly unguarded. Maybe she imagined that moment of brotherhood, maybe she was wronging a man who did his best to be unknowable. One thing was for certain, though: she felt nothing for this man who was so like Gideon, yet so different under those dark good looks. She raised her chin in a silent challenge to mind his own business and let them work out their futures without his interference.

'My nephew has eschewed the bottle, Finch, and you don't indulge, so I'm happy to restrict myself to tea tonight,' Lord Laughraine said genially when it was obvious nobody could eat another thing. 'I'll get Craddock to bring the decanters to the drawing room if you'd like to join us, Winterley, or you can stay here in peace and quiet with your port.'

'I'll give my luckless head a night off from dissipation, my lord,' Mr Winterley said, and

Callie thought he was laughing at himself this time.

A casual observer might think Mr Winterley the perfect gentleman, but shouldn't a cynical beau like him be paying court to the beauty of the moment, attending mills, racing curricles or leading young cubs astray, instead of dining with two soberly married couples and a lord old enough to be his grandfather in the country?

'Well then, my boy, what have you really been up to whilst trying to fool me you were busy out-prosing old Poulson on the lawyer circuit?' Lord Laughraine asked as soon as they were settled in the vast small drawing room again.

'Nothing very momentous,' Gideon said as if saying it with enough conviction might make them forget Mr Winterley's hints to the contrary.

'If you don't let those closest to you into your confidence, Laughraine, the truth will come back and bite you,' that gentleman informed him with a frown that confirmed Callie's suspicions his was a deeper and darker character than he liked to pretend, and one who knew a great deal more about her husband than Gideon liked known.

'And if I do I will be betraying the personal

affairs of some fine people who have since become my good friends,' he protested with a very straight look for his cousin that said this was all his fault, which it was, she supposed, as she listened eagerly for the story Mr Winterley was about to force out of him.

'As they are your friends they must trust you. Tell your family and your good friends here, man, or you might lose everything you hold most dear all over again. I am quite sure anything you may confide in them will go no further and I already know it so you can't hide your adventures from me and I haven't broadcast them in the streets so far, have I?'

Before Mr and Mrs Finch could get up and declare themselves beyond the scope of family, Gideon seemed to decide these particular cats couldn't be put back into the bag now he was more likely to mix with the *haut ton*. He waved them back into the seats they were already half out of and on the point of calling for their gig.

'Winterley is right for once. You are the least likely people to betray a confidence and I should like you to know what I was about so you are as wary of strangers in the Raigne parishes as I shall have to be if we remain here for long periods of time.'

Callie shivered at his implication dangerous characters might want to pursue Gideon for revenge and listened intently to the tale of Mr Peters's adventures her husband told with a determined counterpoint from Mr Winterley when he did his best to belittle his own part in them. It seemed Mr Richard Seaborne had disappeared to protect his first wife and her child by her first husband and his unlucky family, then they spent six years not sure if the man was alive or dead. The adventures the Seaborne family embarked on to try and find their black sheep; Rich Seaborne's adventures and tragedies as he lost his wife in childbirth and three years later chanced upon a fine lady lost in his forest hideaway, then fell in love with her, seemed a wilder story than any Callie had managed to come up with for her books. She was spellbound by the tale and eager to hear the rest of it from one of the Seabornes and sure Gideon had underplayed his part in the happy endings they all seemed to have enjoyed since.

'Oh, my dear Gideon, what an extraordinary tale you have to tell, but what risks you have taken with yourself,' Mrs Finch said as if stronger words might be excusable, but she couldn't come up with them.

Gideon looked sheepish, as if he'd been caught out in something reprehensible, and Callie ached to walk into his arms and tell him otherwise. He had been her hero at eighteen, but it seemed he'd been rashly determined to rescue a good few people from their dragons since then and she wasn't there to try to stop him taking such risks.

'My boy, I'm glad I didn't know the half of it whilst it was going on, or I'd have had you kidnapped and brought back here myself years ago,' Lord Laughraine added in a low, shocked voice that sounded as shaken by the dangers Gideon had faced as Callie felt.

Gideon was staring at her, as if her reaction was the only one he really wanted to hear and she simply didn't have words to let him know. She shook her head numbly and held his gaze with fear and pride in his reckless bravery in her eyes as she did her best not to shake or cry out at the chances he'd taken and how often he could have got himself killed. How many injuries had he suffered that even Mr Winterley hadn't managed to find out about? And then there was the awful suspicion it was her fault he had so little regard for his own skin; that he thought she meant all that nonsense she had spouted on their last day together. She recalled a hysterical rant about it being better for her if he was dead or had never been born rather than see him betray her with her mother's step-daughter.

'I...I... Oh, Gideon, how could you think such a thing? I didn't mean a word of it,' she blurted out in the weak voice she recognised with horror from the day he came back to her and she fainted at his feet. She must be about to do something equally foolish to have said that in front of her grandfather and Mr Winterley.

Gideon looked blank for a moment, which was a good sign, wasn't it? If he had listened to her half-crazed ravings that day, and carried them into every one of those quixotic adventures with him, he would have known what she meant straight away. Then he seemed to cast his mind back to that awful day, as well, and shook his dark head as if she should never have thought up such a silly notion.

'No, it wasn't that. One thing just led to another and I could help, you see? That was all it was, I promise you.'

He understood. Thank heavens for that. She looked up to find her grandfather's eyes on them and realised he did, as well. Goodness knew how, when they might as well be speaking in code. Luckily the Finches and Mr Winterley were making themselves tactfully busy, talking of reforms that needed to be made to the law and better enforcement of it, to notice the byplay between her and Gideon, or they had decided it was none of their business. Lord Laughraine went to join them and stoke the fire as best he could until the two of them had finished washing their dirty linen almost in public.

'Never mind the past,' she managed with a shrug that said it did matter, but she was determined to concentrate on now. 'Promise you'll stop now?'

'That depends on you, don't you think?' he asked bleakly.

'Oh, unfair,' she protested, the tear and fire of her own hot temper threatening to break through her terror at what he had been doing with that whipcord strong body and stubborn, brilliant mind these past few years, when he ought to have been with her. 'And unworthy of you, Sir Gideon,' she added with as much dignity as she could muster when the shock of him risking so much was still making it impossible for her to stand and face him on shaky legs that were sure to let her down.

His gaze was sombre, as if to tell her if they failed at marriage again he couldn't make a promise to stay at home and mope. 'Yes. I'll stay here,' he said with a heavy sigh, as if it was a vow he made very reluctantly indeed.

'Lord Laughraine needs me even if you don't,' he added quietly.

'I'm here, aren't I?' she challenged, because she wouldn't be if she didn't intend to try.

Nine years of letting herself drift without him said trust wasn't one of her strongest suits, so how could she sit here and blame him for lack of faith in her? There had to be a way of keeping her passions under control and loving him from a distance, as a polite couple who agreed to be together for the sake of Raigne and all those who depended on it. Yet it was a poor little shadow of what might have been if the early promise of their marriage hadn't withered away. Didn't a hero deserve someone better than a coward as his mate?

'Why are we arguing about something neither of us wants to happen as if it already has, Gideon?' she asked, still avoiding meeting his acute grey and green gaze because she couldn't let herself admit she still loved him and risk his eyes growing cold and a look of distaste flitting across his handsome face.

'Because we're overtired and intent on running before we can walk?' he offered as if he knew that wasn't it.

'I apologise, my lord, I must be more weary from the road and all these festivities than a self-respecting Corinthian ought to admit to,' Mr Winterley said after an artistic yawn he might be trying to disguise, if he was tired at all, which Callie doubted

'I keep country hours nowadays,' Lord Laughraine interrupted with an intent look that told Callie she looked as wan as she felt. 'Now Finch and his lady have called for their gig and Winterley has been overcome by a rare attack of tact, I shall seek my bed if you two lovebirds will excuse me,' he added with a strong dose of irony Callie tried not to hear.

'I never truly kept anything other than country hours, my lord,' she replied with her best attempt at a smile after a demanding day.

'Once I could dance all night long, then happily come home with the dawn and still be about the estate of a morning as if I'd slept the sleep of the good all night long, but my own Lady Laughraine did love a party, God rest her soul. Consider my house your own and stay awake all night long if you choose to, Gideon, but I'm for my bed. Glad to see you home, my boy, and happy to welcome Lady Virginia's favourite relation under my roof, Winterley, even if you are a resty young devil and I'm not quite sure how she put up with you.'

'Thank you, my lord, but I have a very noble

elder brother who takes most of the accolades in my family, including the position of Virginia's most favoured relative,' Mr Winterley said with his face impassive as a statue's. Callie saw a little way into his true character at last and felt sorry so much bitterness lay between this man and his half-brother, the current Viscount Farenze, for she supposed he had been trying to help Gideon back into his real life with that intervention tonight, hadn't he?

'It strikes me that you two, as Virgil's great-nephew and Gideon as my cousin, are like two peas shucked out of the same pod, Winterley. You both refuse to see where you're valued most,' his lordship said with a direct look at Gideon.

'How ungracious of us,' Mr Winterley said with a would-be careless shrug, but Callie noticed the hot slash of colour across his cheeks and knew those words had hit home.

'It's more important than a little social gaucheness none of us quite believe in, my boy,' Lord Laughraine told Mr Winterley, then offered his arm to Callie as if he knew her legs still felt uncertain after Gideon's latest revelations.

Gideon looked as if he was about to claim the right to escort her upstairs, but she shook her head, so he turned away looking self-contained as ever and she had to bite back an invitation to accompany him wherever he would like her to go.

'Don't suppose they'll come to blows if we leave them to it, m'dear,' his lordship confided when they were out of earshot.

'I dare say not,' she managed to say calmly enough.

'Might have done so a decade ago, of course, but Gideon's not an impulsive young idiot any more.'

'I never meant to hurt him,' she told him impulsively, glad they were between one floor of possible listeners and another.

'We never mean to hurt those we love, Callie, but being frail human beings we manage it, anyway,' he said as if he spoke from experience. 'There's a corner down here where nobody can hear and I think you need to talk to someone who will try to be impartial.'

'Why must we talk about it now?'

'I don't want my granddaughter under my roof at last and feeling as if she's only here because I can't avoid it. Spare me a few minutes and a hearing for your other grandsire's sake, if not for my own.'

'After the plotting you two got up to all those years ago, I'm not sure I want to.'

'So you let that business fester, did you? I never thought you a coward, my dear, not even when you turned the boy away, then punished yourself as well as him by living with your aunt instead.'

Callie flinched at the idea she had been doing just that. Had she been sleepwalking all these years not to realise what she was doing? 'I didn't care where I lived at first and then I stayed because I wanted to be busy,' she admitted.

Chapter Twelve

〰️〰️〰️〰️〰️

His lordship lit a branch of candles from his night-stick as if this might take some time. They were in an odd-shaped sitting area over the imposing Tudor porch. Callie could imag ine the ladies of the house sitting here to read and embroider in the good light from the huge leaded windows, or waiting with over-stretched nerves for their chosen lover to race up the avenue and beg for their hand.

'Habit can be as destructive as active malice,' her grandfather said with a sad sigh that spoke of one or two of his own he regretted.

'Maybe, but if you disliked the situation so much, why did you never make a move to intervene between myself and Gideon years ago?' she asked curiously.

'I may be a bit of a slow-top, but in the end I learn not to make bad worse. If only I had let your father work out his own destiny, we might have been openly related all this time and he could still be alive. I wouldn't listen to his scruples about marrying the good girl his mother and I picked out as ideal for him when they were in their nurseries. Lady Richenda Brierly was and still is a fine girl and I'm fond of her, but she'd have been happier in a convent if she lived in a Catholic country rather than wedding my boy out of duty to her parents and her maker. We thought we were doing our best for them both and served them a backhanded turn instead. It's my belief they were never truly man and wife, because my Will wouldn't bed a woman who couldn't endure the marital act and the poor girl can hardly bring herself to share a room with a member of my sex under the age of seventy even now.'

'It doesn't excuse what he did to my mother,' Callie argued.

'Nothing could, but he was young and weak and must have had doubts about the marriage they sleepwalked their way into, thanks to their bungling parents. I let his mother spoil him when he turned out to be our only child to survive infancy and lacked the will to deny him very much myself, except a free choice of lifetime partner and bedmate—the one choice he should have made by right. My Will never had to fight for anything, so he buckled at the first sign of opposition and did as he was bid. He might have left your mother to starve if Sommers wasn't a good man who wouldn't turn his back on the girl or her babe. I can't excuse Will for that, but I bear much of the blame.'

'I suppose my mother was ineligible,' Callie conceded, feeling disloyal to her very young mother although Mrs Willoughby seemed to have little feeling for the daughter who must be a constant reminder of her folly. 'Grandfather Sommers was the truest gentleman I ever met, but his family struggled to send him to school, then keep him at college long enough to get his degree. The same with my grandmother, I suppose. No wonder you and Lady Laughraine were not delighted when your son declared his intention to wed the vicar's youngest daughter instead of the titled lady you picked for him.'

'Trouble is he never did. The boy muttered a lot of half-formed excuses about a girl who made him feel a better man instead of a monster. He grew up too late to hold on to what he could have had, d'you see? Regretted it to his dying day, but he hadn't the courage to run off with the girl and risk ending up cast off without a penny to bless himself with. Told me later she insisted she wanted to marry a man with his own income and a tidy estate, but if you ask me your aunt had more to do with that statement than your mother. Seraphina Sommers always had a sly look about her, even as a girl, and she used to pinch the other girls black and blue if they were prettier or better natured than she was. Every girl in the parish was one or the other, so I'm not at all surprised she grew up to be a shrew. Should have realised at the time she was up to something.'

'You could hardly do that if my father didn't tell you who he wanted to marry.'

'Maybe not, but upbringing is a curious business, isn't it? You and your mother had the same home and education as Seraphina Bartle and turned out like chalk and cheese. Gideon's father treated him worse than a mongrel dog, yet he grew up a good and honourable man. Can you honestly see him being weak and spineless enough to desert the woman he loved and their unborn child so he could wed a woman who could hardly endure to touch a man simply because someone told him to?'

'No,' she agreed, feeling she'd been trapped by a very cunning opponent. 'He would have made a dash for the border before anyone had time to realise they were gone.'

'So why do you still blame him for your wrongs, Callie?'

'Because I'm weak like my father,' she said as she got up to pace to the now sightless windows and stare out into the twilight of high summer. 'When my world fell apart I sent Gideon away,' she admitted to the night as she couldn't seem to do so face-to-face. 'He pleaded with me to stay close by, even if I wouldn't live with him any more, but I said no and wanted a new start where I could pretend none of it had ever happened.' Callie thought she heard him move, but couldn't turn round and see reproach in those dark eyes so similar to her own. 'Anything that made me feel better was my concern and I wanted him to suffer and grieve and feel dead inside like me, and I succeeded. So, I don't deserve to be happy, you see? I haven't been so for the last nine years and I don't know if I ever will be now.'

'We could be undeservingly happy together,' Gideon's husky voice suggested from behind her and Callie gasped in horror that he'd heard her.

'After all I've done and said to make you turn away from me?' she asked steadily, eyeing his reflection in the dark glass as he moved closer. Her skin prickled with goosebumps and her nerves shivered in that old familiar dance of sensual awareness, despite the fact she was holding her breath for his reply.

'If I had been stronger back then I would have camped out in the hills when you refused to have me in the house,' he told her as he came to stand beside her. 'We had a lot of growing up to do, though, didn't we, Callie?'

'You appear to have done yours,' she said, and found the courage to turn round and face him again. Lord Laughraine looked almost as shocked as she felt that Gideon had managed to appear without making a sound. She acquitted him of getting her to speak about feelings she would probably have kept hidden if she knew Gideon was there and her grandfather shifted and cleared his throat as if speaking came hard when such raw emotions felt almost tangible in this gracious old corner of the house.

'Time I was in bed,' he said gruffly, and waved away Gideon's offer of help. 'We can talk another day, my dear, but Gideon has waited too long to have his say. Remember that nephew of Virgil's will hear more than you want him to if he can, though, won't you?'

'Goodnight, Grandfather,' Callie said with a shrug and a wry smile to admit it wasn't the best time to call him so with that warning in the air.

'Goodnight, child,' he said huskily and went to his rooms looking as if he thought something momentous had happened today and he was very happy about it.

'I was wrong about him,' she admitted for Gideon's ears only.

'He's pleased as a dog with two tails to have you here, but you're weary half to death and we don't need to talk now if you don't want to. Will you trust me to escort you to your room and help you as best I can, since I heard you tell Biddy not to wait up?'

'Yes, I've been lonely, too,' she agreed with a heartfelt sigh. 'And I do trust you.'

'For now,' he added for her. 'You certainly didn't at Willoughby Manor.'

'Why did you have to remind me of that? I had almost forgotten the real reason we parted all those years ago in my shock at Aunt Seraphina's scheming.'

'All these little, locked places in our lives will wreck us again if we let them, Callie,' he said flatly, and, of course, he didn't relish dragging such a painful subject back out into the open, either.

'Perhaps you're right,' she said with a sigh as

he finally ushered her safely into the lovely sitting room that led off theirs and she wondered if she would ever find her way round this huge old house without a map.

'This suite proves to me how delighted his lordship is to have his grandchild under his roof at long last, Callie, for I certainly never warranted such gracious rooms on visits to Raigne in the past,' he said to lighten the atmosphere between them.

She frowned as she realised he was taking another step back from those who cared about him and refused to let him. 'He loves you, Gideon,' she said.

'Lord Laughraine is a realist. He makes the best of a bad hand.'

'And you think *I'm* blind?'

'What I think is I was too young to make a good fist of what we had and we let it die between us. Your grandfather knows what a poor husband he inflicted on you.'

Callie watched the guarded shine of his eyes in the mellow shadows of the candlelight. She wanted to be aware of every beat of his heart and was curious about each thought in his handsome head, but did she dare let herself care so much for a man who didn't seem to want to love anyone these days? Untrue, he obviously loved Lord Laughraine and she suspected he could be a steadfast and loyal friend, but when she looked back at the wild and passionate boy he had been she longed to find a trace of that pent-up yearning in the man she had helped make him.

'We were painfully immature, weren't we?' she asked as she considered his headlong loving of once upon a time.

'Aye,' he said heavily.

'And now we have grown up apart,' she said sadly.

'Maybe, but I never gave another woman more than a passing look from the moment we two first kissed, Callie. You have to believe me about that, even if you think everything else I have to say is a lie.'

'How can I?' Callie held up a hand to stop him. She recalled the horrifying sight of Cecily Willoughby scuttling away from a half-naked Gideon, all ruffled loveliness and almost guilty, as if it happened only a moment ago. 'I knew it was my own fault even when it happened, you know? I refused to let you share my bed and even my mother warned me a man can't resist temptation for ever. I had to keep you at arm's length because I felt as if I'd break in half if I let you back in. I couldn't tell you that back then, but I have the words to say I wasn't strong enough to let your grief in, Gideon, and I'm sorry.'

'Don't be, I deserved for you to shut me out. You were right not to listen to my abject apologies for saying you manipulated me into marriage at your grandfathers' behest. I was a damned fool to let my wretched father drive that particular wedge between us. He gloated that I'd been used as a stud to put a real Laughraine heir in the nurseries at Raigne.'

'Was that why you listened to me when I insisted on living in London with you?' she asked, feeling a new level of betrayal threaten and wishing it didn't sting so sharply. 'So our child couldn't lie in the Laughraines' cradle and make his twisted tale come true?'

'No, I couldn't endure parting with you, even when it would have been far better for you and the baby to stay in the fresh air and live at Raigne while I continued my education so I could support you properly one day.'

'I wish you'd told me so at the time.'

'You see what I mean about all those petty little secrets that kept us estranged?'

'Some weren't quite so little,' she said bleakly.

'You mean the silly chit who wrecked our

marriage?' he said with a grimace of distaste she still refused to find convincing.

'Maybe we were already floundering, but we would have come about if not for her.'

'Would we, Callie? I would have fought a pack of hungry wolves for you, walked a continent if you had asked me to prove how wrong I knew that tale of my father's was, but you refused to share a meal or a room with me. Then that lying little doxy pretended to be caught in my bed and you believed her. I never laid a hand on her but to push her away, I promise.'

'Her blonde ringlets and wide blue eyes could have taken in a far cannier gentleman than you were then,' she objected weakly, because she couldn't quite let herself see that she had allowed so much time gape between them for the sake of a lie.

Cecily Willoughby had been as lovely as a spring morning back then. Callie had felt so dull and uncaring of anything but missing her baby at the time that she could hardly endure looking at her own face in the mirror. Of course, her husband preferred a lovely and forbidden bedmate to the one the law and the church sanctioned. To believe otherwise would make Gideon's love greater than hers and she couldn't let herself admit responsibility for nine years of empty loneliness.

'Not for me, she was easily as heartless as your aunt and I wouldn't touch her with a nine-foot pole even if I wasn't married to you. If you won't grant me faithfulness, at least credit me with some taste, Callie,' he said coolly, and watched her with that lawyer's gaze of his— guarded, wary and unreadable.

'You blame me for everything, don't you?'

'No, I curse myself for pushing you to let me share that visit to your mother's home with you. I wanted to take some of the hurt and grief and rage off your shoulders, but I'd caused most of it to begin with.'

'No, but I didn't want to share it. I would have to admit you hurt as much as I did and grief was all I had left to give our child, you see? I was a miser with it.'

There, she'd said it at last. She expected his grey gaze to harden and for him to walk away in disgust. He shocked her by nodding as if he understood and staying.

'You were eighteen years old, Calliope. You had lost your grandfather one week and our baby the next and all I could do was drink and damn the devil, then ride out in a temper because I couldn't seem to find the right words to comfort you. If not for that selfish little harpy getting between us, I would probably have broken my neck on one of those midnight rides, or forced my way into your bedchamber to beg to share it and you would have hated me even more.'

'I might not have and I didn't hate you, anyway. I needed to realise you hurt, too—even if I cursed you for being such a reckless idiot in the same breath.'

'I still miss little Grace, you know,' he admitted as if he was embarrassed about it and wasn't that her fault?

He had every right to mourn their daughter and he thought she would resent him for doing just that. How could she have doubted he'd loved their baby, after what they did when she died? He was her fellow conspirator against the laws of church and state that said an unbaptised child couldn't be buried in a Christian burial ground. By the time they took in the idea of burying their little girl in unhallowed ground, Callie was struggling against the pall of indifference that seemed to wrap her up against the world, but Gideon was right when he said Reverend Sommers would welcome his great-grandchild into heaven, happy to embrace her in death as he couldn't in life. They put a bundle of rags and stones wrapped in a tiny shroud into that dank hole on the wrong side of the churchyard wall and set off to furtively bury Grace in King's Raigne churchyard with her great-grandfather.

'Neither of us will ever forget her,' she admitted as she recalled how stalwart and kind he was throughout that nightmare journey.

Why could she only admit that now, so long after the event? Then the world seemed to be going on as if nothing momentous had happened and it felt like an insult to Grace's unlived years, but why had she blamed Gideon?

'What do you think she would make of the way we are now?' he asked.

'We would be different if she was still here. I failed you both.'

'No, Callie, her death was an act of God. Go on blaming yourself, or the fates, or the time of day, or month, or year and you will never escape the past, or be the woman our girl would want her mother to be.'

'How could she want me to be anything?' she burst out with a flash of her old, impotent anger with him and the world. 'She's dead, Gideon. Gone, blank, absent and any other definition of the word you can add. I try to feel her near and she's just gone. Like you for the last nine years, she simply isn't there.'

She blinked away a tear and got her temper and grief back under control just in time to see him flinch as if she'd hit him. Sensitive, passionate Gideon was there under all that frost and she'd hurt him again. 'I know you went at my bidding, Gideon, and I'm sorry. I took an easy way out because it was less trouble than fighting for our marriage and everything else we should have been able to have together, even without our little girl.'

'Cecily Willoughby couldn't have driven us apart if I hadn't already blamed you for your grandfathers' schemes to throw us together,' he said bleakly.

She couldn't deny it because he was right. Mistrust had already been too strong for comfort between them and Cecily's spite had done the rest. 'I suppose not,' she said wearily and felt as if they were half a continent from each other rather than a few yards.

'You're tired half to death and I'm a villain for promising you peace, then dragging all this up again. This clearly isn't the right time to talk about any of this and I'll bid you goodnight now, as I clearly can't be rational around you right now. You can rest easy in that splendid bed knowing I won't trouble you unless you actively invite me to, by the way,' he said stiffly, all his defences firmly back in place.

'Goodnight then, Gideon,' she said softly, because she couldn't bring herself to brazenly say she didn't want to sleep alone any more. She watched him walk away in the reflection of a beautifully wrought mirror and all the hopes and dreams that kiss had started up in her secret wanton whispered she was a fool.

'Goodnight,' he murmured and left her, the complicated great idiot.

Had she believed anything he said? Gideon shook his head and realised he had no idea if his wife still thought he'd taken her stepsister to his bed or not, so he wasn't the only one who had learnt to guard his thoughts during their years apart. Little wonder after what they had to do to bury Grace with the whispered rites of the church Callie managed to recall even through her haze of grief. What a fool he was for expecting her to take him back as easily as if she'd never suspected him of adultery. She had been broken-hearted over their child when it happened, so no wonder, after endless miles of holding their precious, perfect baby in her arms so they could bury her in secret, she almost lost her reason for a while.

Gideon rubbed a weary hand through his severely styled dark hair and felt impatient of the tight self-control he'd learnt to live with as Frederick Peters. It was the best he could do with the life he had then. But now it felt as if Peters's shell was too small and his essential self was locked inside a hard prison he had to break out of or be crushed. He paced the lovely old room adjoining his wife's; the stark emptiness of the opulent bed about as tempting as a hollow under a hedge. She had kissed him back, though; he recalled the feel of her lips, familiar and eager under his, and moaned. The grind of endless need tightened and had to be reminded more than that hot, sweet kiss was a fantasy it was best not to dwell on right now.

He ignored the feather softness and clean luxury of the heir's bed and stripped off in an attempt to fight his body's ridiculous state with cold water from the pitcher he'd ordered earlier against the trial he knew was coming. As well to be prepared for this familiar demon, yet this time it felt as if the devil himself sat on his shoulders and whispered temptations he had to find a way to ignore, somehow. He eyed the fact of his sex, rampant and stubbornly ready for action the instant he thought of his wife a mere few inches of carved oak away, and wondered how it could be so blindly stupid.

He groaned again and hoped that oak was thick enough for her not to hear. If she came in to find out if he really was in mortal agony, he wasn't sure he could restrain the beast inside him any longer. He reminded himself it was an agony he'd pay over time and again to get his wife back, then redressed and took himself and his sex off to a hard bed in a forgotten attic where they might find an hour or two of forgetfulness of this old, familiar torture. He had something he hadn't enjoyed for years tonight, though, for all the gnawing frustration and fever of dreams and nightmares he was about to endure. Hope. Even the slenderest form of that was pure gold to a man who lived without it for so long.

Chapter Thirteen

'Good morning, Lady Laughraine,' Mr Winterley greeted Callie the next morning.

'Good morning, sir. It promises to be a lovely day,' she said, and slipped into a chair by her grandfather with an ease she would never have dreamt of feeling yesterday morning. 'We have been most fortunate in the weather, have we not?' she said, absently looking for a sign Gideon had been here, or was yet to emerge from his bedchamber.

'Good morning, my dear. We need rain.' Lord Laughraine objected to her topic as if he was wondering why they hadn't arrived together. She blushed as the wish they had slipped into her head and refused to go away. 'Your husband has been and gone,' he finally informed her gruffly.

Did he know she and Gideon had not slept

in the same bed? After all, she *was* his only hope of a great-grandchild and was that all this grand family reconciliation was about? The Laughraine succession was the rock that had wrecked her marriage the first time and she refused to let it destroy any second chance she and Gideon had of remaking their marriage. No, she had to stop this and learn to trust again. Aunt Seraphina had proved herself a stony-hearted villainess, but that didn't mean every person she was related to by blood was cast in Mrs Bartle's image. Maybe her grandfather was simply a man of few words before he had broken his fast and was ready to face the day.

'That was a fine animal you rode in on yesterday, Winterley,' Lord Laughraine pronounced after a while as if to divert all their attention from that empty place. 'Must be some Arabian in him.'

'The rogue who sold him to me swore a sultan's favourite stallion got him on his pack horse. He was a French deserter, though, and I'm not sure he'd know the truth if it stood in front of him with a cannon aimed towards his vitals.'

'Sounds plausible enough. Looks as if there's plenty of strength in the animal's hocks as well as show and good looks. Deceptive beast, but the real thing at bottom,' his lordship concluded with a straight look at the animal's owner to say like master like horse.

'He suits me well enough, anyway. I'd like to breed him if we ever find a place to build a fine stable block to house him and his harem,' Mr Winterley said casually, as if not quite able to admit it was a dream he'd had since he first found the animal and realised his promise.

Callie was almost shocked at his casual reference to setting up a stud and using that fine stallion he'd been controlling with such casual ease yesterday to found it on, before she remembered a married woman could safely hear such plans, even if her aunt might try to hustle her out of the room if she was here, and wasn't that a dreadful thought?

'Are you visiting the area to search for a suitable home for your horse then, Mr Winterley?' she asked, reminding herself it was high time she cast her aunt's narrow morality aside and became her own woman.

'That's an odd way to put it, Lady Laughraine, but you could be right,' he admitted as if it had only just occurred to him he could have a home, as well.

'You could found a fine stud with that beast and I can point you to a few promising mares if you seriously want to settle down and breed from him, Winterley. Virginia used to fret over your restlessness whenever you were off on one of your adventures.'

'She certainly didn't let it show. I always thought she was glad to see the back of me. Before he wed again and found other ways of putting all that tiresome energy to good use it was as well to make myself scarce before my brother and I argued so hotly we managed to kill one another.'

'I doubt it would have come to that, but Virginia worried whenever you disappeared to one of those outlandish countries you kept running off to when her back was turned. She cared about you, boy, whatever you've convinced yourself to the contrary.'

'So it would seem,' Mr Winterley said, and did his best to pretend he was too absorbed in his breakfast to find that revelation surprising.

Callie felt a moment of camaraderie with the man. She had half-sisters and a half-brother she could never be close to, as well, mainly because she was a mistake it was better they didn't know about, but a respectably born aristocrat must have a different reason to be estranged from his kin, and something told her

he was as far adrift from them as she was
from hers.

'Might be worth you taking a look at the
Saltash place,' her grandfather suggested,
seeming determined to get his guest out of the
house while Gideon was away from it.

There was no need to do so on her behalf.
All Mr Winterley's dark good looks and raff-
ish charm couldn't distract her from her husband, but she supposed her grandfather didn't
know that, since she did her best to disguise
her obsession. Her heartbeat scurried even at
the thought of Gideon, though, and she felt almost as breathless and silly as a young miss
gasping for love. And where the deuce had he
got off to this morning? At this rate she'd only
see Gideon at the odd meal and for some reason urgency drove her this morning, as if this
chance for them was fragile and elusive as a
bubble and needed to be caught before it burst.

'Where and what is this Saltash place of
yours, my lord?' Mr Winterley asked with the
resigned look of a man who had his morning
mapped out for him, whether he wanted to in-
spect a potential stable or not.

'Must be about ten miles across the other
side of the Raigne valley and further into the
hills, but my stableman will tell you more if

you ask him. Dare say he has a groom he can spare to show you the way at this time of year, as well. Most of the house needs rebuilding or knocking down, but the land is good and there's a fine spread of woodland and arable and pasture to keep the estate right, if only someone would see under all the neglect and take it in hand. Might suit a restless fellow like you, a challenge like that.' Lord Laughraine trailed the task like a huntsman laying a tricky scent to keep his hounds busy.

'I'm no farmer.'

'Afraid you might fail, Winterley?'

'Not sure I even want to try,' the gentleman returned as if his good manners and patience were both near the end of their tether.

'Think of it as a good ride on a fine day then,' his lordship said ruthlessly, as if he had no idea he was being a managing host. He then ordered the butler to convey his orders to the stables that the best hack in it should be made ready for Mr Winterley while his own rested and young Bradley could take the second-best one in order to keep up with it.

'Sir Gideon took the tempest out hours ago, my lord,' the man said so at least Callie now knew her husband had gone out before she was up, let alone at the breakfast table, and she wondered uneasily if he'd slept at all.

'Mr Winterley must make do with the Dancer and Bradley can have that new gelding and tell him to let me know how he goes.'

Mr Winterley made an elegant bow to his host, planted a brazen kiss on Callie's hand and bid them both good morning as if he hadn't a care in the world.

'Impudent young rascal,' Lord Laughraine observed mildly and Callie concluded he liked the late Lady Farenze's problem nephew, despite his ruthless determination to keep him out of her orbit as often as he could manage it.

'I'm quite capable of seeing through a rake nowadays,' she told him, in the hope it might stop him fighting dragons that didn't exist.

'Maybe so, but I'd avoid giving Gideon an excuse to lose his temper over that young rascal if I were you.'

'Has he still got one?' she asked a little wearily.

'Aye, and take the advice of one who's had to watch that boy brought up by a pair of idiots who didn't deserve him and avoid giving him an excuse to lose it. Gideon doesn't think he's worthy of being loved, d'you see? Might admit he's well enough looking if you catch him at the right moment. Can hardly deny it when the rest of your sex seems to find him very presentable indeed, but he's not confident of his own attractions with someone who matters to him like you do. I've done my best to show him I prefer Virgil's grandson to any my uncle could have had if his true sons lived, but the boy thinks of himself as a cuckoo in my nest and that's that as far as he's concerned.'

'He's still a stubborn idiot then?' she asked with a wobbly smile.

'More or less, for all he thinks he's such a cold-blooded man of the law. I suspect he's got that wily senior partner of his to thank for making sure he doesn't give away more than he makes at that lawyering he's insisted on doing, although I told him there was no need and he should stay here and learn to manage the estate. Of course, he'd sooner starve himself than see you want for anything, as well.'

'Truly?' she asked wistfully.

'What fools love does make of us, Callie girl,' her grandfather said with a wry smile and tried not to look smug about it.

'I never said that I still love him,' she argued.

'I dare say Gideon's the only one ignorant of that particular fact. You hardly know the rest of us are in a room the moment he steps into it.'

'How ill mannered of me,' she managed weakly and wondered how to cope with the idea everyone except her husband knowing how she felt about the great dunce. 'It sounds as if he could be a rich man, though, if he exploited those connections you and Mr Winterley claim he's made in the last few years,' she added, because she might as well find out what she could about Gideon's new life and she couldn't give herself away twice, could she?

'I dare say he does well enough for himself, but I doubt the great and the good would trust him if he trumpeted his dealings with them like a cock in his own hen yard.'

'How would I know? I'm as ignorant of the *ton* as they are of me, thank heavens.'

'If you're willing to admit you're married to Gideon at last you won't be able to remain so for long, child. It's the world his friends belong to, whatever stable they come from, and they'll stand by him just as he stood fast for them when they needed him to.'

Callie heard the note of warning in his voice and shivered. 'My mother and her family will suffer if the tale of my beginnings ever gets about, though, won't they?'

'Then we must find a way to include her sad tale in our plans for the future. No, my dear, don't shake your head and try to deny it. Now your aunt has no reason to keep silent about it that tale will soon get out.'

'Gideon threatened to pursue her with every resource available if she so much as whispered it,' Callie protested.

'And how would he prove she was the source of any gossip? That's the beauty of scandalmongering—it only takes a few judicious words dropped in the right ears for it to spread like the wind and who is to say who began it, let alone prove it? Sooner or later we will have to tell that tale first, so she can't blackmail anyone else with her nasty little half-truths embroidered with lies. Anyway the real choice is for us to leave things as they are to avoid a scandal now and risk a never-ending lawsuit over the Laughraine succession after I'm gone, or tell the truth and dare the devil. If I make you my heiress, no court in the land could deny me the right to pass Raigne on to my only grandchild, whichever side of the blanket you happen to have been born on.'

Callie would have spoken, but he seemed determined to have his say so she let him; she owed him that much and perhaps a lot more if this second-chance marriage of hers and

Gideon's actually worked out as she was beginning to hope it might.

'I know you loathe the idea of your true birth coming out and I dare say you consider that scheme your other grandfather and I dreamed up when you were a mere babe ruined your happiness with Gideon, but think, Callie, how much it will save him going through one day if we tell the truth now. He might have to face a court and admit he's the progeny of my aunt's by-blow and not the legitimate heir to the Laughraine estates and titles as the bare facts seem to declare him one day, if you don't let the truth come out.'

She shuddered at the idea of Gideon's legal adversaries publicly humiliating him. However hardened he thought he was, however little he believed he cared for the good opinion of his fellow aristocrats, he'd be hurt and ashamed as he told a truth he didn't have it in him to lie about. How could she let him go through that ordeal if there was an alternative?

'What about entails and legal caveats?' she asked warily.

'My father and grandfather trusted me to leave what they passed on to whoever would care for it best. For all its age and splendour it's only a parcel of land and chattels, Callie.

When you reach my age you realise it's not the things you have accumulated that make a life, but those we managed to love along the way.'

'So now you're telling me not to put a high value on names and acres and accusing me of being taken in by them? I thought I was doing the exact opposite and you really are very like Gideon in some ways, my lord, or perhaps he's like you?'

'I truly hope so, he's a fine man.'

'Yes, he is, and a far better person than I deserve. But how am I to discuss all this with him? We can hardly talk about our future when we don't have a present.'

'I suppose you must come to terms with one another then. I suspect his absence this morning has more to do with too much avoidance in the past than any desire to avoid you now. He is a man, after all, my dear. I'd be a fool not to have noticed how slavishly he follows your every step and gesture when you're together and draw my own conclusions about how much and how urgently he wants you as a lucky man always wants his wife. Perhaps it's time you let yourself see how surely you could drive him mad waiting for you to admit you want him back, since the rest of us have already noted it. Even young Winterley knows you are an impossible cause now he's spent an evening in your joint company, but he's a wild one, is Master James. You'd do well not to give him an inch of rope to tangle you and Gideon up in. It might save us all a lot of trouble if you admit to feeling something powerful for Gideon before he can try it.'

'Even though you sent Mr Winterley off for the day as if you didn't trust me to repulse his half-hearted attentions?'

'He has a dangerous reputation and a reckless spirit. If he thought he could stir up trouble between you and Gideon, he'd do it for the fun of seeing what happened next.'

'And you invited this man to stay under your roof, even though you knew your friend Lady Virginia was about to interfere in all our lives and try to throw Gideon and myself together again?'

'How did you know about that?' he said unwarily, then looked very conscious he'd confirmed what was only her suspicion about this business.

'I wasn't sure I did, until now.'

'Ah, well, it was fairly obvious, I suppose. Virginia loved Gideon and only wanted him to be happy, so don't make her interference another reason not to be reconciled with him, girl. I know you're a Laughraine and can't help being contrary, but it really would be cutting off your nose to spite your face if you let Virginia's notions of doing good to both of you send you running in the opposite direction out of sheer stubbornness.'

'Is that what we do?' she asked, thinking if Laughraines were stubborn then the Winterleys took the palm for sheer perversity, if Gideon and his cousin were any indication of the breed.

'Who does what?' Lord Laughraine asked rather absently.

'Laughraines,' she explained patiently. 'Is that what they do? I really have no idea. Until the day before yesterday I thought I knew how the Sommers family worked, but it turns out that I was wrong, so I should like to know which of my virtues and vices I get from the other side of my family,'

'According to my late wife we're born stubborn to a fault and about as easy to lead as an army of farmyard cats, but she could hardly be considered an unbiased observer as she was easily the most determined woman I ever had the good fortune to encounter,' he said with a fond smile at the portrait of his late lady in her prime over the mantelpiece.

'I don't have much hope of turning into a meek and mild lady of leisure then, do I?'

'None at all, I should imagine, and I doubt Gideon would want you to if you did. I should think it's about as boring as day-old rice pudding to live with such a milk-and-water creature for life.'

'But you wouldn't know, would you?' she said, eyeing the stunningly beautiful girl in that picture. Despite the comical effect of powdered hair and skirts as wide as she was tall, the vivid face under the towering hairstyle of the day was unforgettable and she suspected the lady herself was every bit as fiery and full of character as his lordship was implying.

'She had fair hair under all that powder we all insisted on dousing ourselves with in those days, but apart from that she was the image of you when she was young.'

'I'm not a beauty,' Callie disclaimed as she looked for the likeness he claimed to see in that magnificent portrait. She saw something of herself in the lady's large dark eyes and heart-shaped face and for a moment wondered if he could be right, but surely not; she had gone unnoticed for years at Cataret House so she must be a nonentity, mustn't she?

'Such a marked contrast between blond hair and dark eyes and brows must have made her very striking when it wasn't powdered,' she said, and her hand went up to touch her own irrepressibly curly dark hair and how she wished she took after her ancestress in that aspect, as well.

'It was, but she considered her hair insipid and would have envied those raven-dark Laughraine curls of yours, m'dear. Only goes to show we're human and never quite satisfied with what we have, I suppose.'

'True, my father had them then?'

'Come to the picture gallery and find out. It's about time you were introduced to your family and we must see about getting your portrait painted soon, as well. Not sure there's an artist about who can come close to Gainsborough's ability at capturing a likeness nowadays, but we can but try and if we can persuade Gideon to stand still long enough he ought to be added to the line, as well.'

'What do you think a fine artist would make of me in my schoolmistress's morning gown?' she said with a rueful look at the plain cambric Biddy had ironed so carefully she must have been up with the lark.

'That the jewel outshines the setting, I imagine. You are a lovely girl under all that tightly wound hair and you can't see me get up, you know? It's time you forgot your aunt's notions of proper dress and learnt what suits you. A lady of Raigne needs to be sure of her own style and not follow the herd and I suspect your aunt has spent the last decade telling you that you are plain and nothing out of the common way when the exact opposite is true.'

'Is that what you do, make your own style?'

'Always,' he said proudly.

'I suspect you and the late Lord Farenze of being a fine pair of arrogant and devious bucks in your heyday, Grandfather,' she observed coolly.

'I can't tell you how it gladdens my heart to hear you say so, Granddaughter,' he told her, and stood up to escort her to the gallery and all the ancestors who would have disapproved of her so deeply if they were still alive.

By the afternoon Callie felt restless and Gideon still hadn't come home. After a brief lunch she went upstairs to discuss her woeful wardrobe with Biddy and the housekeeper. The ever efficient Mrs Craddock produced an array of fine materials and fashion plates by some sleight of hand and Callie's head was soon buzzing with the endless quantities of gowns and accessories she seemed to require. Apparently two muslin gowns and a calico print for summer plus three wool day dresses for winter wouldn't even clothe a governess properly. So a single plain silk evening gown for summer and a velvet one to keep the cold out at Cataret House were laughable even to Biddy, who was learning to be a superior lady's maid at an alarming rate. Lady Laughraine must have enough clothes to turn out several young women in style and it almost made Callie long for the days when she could put on her chosen plain gown for the day and forget it until she took it off at night.

Her grandfather's words about making her own style echoed in her head as she flicked through images of gowns that looked wonderful on the tall and slender creatures depicted, but might not on a shorter and more curvaceous woman who wanted to live a real life. In the end they chose a dozen of the simplest styles and flimsy fabrics in slightly richer colours than the current mode to be going on with. The local dressmaker could make them up and they would do Callie very well, until she had chance to visit a fashionable London modiste and endure her shortcomings being picked over by a professional. For now it was all parcelled up with instructions on which style went with which bolt of fabric and every measurement the seamstress could possibly need taken so she could begin her work. Callie sighed with relief and rang for tea then insisted her maid share it with her.

'Ah, that was proper lovely, but whatever would Cook say if she could see me sitting about with my lady in the middle of the day?'

'Being a fair, as well as patient, woman I'm sure she would be pleased you have a job that doesn't mean scrubbing and stoking a fire and doing whatever hard work needs doing on such a hot day.'

'Do you think she'll find another job, though, Miss Sommers? She was as good to me as Kitty or Mrs Grisham ever let her be.'

'I suspect Sir Gideon paid everyone's wages until quarter-day and I promised Cook and Jane and Seth a good reference, so I'm sure they will find something to suit them.'

'That Sir Gideon of yours is a good man, though, ain't he?' the girl said with a sharp look.

'Yes, he is,' Callie agreed meekly.

'Can't imagine why you ever let him go then, miss.'

'Neither can I, not that it's any of your business,' Callie told her in an attempt to remind both of them she was my lady now.

'Of course not, I beg pardon, ma'am. Are you wanting to rest now, miss, I mean, my lady?' Biddy asked brightly, as if she rather liked the idea herself.

'No, I want to explore the gardens before a storm comes along and batters the flowers to the ground. Lord Laughraine thinks the weather will break today, for all the sun seems bright as ever at the moment.'

'It's terrible hot out, though, miss. You'll melt in the open on a day like today.'

'Not I, but I don't intend going far and will stroll about like a lady of leisure under a parasol. Once you have my best silk properly shaken out and almost smart enough for dinner tonight you can do as you please until the dressing bell rings.'

'I should come, too,' the little maid said doubtfully. Being outside on a day hot enough to fry an egg on the more exposed stone pathways clearly wasn't her idea of enjoyment.

'Nonsense, I won't come to any harm in his lordship's gardens and I don't intend to leave the grounds,' Callie said, and left the room before Biddy's conscience could nag her into coming as well when neither of them wanted her to.

Chapter Fourteen

It was hotter than ever out of doors and Callie supposed it would be sensible to find somewhere shaded and sit still and hope for a cooling breeze, but she was far too restless to do that. Raigne felt too grand for Miss Sommers of nowhere in particular at the moment, despite Mrs Craddock's efforts to bring her into fashion. Biddy had done something to the plain muslin that Callie had unwarily changed into after their exertions with the tape measures, as well, and she doubted the girl would do that without the housekeeper's say so. The gown was cut lower and a layer or so of stern petticoats had mysteriously been lost in the wash. Since it was cooler without the lawn undershirt made high to the neck and even a fine shift seemed more than enough today, maybe she should get used to being more fashionable.

She put aside worrying about taking on Lady Laughraine's outer trappings without sharing her husband's bed and let herself marvel at the beauty of nature, subtly controlled by man. Weeks of relentless July heat meant most of the roses had all but done with flowering, but vast old lavender bushes still hummed with sleepy-sounding bees. Daisies and lilies, hyssop and Sweet William bloomed among the shaped yew and tidy box hedges and knots of the older parts of this great whole and suddenly she passionately wanted her children to grow up here.

Her eyes went dreamy and her steps slowed as the sounds of them laughing and racing along these old brick-and-stone paths echoed through her as if they were already real. Gideon would make a wonderful father; all the more so for the barren years of loneliness she had inflicted on them after they lost Grace. He would contain his wild offspring when they were at the edges of what was acceptable, but he would also give them all the love he was denied as a boy. She must make sure she found time to watch them rough and tumble and argue and laugh, then she could thank God that she tumbled headlong in love with such a wonderful man when she was far too young to tell a hero from a fool. Calliope Sommers was so much luckier than her mother and had found a good man to love when she was still in the school-room.

That was something else the gossips would whisper over their teacups. They'd say young Calliope Sommers saw what a promising youth Gideon Laughraine was and grabbed him before he was old enough to know better. Some would tut and frown and secretly resent her for catching a man who would do their own girls very nicely, thank you. They were sure to pick apart their long estrangement and find it too delicious to keep to themselves and she sighed at the thought of the stories that would race round the Mayfair drawing rooms at her expense. It didn't matter next to the hope she and Gideon might be happy at last and she hardly let herself believe that could happen, but it seemed as if it just might, as long as they were very careful with each other this time and she didn't believe any more lies.

'I was beginning to think I'd never catch you alone,' a voice she never wanted to hear again said coldly. Callie realised she had wandered down a path that looked over the park and lingered a little too long staring sightlessly at the view beyond the gardens.

'You have been watching then?' she asked

as her mother's stepdaughter eyed her as if she were an unsatisfactory cabbage being offered for sale by an impudent market trader. 'What on earth for? We have nothing to say to one another and you have no business here, Miss Willoughby,' she said distantly, shocked to see the woman she would have done a good deal to avoid if only she knew she was coming.

'I am Lady Flette now,' the wretched female corrected her with a snap, as if the whole world ought to know Miss Willoughby had netted herself a title.

'Then I hope you are passing through King's Raigne on a long journey to the distant home of your noble husband, because you are not welcome here.'

'That's why I had to wait until I could see you alone. I knew you would refuse to see me and everyone knows we are related in some way and it will cause a scandal if I am not received here. Sir Roger and I live a few miles east of here and as his family can trace their line back to a Conquest knight, we will not be going anywhere and we have a right to be known as your neighbours at the very least.'

'So you have been spying on me in order to inform me of these facts you seem so sure of?'

'Not spying, just waiting for the chance to make you see reason.'

'I hope you had a very uncomfortable time of it, then.' All the same Callie was shocked to see how thin and careworn the woman was when even she had to admit she had been a rare beauty in her youth. Perhaps her real character was beginning to show through the mask of angelic innocence she once wore so perfectly. 'You boasted how you would spend all your time in London or Brighton once you were wed and never set foot in the country but to stay with princes or dukes, and now you are happy to impose yourself on me when I sincerely wish you had gone to one of those fashionable places and stopped there.'

'Sir Roger prefers a country life,' the confounded woman said as if that explained everything, and perhaps it did if Cecily Willoughby had truly met her match.

'And you oblige him? You *must* be a changed creature.'

'I have no idea what you mean.'

'Then your memory is at fault? You seem very young to suffer such an affliction.'

Lady Flette stopped looking down her nose at Callie's simple muslin gown and old-fashioned parasol and simply looked sour for a moment. 'Sir Roger has told me I must make peace with my stepmother's cousin, whatever quarrels we had as girls. Since you were brought up by a vicar you must be ready to turn the other cheek.'

'No, and isn't the local gossip efficient for you to even know I am here so soon after my arrival? I dare say you know my husband is Lord Laughraine's acknowledged heir and I will be lady of Raigne one day, as well. I can't imagine any other reason for you to come here and pretend either of us has the least wish to know the other.'

'Your aunt kindly sent me a message to tell me you and your husband would be arriving any day and had been accepted as the proper heirs to Raigne Place for some odd reason known only to Lord Laughraine. My husband was most grateful for the warning, for he likes to be on good terms with his neighbours and Raigne is the most important estate in this part of the world, after all, so who can blame him?'

Was there no end to Aunt Seraphina's malice and clever little twists of the knife even now Callie had thought her out of her and Gideon's lives for good? As well to know the woman would always do what she could to make the lives of those she ought to love most as miserable as possible, she supposed, and resolved not to let that happen again. She had no idea what had occurred to make Aunt Seraphina and Lady Flette believe they had a right to push anyone who got close enough about on a board like so many chess pieces. It seemed to her there were some sorts of human mind it was better not to understand and deplored Gideon's experience of even more malicious and ill-intentioned souls than Aunt Seraphina and this self-serving creature on the darker side of the criminal underworld.

'What a pacific gentleman your Sir Roger must be,' she said so blandly it must be obvious even to the self-absorbed Lady Flette that she thought exactly the opposite and still didn't intend to make the woman's life easier for her.

Callie thought she saw her foe shiver in the sticky heat and concluded Sir Roger Flette was indeed the very opposite of a peaceful husband and possibly even a cruel one. She might feel enough sympathy for any other woman who went in fear of her husband to pretend an amity that didn't exist to make her life easier, but she wasn't saintly enough to pity this one. 'If I was weak enough to welcome you to our new home, do you think my husband would tolerate your presence under any roof he lives under after what you did?'

Lady Flette looked a little conscious and refused to meet Callie's eyes. 'That was years ago,' she said weakly.

'If a century had passed I still wouldn't forgive you for sneaking into my husband's bed as soon as my back was turned.'

'Oh, don't be ridiculous, even a prude like you ought to have got over a girlish practical joke like that one by now.'

Callie stood speechless for a long moment and half wondered if she had fainted again and this was really a bad dream. 'A girlish joke you were lucky didn't get out and ruin your chances of any sort of marriage, let alone one that made you a lady in name, if not fact,' she finally found the words to snap. 'I know there's no point appealing to your better nature, since you don't have one, but how would you like it to be widely known what you did to get me out of Willoughby Manor that day? Is your husband aware you lay in another man's bed before you got to his, madam? No? Then perhaps it's time he found out. Or maybe you would prefer to simply leave Raigne and never bother either of us again?'

'He won't believe your spiteful tale bearing

because he's in a very good position to know it's not true,' Lady Flette said scornfully. 'Have you never let that poor wretch you eloped with off that fine drama your aunt and I set up so I could be rid of you? What a poor henpecked specimen of manhood he must be by now if he's had to live with you throwing that piece of playacting at him all these years.'

'It was a lie?' Callie asked hollowly.

'Of course it was. I knew there was something off about that tale of a poor little cousin bereaved of her guardian and child all in one week. My stepmother would never have taken a step out of her way for a worthy distant relative and when your aunt told me who you really were, I had to get you out of the house before someone put two and two together and made a scandal. If it got out that my father had wed a whore back then I'd have lost any chance of a good marriage, so you obviously had to go, and your aunt wanted to set up a school, but all she ever wanted was to get away from her father's stuffy lessons that you soaked up as if your life depended on it. If she could get you away from your disreputable husband, she would have the perfect teacher to help run her school, and it seemed to me that was about your true level in life, so we agreed to help each other. In the end Mrs Bartle came up with a plan to make you think your husband was my lover without much risk my father or his wife would find out. They would have refused to frank me for a London Season if they knew, but I certainly wasn't fool enough to give my maidenhood to that handsome brute you married. I needed it to hook a wealthy husband and he didn't want it even if I hadn't.'

'How cunning of you,' Callie managed to say as if it was an unimportant tale from long ago.

'Yes, your aunt and I got on well, although a country school and you to run it for her seemed to be the beginning and end of her ambition. I suppose a quiet lie endures longest. She must have found some other fool to teach her brats and run her house since you're here with your husband and Sir Roger says you must have lived together incognito all these years.'

'You may tell your husband I am unsure if I wish to recognise a remote connection. I will consult my husband and perhaps your father and stepmother about the matter.'

'That's not what Sir Roger wants.'

'How sad,' Callie said distantly, her gaze chilly as a distant rumble of thunder growled in the heavy air and a line of dark cloud blurred the parched horizon.

'I rode over. I shall be soaked through if I get caught in a storm.'

'Oh, dear, you had better hurry home then, hadn't you? You will beat the storm if you are lucky.'

Lady Flette looked as if she would like to demand the use of a carriage to go home in style, but Callie's bland challenge made her hasten off without a goodbye on either side. At last the impractical sky blue of her ladyship's summer riding habit was beyond her view and Callie pitied the poor animal she would whip into a gallop to get home in time to avoid a soaking. She almost shouted after her that she could take a carriage, after all, but managed to bite her tongue. Give that one an inch and she would never be out from under their feet, however unwelcome she knew herself to be.

'What the devil was Cecily Willoughby doing here?' Gideon demanded the moment Callie stepped in through the long windows to my lord's library, feeling pleased she had managed to find her way round one part of the huge old house and its vast gardens.

'You saw her?' she asked numbly. She should tell him straight away that she knew he hadn't been unfaithful to her, but the words just wouldn't come off her tongue.

'No, I just got in and Craddock told me she had been asking for you, but where have you been since she left, Callie? I was about to turn everyone outside to search the house and grounds in case she hurt you.'

'Oh, no, she's far too much of a coward to risk a fight, and I have the upper hand this time, or should I say the greater expectations? Her husband sounds as if he is obsessed by rank and wealth,' Callie said as steadily as she could, then went to examine her reflection in the watery Venetian glass mirror that told flattering little lies she needed right now.

Considering the upheaval her world had just gone through, she thought she looked remarkably calm and collected, so appearances really were deceptive then. The low rumble of thunder in the distance gave way to a mighty crash right over Raigne. From Gideon's tight expression it didn't bring a release of tension with it. Unable to face telling him what she knew right now, Callie clenched her shaking hands and tried not to flinch as the boom of that first peal of thunder rolled into a constant clash. Lightning ripped the sky so close it seemed all around them rather than a streak across the heavy clouds. She shivered convulsively and Gideon cursed softly and rang the bell, but she couldn't tell him it wasn't the coming storm that made her shudder, but the thought of all she had done to both of them by believing yet another lie. She had been wrong about the words not coming out, there just weren't any words in her head right now that felt good enough to work with.

'A shawl for my wife, if you please, Craddock, and would you like tea, Callie?'

'Yes, perhaps it would help,' she replied absently, feeling as if her composure was about to shatter like glass.

'The cure for all ills?' he said with a shadow of his old smile.

'You really are a good man, aren't you?' she said more or less at random, although it was true, of course.

'What has she said to you?' he asked apprehensively, as if he thought his world might be about to tumble round his ears all over again.

How could she have done this to him? And why couldn't she just come out and admit what a credulous fool she was? A hard knot of misery seemed to have taken up residence in her belly and she doubted any tea could get past it, but he looked so anxious about her now that she hated herself and if feeding her tea made him feel better, she would do her best to down it and pretend it was what she needed. 'Far too good for me, I think,' she added as if he hadn't asked that question about Lady Flette and she really must pull herself together.

'What nonsense is this, Callie?' he asked impatiently. 'Have I gone from devil to angel in the space of a day now? I must tell you that I'm not very fond of either role.'

'I never really thought you a devil,' she told the clammy air by one of his finely moulded ears and this wasn't the time to remember exploring it in slavishly intimate detail when she hadn't yet discovered the meaning of reserved where he was concerned.

'That's not how I remember things,' he argued, the dark times after she lost their child bleak in his gaze.

All those days of her weeping and simply wanting to be left alone sat in the heavy air between them. Then his eyes warmed with curiosity as the hot flash of colour she could feel burning across her cheekbones as they talked of serious, important things refused to chill with the subject. Could he tell that three parts of her thoughts were on how it once felt to love him with everything she was right now? 'I wasn't rational,' she offered with a shrug to admit it wasn't much of an excuse for turning away love.

'And I should have been more patient, more understanding of what you were going through. You were in such terrible pain that I didn't know how to make the world right for you, Callie. The harder I tried, the worse you seemed to feel.'

'And I hurt you deeply, didn't I? I'm so sorry, Gideon, words aren't good enough to say all they should at times, are they? All I can manage is that I just couldn't seem to let you in because my grief was too big to share. I did say I wasn't rational, didn't I?'

'Of course you weren't. Why should you be at such a time?'

'Aunt Seraphina pointed out she had lost her father and her husband within a month and *she* wasn't crying and moping and damning the devil.'

'To do that she would have to possess a heart and I thought she was out of our lives at last. Did Lady Flette's arrival on the scene bring that business at Willoughby Manor back to you again? Is that why you're looking at me as if I have grown two heads? I knew I shouldn't have abandoned you again today, but even I didn't expect your aunt to send her witch's apprentice to stir up trouble between us in her stead.'

'She didn't and I'm not made of glass. You didn't abandon me last time. I told you to go. If you turn all this around so everything becomes your fault, we will never be able to work our way past what I did to you all those years ago, Gideon.'

'Very well, how much of the blame would you *like* me to shoulder?' he asked with a teasing challenge that woke something euphoric and youthful in her she didn't think would ever live again before he came back into her life. 'This much?' he asked; arms wide open as if he'd encompass half the world if he could. 'This?' he added; a tiny pinch of space between his first finger and thumb. 'None at all?' was the next question as he put his hands behind his back and pretended to be far too angelic to know how to sin, let alone actually do it.

'Idiot,' she said, and laughed out loud when he managed to look injured and handsome and nigh irresistible all at the same time.

'Give me a clue then, Wife,' he protested, but there was hope in his eyes and a smile on his lips as he did so and if only they could get past this there was a chance for them, wasn't there?

'Oh, Gideon, I was wrong,' she told him at last in a rush.

'In what way?' he asked warily and she had done that to him, made her impulsive, passionate and hopeful young love wary of every word that left her lips.

'Every single one I can think of right now. Cecily admitted to me today that she lied that morning and my aunt put her up to it.'

'I know,' he answered steadily, and of course he had worked out their complicity a lot sooner than she had. He wasn't a gullible fool, always half ready to believe nothing as wonderful as true love could happen for her. 'It doesn't come as a surprise to me, love.'

'How can you call me so when I was such an idiot? How can you calmly stand there and watch me as if nothing has changed between us?'

'Because it hasn't, has it? I always knew I wouldn't lay a single finger on that little termagant in lust if we were the last two people left on earth, so it's not news to me that I never did.'

She made herself meet his gaze and wondered numbly why he wasn't walking away in disgust. 'I should have trusted you.'

'Why? I was a hot-tempered boy who thought himself hard done by. Why would you take my

word on my love and loyalty to you over your
aunt's? Oh, don't look at me like that, woman, I
haven't grown wings or become a saint. I raged
at you every time a letter pleading for mercy
fell on deaf ears. I hated you when I lay on the
rack for the pain and emptiness of wanting only
you night after night and month after month
and not being able to have you in my bed. All
that stopped me finding you and telling you
how aggrieved I was, and how wrong and mis-
trustful you were, was the thought of you so
emptied out and broken as you were after we
lost our child. You were too young for me to
need you as much as I did, Callie, too close to
being a child to carry one yourself.'

'And you were so old and mature yourself
at eighteen years old, were you? Oh, Gideon,
perhaps you are the bigger idiot out of the two
of us, after all,' she told him as she saw all that
frustration and agony in his gaze and too much
hurt for a man of eight and twenty to carry as if
it was his lot in life. 'Instead of expecting you
to be strong and certain for me I should have
been less unsure of myself. I was taken in by
my mother's family and loved and looked after
as if I was the most precious being on earth by
my grandfather. Given what I've learnt about
my aunt lately, perhaps he had reason to be

wary of loving her wholeheartedly as I know he wanted to, but I was cared for and encouraged even as you were neglected and blamed for the fact your parents had to wed in the first place.'

'I wasn't some innocent victim, though, was I? I grew up wild and angry and bitter and even when I fell in love with you and you loved me back I refused to see how lucky I was. Instead, I railed at the faults in my destiny and hated my supposed grandfather for making me learn the law instead of sending me to Oxford. Raging at you when I found out who you are put all those doubts about my love for you in your head, Callie. How could I blame you for believing in the woman who helped bring you up when I treated you like a traitor who had been foisted on me by your grandfathers?'

'Is that why you never took a mistress, although you must have been almost as desperate for her companionship as the physical release of taking a lover? You stayed faithful to me because you felt *guilty*?'

Callie felt revolted by the idea he kept his marriage vows because he felt uneasy after accusing her of using his passion for her to scurry him into marriage and solve the puzzle of the Laughraine succession. The thought of him in another woman's arms, let alone her bed, made her feel sick and furious and wildly jealous all that the same time, but guilt? Even for the sake of loving him at a polite distance she couldn't stay here and be his penance.

'No, damn it. I love you.'

'You can't,' she whispered, all those years of longing and hopeless regrets like a weight in her chest she had to squeeze the words past. 'I sent you away. I believed a woman who obviously hates me even when you vowed on everything you held sacred that you were innocent. I can't believe you don't hate me, let alone love me.'

'Can't or won't?'

'No, I want to, heaven knows I want to, Gideon,' she managed to say huskily. 'I just don't see how you can love a woman who put you through hell and then ordered you to leave. In your shoes I would have drunk and caroused my way round London and made certain it got into the scandal sheets so you must see it and know it was all your fault. I deserved to live like a nun for being such a fool, but you didn't need to be a monk to prove it.'

'I did, because none of the women I could have were you. I deserved it because I was furious and hurt when I found out you were the true heir to Raigne and I took the sins of our parents out on you, instead of raging at those who made that mess in the first place.'

'I'm sure you had enough to go round them, as well,' she couldn't stop herself saying with a wry sort of tenderness as she pictured the angry young man she married and wondered how he was so different now. 'Where did all that pent-up anger go?'

'For a month or so I drank myself into a stupor every night and raged at you like a fool with every other sentence, then Poulson, my mentor and now senior partner, and Lord Laughraine hauled me out of my lodgings, put my head under the nearest pump and told me to prove myself a better man than anyone thought me instead of confirming their worst suspicions. It took a great many false starts and a lot of patience on their part, but in the end I learned to pour my anger into what I saw as a fight for justice. A lawyer doesn't need to look far to find one and it took me to some surprising places. There was never a more driven seeker after truth and what I wanted to call justice as I was during the first few years of my legal career.'

'You speak as if you are halfway to your dotage now,' she said with another half-smile for this new sort of intensity in him. It made perfect sense. His exploits as a seeker after truth chimed with the restless Gideon of their youth with so much misdirected energy she was surprised none of them realised how much he needed a worthwhile occupation. Her driven young lover was alive under Mr Peters's cool self-control and her heart raced with joy and something a lot more personal at the thought of all that fire and urgency lying under the disguise of cool reason he now showed the world.

'Of late I sometimes feel as if I am,' he said with one of those self-deprecating shrugs that made her long to explore the new breadth of his shoulders and the tight muscles lower down she was no longer surprised a lawyer managed to maintain. 'But if we stay here that part of my life is over. I couldn't live in danger with a wife waiting at home for me. It wouldn't be fair to you.'

Chapter Fifteen

There was the reproach she almost needed to hear at last. He had a wife who refused to be one during all the years he was risking his body and that tender conscience of his for others. Still he took the risks he must have taken, because she wouldn't listen when he swore he was innocent. What else could he do but help the innocent in his own way; being so had not got him an iota of justice from her, had it?

'And if we don't?' she asked, because she couldn't help herself and maybe she hadn't changed as much as she hoped either. How awful if they were locked into the insecurities of their birth for the rest of their lives.

'Then we must learn to live together somewhere else, because I can't endure being wed and not wed to you any longer.'

'What about love?'

'What about it? I've just nailed my colours to the mast, but if you can't love me back I'll take a marriage of amorous friends if that's all you can offer. I'm not proud any more, Callie, but I am your husband and willing to take unfair advantage of the fact church and state bind a man and wife together unto death.'

'I…' Callie tailed off before she could send up her own colours when her grandfather opened the door and blinked.

'Ah, there you are, m'boy. We've been worrying ourselves to flinders about you all day,' Lord Laughraine exclaimed as he came into the room on another peal of thunder, then stood looking at them as if he felt the charge of emotions in the air instead of the vitality of the storm outside. 'Oh, suppose you're having lovers' quarrel and I've interrupted? Leave you to it, then, and see you at dinner,' he said and almost closed the door before he turned back. 'I gave you that suite so you could have some privacy whenever you need it, you know. You could make use of it and let Honey and Bramble hide under my desk in peace. They're gun-shy, but I can't bring myself to think any the less of them when I'm not a great one for slaying innocent creatures, and they feel safe under there in a thunderstorm.'

'Of course they do,' Callie said, and laughed, despite the poor timing of master and dogs, as two spaniels shot out from behind their beloved master to take refuge under the wide and rather ponderous oak table he used to spread his papers. 'Perhaps we could find a guard dog to protect your guard dogs, Grandfather?'

'Perhaps we should, but right now Gideon is frowning at me like a gargoyle and you were enjoying a stimulating discussion, weren't you? Lady Laughraine and I often used to fight like cat and dog in the run up to a storm, seem to recall making up afterwards was a lot more stimulating, though.'

'I could easily love you, my lord,' she said gently, practically feeling Gideon's driven impatience at her shoulder as he glowered at both of them and the dogs for socialising when he was teetering along the edges of reason.

'Good, good, probably don't deserve it, but always wanted to love you, my dear. Sommers didn't think it advisable for the world to know who you were while you were growing up, though—gossip and all that.'

Callie stood on tiptoe and kissed his cheek. 'Thank you for letting him do that then and allowing me to grow up in peace, but right now I really have to go upstairs and quarrel with Gideon, so you will excuse us, won't you, my lord?'

'Aye, minx, take your time,' he said with a gesture of dismissal and went to his desk with the rest of his assorted pack of hounds at his heels and pretended he was deaf to hers and Gideon's hasty farewells.

'Just as well he came in when he did, I suppose,' Gideon said gloomily as he finally followed her into their vast sitting room and she made sure Biddy wasn't waiting in her bedchamber or dressing room to frustrate them again.

'Yes, we could hardly make love in my lord's library now, could we?'

'Don't, Callie,' he rasped in a voice that sounded scraped raw with emotions he'd held in too long. 'Don't offer water to a dying man and not expect to be pounced on as if you're my last hope on earth.'

'I want to try again, Gideon,' she whispered, and looked into his eyes although it cost such an effort. She winced when she saw the guard that he kept on his thoughts was still there like a barrier against the world that he couldn't bring himself to drop. 'I want it so badly it hurts.'

'Oh, Callie, you have to be sure before you

say such things to me. I can't draw back and play the white knight if you change your mind. It's been too long since I had a wife. I'm too dangerous to play games with right now.'

'Do you think I haven't longed and ached and hurt for you, too?' she asked in a whisper that felt more like a long gasp of need more than words. 'I've burned. I've needed. I've yearned for you, Gideon, night after night and week after week every year since we parted. It was only ever you for me, will only ever be you. I'm blind to all the rest of mankind because of you.'

'You sent me away, Callie, you couldn't endure to so much as look at me,' he said with a visible shudder.

'I know. I'm so sorry. I hurt so much I wanted you to hurt, too, and that was cruel and little. When I sent you away I thought all the guilt and fury and hurt of losing Grace would go with you, you see? But it didn't go anywhere and it was easier to think that was your fault as well than to see what a silly, jealous little fool I'd been.'

'I should never have gone,' he said bleakly, and for some reason that made her angry.

'Why not? I told you to, so why would you

stay when I couldn't do anything but hurt you over and over again?'

'So that's why you turned your back on me?' he asked as if the words tasted bitter. 'To *protect* me? What sort of marriage did we have if you thought you must guard me from your deepest feelings as if I might break?'

'Don't go,' she gasped from the heart. He seemed about to turn away, go downstairs and order a horse to ride back to London despite the still-grumbling storm and the relentless lash of what sounded like all the rain they hadn't had in weeks.

'I have to. You'd best stand aside, Calliope, because I'm not safe right now.'

'No, I won't let you leave and not come back for years. We have to talk about it all. I didn't stump about half alive for the last nine years to carry on doing it a different way when you recalled you had a wife and came home.'

'I knew I had a wife every second of those nine years, Calliope. If you have any sense at all you'll step aside and recall how long it is since I enjoyed the fact of you in my bed. I'm not going to run back to London like a whipped boy, but you really don't want me to stay in this room right now, I assure you.'

'Of course I do,' she argued furiously, confronting him with her hands on her waist and arms akimbo like an angry fishwife. 'I'm a woman. Apparently you can manage without one, but I can't wait another day for a man. I want you. See?' she said with a fierce gesture at the way her nipples had pebbled against the muslin of her much-altered gown.

'Do you think I'm blind or daft, woman? Of course I see.'

'Then why do you only look, Husband?' she snapped as if it was a commonplace thing to have him watch her with such sizzling heat in his eyes they looked like melted metal instead of cool grey with those intriguing blazes of green shot through them. No, they looked like Gideon's, full of lambent promise and heavy-lidded with sensual need. He was here and her heart was racing and her body tight and loose with need all at the same time. How desperately she'd missed him and he was only *looking* at her? 'Never mind what I said,' she added. 'I don't care if we fly blind into passion, after all, Husband, just stop looking and start seducing me, for goodness' sake.'

'We're more like to hit a wall at breakneck speed than fly anywhere,' he protested unsteadily, but his gaze was fierce and his mouth set like an invitation to pure sin as he focused everything in him on her and fire trailed over her body with every hungry place his gaze lingered. Each look set another spark to the blaze flaring between them and they hadn't even touched yet.

'I only want to hit it with you, Gideon,' she said with the fierce heat in her core frank in her gaze and all she'd missed so desperately about him coalescing into pure longing at the heart of her.

One more fractured sigh and she was done with the gap he'd insisted on keeping between them. So close she felt the fine shake of his leanly muscled body before they brushed one on the other and all of a sudden they were melded skin on skin, as if any other sort of existence was impossible and each saw the world through the other.

'Kiss me, I'm not made of glass,' she managed to gasp as the stretch of his body under hers overheated the need inside her to melted honey.

'I can feel that for myself,' he rasped, and she felt his breath on her cheek and wriggled shamelessly to inch higher and offer up her mouth.

Here was her Gideon, her love, home again with her. She shook like an aspen as his mouth took hers. At first a little clumsy and unpractised, then urgent as they learned all that was heart-achingly familiar and all that was new about each other. Impatient, she opened her lips to lure him in, gasped as pure need, total demand thrust and teased her when his probing tongue delved inside and imitated the beat of life itself, reminding her where they were going. He gasped in much-needed air to trail kisses frantically along her jaw and linger on the line where it met her slender neck before racing his mouth to her ear to learn it again. She was so shaken by the memory and newness in his touch as he found the places he knew would drive her wild, yet seemed to linger in wonder over all that was the same as well as the new maturity of her womanly curves. Was it possible to reach a wild climax simply from the feel of her lover's urgent, sensuous touch on something as every day as her earlobe? She keened a protest, because if she was to fly she badly wanted to do it with him.

His breath was unsteady against her skin and he seemed to fight the same urge to an unconnected climax as she forced herself away from a second ago. His hands were urgent and a little clumsy on her laces and she smiled her approval, although she sensed his gaze had gone as unseeing as her own at this driving urge to mate until they were both utterly undone.

'Never mind them,' she urged, directing his hands instead to the front of the fragile stuff and sighing with delight when the material ripped from stem to stern. She had no real interest where it ended up. This was their now and their next.

Now his hands were busy snapping the ribbon of her shift and who would have thought a woman's corsets could disappear so fast she had no idea how he did it? A brief moment of doubt that he wasn't more practised at this than either of them remembered and she called on her faith in him and ordered it not to fail them this time. Busy about his coat and waistcoat as he had been about her gown, she supposed eagerness and extreme need were all it took. There, it was off in one powerful shrug and they could deal with his neckcloth and fine linen later. She felt his hands, unexpectedly calloused from hard work and long hours in the saddle, revelled in the contrast between the firm touch on the soft skin of her breast as he cupped it, then he dipped his dark head to explore more intently with his mouth and she gasped her delight.

Now she was so glad to be more luxuriant there than she was at seventeen. Her breasts shamelessly revelled in his would-be reverent touch and raised and rounded even more under his fascinated gaze. There, oh, there, he settled his hot mouth on her pleading nipple again and ran his tongue about the tight core, then suckled, and she heard herself moan with the pleasure and need. She was so hot and wet she writhed against his mouth and he made an inarticulate sound of approval and racked up the hot rhyme of his mouth on her to an even more driven and deeper need. She clasped his dear dark head to her and groaned out her pleasure and her driving, galloping need for his hardness inside the hot wet core of her and driving them both insane with completion.

'Oh, love, I need more of you. I'm so ready I'll melt if you don't get on and give it to me,' she whispered into the dark curls under her shaking hand as she rediscovered them and raked her fingers through memories of her wild-haired young love and felt a fleeting sense of smugness that this was another part of him that was only for her nowadays.

'You don't know how ready I am,' he gasped on half a sob and half a laugh.

'Oh, I think I do,' she argued as she wriggled wantonly against the iron-hard fact of his need and gave him a wicked, self-satisfied smile as it leapt even more eagerly under her invitation to set it to work as hard and fast as they could be together again in the most intimate way possible.

'Witch,' he whispered as he managed to steady himself enough to explore her welcome and found it every bit as eager as his need to be inside her for the first time in so long the thought of it made her sob with wistfulness and self-pity. 'Nearly there, my Calliope,' he murmured as if he understood why she felt a moment of acute sadness, even as the joy of being one with him was so close it set her heart racing ever faster and her breath fighting for space in her lungs.

'I missed you so badly, lover,' she confided against his bent down head as he took all the time and restraint he'd found from somewhere to ease her into a position so she could take his rampant need of her little by little, instead of in the frantic rush she could sense he was fighting with every gallant nerve and sinew in his body.

'You're in my head and my heart, always, love,' he told her as he was there at last, first a little intimidating and even harder and bigger than she remembered. She refused to doubt he'd slide home and let them dance to the old familiar beat of this truest and deepest of intimacies.

'Trust us, Callie,' he urged as she gasped in a breath against the undefended state the ultimate act of love gifted to lovers.

'I do,' she told him and met his eyes to let him see it was true as she relaxed and took him in inch by precious inch.

'Ah, love,' he gasped as if he meant it.

She let a pinch of sadness in at the gap of time since they had loved, then let it go to live now. A very fine now it was as he stilled as best he could to take account of it being so long since they had loved. She felt the effort it cost him to hold back in the newly sleek power of his buttocks tense under her touch and the shake in his breath and his touch. Exploring his narrow waist and satin-smooth skin over taut bands of hard muscles, she moved her hands up his back under that confounded shirt they hadn't managed to rid themselves of yet and leaned in to tweak a hard male nipple through the finely woven fabric.

It worked and she felt wickedly triumphant as something broke inside him and he seized her narrow waist to tug her closer to the edge of her perch and thrust so far into her he was fully seated and she could glory in every rampant inch of him, then he stood with her at his level on some convenient surface she had no time to think about now as he withdrew nearly all the way before another deep thrust drove her to hook her legs about his narrow waist and try to urge him to go faster and deeper, before she'd fully taken in the fact they were really lovers once more. Now she was shaking and on the edge of begging when he did it again. She broke into those high, hard spasms of absolute pleasure she remembered and beyond to somewhere new they'd never gone before, even at the height of their youthful glorying in each other's bodies. At the very moment she began to writhe and moan under his bucking body she felt him fly with her as if he couldn't control the desperation in him any longer.

It was glorious and huge, limitless and yet it contained only them; it was their world and their reality. They gasped and bucked together and touched each other tenderly, as if the heat and fire and wonder in their skin and sinews and racing hearts and minds must be shared through every sense they had. Huge spasms of ecstasy raged through her and she lost herself in him. Amidst the heat and hammer and glory was absolute satisfaction and a heady sort of peace. Such exquisite pleasure—she was shocked somehow to find it waiting for them after so many years of drought. Yet also such novelty it was as if they'd never got so far nor been so close until this moment.

Callie still felt delicious little quivers of pleasure echo through her body into his as they calmed and revelled in the warmth and bliss of being together like this again. Once upon a time this had been their time to outbid each other with words and promises. They would laughingly compete to come up with the most outrageously overblown endearments for each other, the richest and most inventive of poetry to murmur in praise of one lover for the other. Now they were silent and waiting, a little bit wary again as all the years apart slotted back into their minds and they discovered how to be a little shy of each other in the most unlikely of circumstances.

'You haven't spent much time in your office reading dusty tomes these last few years, have you?' she half asked, half observed as she let her hands show how much she liked the feel of all that intriguingly arranged muscle and bone under his bronzed and now-cooling skin. The race of his frantically pumping heartbeat was slowing and his breathing almost normal as she ran her hand over his clinging lawn shirt and let out a wifely tick of disgust. 'And you still haven't taken this confounded shirt off,' she admonished him with a shake of her head she hoped he realised was nowhere near the scold she pretended.

'My wife is too hungry for my body to give me time for niceties,' he drawled as if very happy to report that state of affairs.

'Your wife feels it's high time she had a chance to examine that body you are so vain about in detail,' she managed to say solemnly as she tugged and prodded at his prone form until he gave in and heaved himself up from the sprawl he'd slumped into when he carried them into her grand bedchamber and rolled them on to the bed so she rested over his torso and they could lie and wonder at each other all over again.

'Whilst your husband could gaze and gaze at his naked wife for hours on end, if only she would let him,' he retorted huskily and, even as he unravelled the chaos they'd made of his cravat between them, then heaved his shirt over his head to throw into some unloved corner of the room, he was doing exactly that.

'As it's high summer and no hardship to lie about naked with you, I might do that,' she said with a complacent smile for the sheer joy of being on this great bed with him and hours of looking and feeling and touching to gloat over and store up against the day.

'Perhaps not,' he said hoarsely and she laughed as the effects of simply watching her stretch sensuously against the linen sheets left his sex far more rigid than either of them had thought possible only seconds ago.

'We *are* married, after all,' she told him daringly, finding out that all those years of lonely self-denial left a woman a lot more frank and open about her physical needs than even his besotted and passionate seventeen-year-old wife had been.

'We are, but what has that to say about you lying there flaunting yourself like a houri?' he teased as he propped himself up on one elbow to do as she'd invited him to and watch every curve and pulse in her revel in being his lover again after so many years of being so buttoned up and lonely she often wrote into the night just to block out the lack of him in her narrow bed and the terrible gap in her heart.

'That I was so lonely it was hard to tell where I hurt most, Gideon. I missed you—missed this—but having you here, with me, ah, I missed that most of all. I sometimes thought it might be better if I was dead rather than half alive without you.'

'Don't, Callie, I can't endure it,' he said harshly and turned his head away as if to hide from her and how could he do that when they had just made such wonderful love every inch of her sang with satisfaction and joy?

Chapter Sixteen

'I'm sorry, that was a silly thing to say,' she argued against herself and tried to soothe his shivering body even as he did his best to hide his tormented expression and seemed ashamed she might see into his heart this time.

'You don't understand,' he grated as if half the demons in hell were sitting on his shoulders and might drive him mad. 'You don't know,' he added under his breath.

'Stop it,' she ordered as she knelt up to pull him back into the soft cocoon of the great bed to simply lie here together as rain beat on the parched ground outside and the rest of the world seemed a long way off. 'Tell me, Gideon, whatever it is that puts shadows in your eyes and tortures you. I have to know about it this time. We can't have those dark little patches of mystery waiting to come between us if we're going to do better at marriage from now on. Don't you see we can't risk hiding our thoughts and fears from each other again?'

Shaken and suddenly terribly anxious about the suppressed emotions raging under his front of calm self-control, she shook his shoulders and glared at him as a real threat to their marriage seemed alive and terrifying. 'Listen to me, you foolish man,' she snapped as she physically made him look her in the eyes and see how deeply he'd worried her.

'If I tell you, you won't want me near you,' he said, agony in his complicated gaze as he made himself meet hers as if it cost him half a lifetime to do so.

'You did what we did just now with another woman, didn't you?' she accused him bleakly, a stab of that agony sharp in her heart before fury could lash out at him and make him hurt even half as much as she did.

'No!' he gasped, then stared back at her so solemnly she believed him. An almost smile lifted his mouth as he added a caveat, 'Not since I was sixteen anyway and even then it was nothing like we ever had.'

'One day I will have all the details out of you, before I make sure she is living in another country and you solemnly promise me you'll never want her again,' she threatened direly, but still there was that terrible sadness and a refusal to let her all the way into his head in his gaze. She recognised the bleakness in his eyes from the time after they lost their daughter and realised she'd been too wrapped up in her own terrible grief and despair to see it as the strangeness it was, even for the loving father he would have been to their little girl, if he had been granted the chance.

'As if I could want anyone but you,' he said, almost as if he was saying goodbye to a lovely fantasy of them being back together and willing to admit they still loved each other.

'Tell me, Gideon,' she demanded softly, matching him eye to eye, refusing to be fobbed off with a marriage where neither asked the deepest questions in their hearts.

'You will only hate me again.'

'I never hated you. Even under all that darkness and despair I only ever loved you,' she confessed huskily and bravely kept her eyes steady and did her best to show him all she felt for him, then and now, at last. 'If we'd been older, we would have known all we needed was a little time for our world to right itself. Our lives would have been lived well together despite our grief, if my wretched aunt hadn't interfered and I wasn't stupid enough not to see her for what she is. I was such a fool.'

'Not that, my love, never that,' he protested, and paused as if he needed all his courage for the last and biggest secret in his stock of them. 'I was the fool, I simply couldn't stay and keep facing you when I knew you were right and I am a monster,' he confessed on a deep breath, as if owning up to a capital crime.

'I wouldn't blame you for not wanting to be with a woman so mad with grief I didn't even want to live with myself, but I was the one who told you to go, Gideon, not the other way about.'

'I couldn't face you then and I'm not even sure I'm worthy of a second chance at marrying you now,' he admitted painfully.

'Stop it,' she protested as forcefully as she could when she was on her knees facing him in the same naked state as he was. A shiver of awareness and longing for his touch ran through her and there was no disguising she wanted him, whatever he had to say. 'Don't you dare put me on a pedestal Gideon Laughraine. I'm not a goddess to be worshiped or a serene saint to be revered and never touched, lover. I'm a woman and a very fallible one at that.'

'You're certainly not a shy little siren any

more, are you, love?' he asked so tenderly it had to be love warming his grey-green eyes.

'No, now get on with it,' she demanded.

'Very well, but you might want to be further away when I tell you.' She shook her head impatiently and refused to let him off a single inch of intimacy. 'When they said Grace was dead I was so relieved I thought I might faint,' he confessed in such a raw voice she hardly recognised it as his. 'When everything went so quiet in that infernal room nobody would let me into while you gave birth to our child and I wasn't allowed anywhere near, I could tell something had gone terribly wrong and I thought you were dead, Callie.'

He raised his eyes and faced her steady and composed and utterly serious, as if awaiting a verdict of death from a hanging judge. 'I wanted to rage and weep and argue with the angels over our perfect little girl and how her life hadn't even begun before it ended, but all the while I was blind with relief and ecstatic that you were still alive. They even said it was an easy enough birth for a first-time mother and I was happy you hadn't suffered as much as I know a very young mother like you can in childbirth. All the time you were so quiet and sad and not my Callie at all, I knew that I'd thanked God on my knees that night because you were still alive. It was a terrible price to pay for you, but I paid it willingly, Callie.'

'Oh, Gideon,' she said with a hard sob as she looked back at that passionate and suffering young man and felt only compassion for his conflicted soul. 'Oh, my love,' she managed as she put her open hands against his hard cheekbones and made him meet her eyes even though they were spilling over with tears. 'What a mull we made of it all between us, didn't we?' she whispered as she explored his dear features with trembling fingertips, as if she had to learn the map of her lover by heart all over again.

'I can't deny that,' he murmured and yet he looked like a man on the rack with suppressed agony, as if he still expected her to turn away and admit she couldn't live with him, after all.

'If you were the one in danger and I had to choose, I would have thought the same and felt as you did, Gideon. It makes no sense at all to me now, but back then it was the very fact I couldn't endure the thought of life without you that made me turn away. It certainly wasn't because I loved you too little, but it felt so deep and dangerous I thought it easier to lose you in the now than spend my life dreading every minute we were apart. You have no idea how bitterly I hated every passably pretty female you set eyes on, or dreaded any of the seductive gestures or looks I knew would come your way as you grew into yourself and made a place in the world apart from me. I was a coward, Gideon. It was better to lose the one person who meant the world to me, rather than risk living like that for the rest of my days and driving you away with too much love for a young man to live with.'

'Love,' he said softly as if it was all he could summon on to his tongue right now. 'Ah, love,' he added shakily and put his hands out blindly to echo her need to feel beloved skin under a butterfly touch.

'Yes,' she agreed on a whisper nobody a breath of listening further away could have heard. 'Yes, Gideon, I do,' she told him bravely, throwing all her defences away and admitting it with all that was once between them and this new love she'd discovered, as well.

'Marry me?' he asked with a parody of James Winterley's one crooked eyebrow that made her want to laugh at just the wrong moment.

'We spent weeks on end dashing about the countryside at great expense so we could wed without let or stay all those years ago, why would we do it again?'

'First, I want to say all the marriage service to you in public,' he counted off on his index finger. 'And I love you so much it hurts.' He spared his touch from her long enough to list on his second finger. 'The world needs to know that us being man and wife is all that matters in the fine tangle our parents and grandparents made of things.' He ended on his ring finger and even the thought of placing a heavy gold band there made her smile like a moon-mad idiot. 'And did I remember to say I love you?'

'I believe you might have done, but it won't hurt if you repeat it at regular intervals for the rest of our lives. So, yes, I will. We'll be written off as a pair of lunatics, but it's a well-known fact they need humouring, isn't it?'

'Indeed it is,' he said with a smile that felt warm and open as the first day they met as almost adults and he dazzled her with it and put himself in her heart for all time as the only lover she would ever contemplate having. 'Are you sure?' he asked, letting her see all the vulnerability and self-doubts he must have struggled with as a boy and young man.

'Do I look as if I have any doubts? Of course I'm sure, Gideon, and we will do better at being man and wife this time, I promise you,' she said solemnly. She had proved life without him was possible, she supposed, but it felt as if she had been wandering for nine years in a barren wilderness now she looked back. 'I learnt a lot while we were apart and I do have a new love in my life, as well,' she told him with a sweet, blank smile and a provocative look.

'He will have to accept banishment to a far-away shore or accept his days are numbered, then, won't he? Please don't run away with the idea I could ever share you, Callie, it would be a very bad mistake.'

She eyed the rock-steady facade he seemed able to throw up between himself and even her when he wanted to hide the passion and fury under the skin of a man of law and took the warning in it with a well-hidden shudder. No, she could never risk being on the wrong side of that wall ever again and shook her head at the very idea and her own stupidity in risking it in the first place.

'It's not a man, it's only my novels that you need worry about taking up my time,' she confessed. 'They made the loneliness of living without you almost endurable and I don't want to give them up even now I have you back in my life, Gideon.'

'Then I shall have to regard them as mixed blessings, since you might have taken the obvious remedy for that solitude and found me out if you hadn't been otherwise occupied.'

'Maybe, but we had a lot of growing up to do. Could you have taken me back without hating me for making you go, love? In your shoes I'm not so certain I could.'

'My life was bare and barren and dry those first few years, Callie,' he said a little too seriously and she wanted to turn away from the bleakness on his dear face and be ashamed of herself for putting him through purgatory on the contrivance of a pair of liars without a conscience between them. 'Don't hide your face from me, my love. I've got years' worth of gazing at you to gloat over now I've finally got you in my bed again,' he argued as he cupped her chin with a gentle hand and made her look at him again.

'I'm so sorry,' she said seriously, no thought of joking them back into laughter and heat and passion in her head this time as she let the bare facts of their split lives into the open. 'I can't even think of the lonely and rootless young man I made of you without wanting to go back and rage at the idiot I was for doing that to us.'

'It wasn't so bad, my darling,' he soothed

as his touch went absently sensual again and his fingers began to explore her soft skin and finely boned cheeks.

Heat and longing shot through her body like the occasional darts of summer lightning still left over from the storm outside as steady rain beat against the windows and she felt safe and loved and warm in her lover's arms.

'I found ways of using the law to chase justice and one night I helped save three lives all at the same time and thought myself the devil of a fellow for a while,' he joked and seemed to realise what he'd been about while his mind told him it was busy remembering. His gaze went silver and hot again and she wanted to simply enjoy all they could have in this glorious old bed once more, but that story sounded too intriguing to quite let go.

'Who were they?' she asked rather breathily as his exploring fingertip trailed slowly down her jaw to explore the smooth skin of her neck and rest at the pulse at the base of it and linger like a kiss.

'Hmm?' he asked as his hot glance followed his touch to gloat over that racing little giveaway, even if her skin wasn't glowing with desire and her body very obviously aroused. 'Oh, them, that's Rich Seaborne's tale. You'll have to wrench it from him some time if your writer's curiosity won't rest now I've woken it up again.'

'Heavens,' she murmured with as much of that quality as she could spare. 'I wouldn't dare,' she whispered with a preoccupied gasp as he stopped looking and set his wicked tongue to that hasty pulse of hers and added fuel to the fire.

'Good,' he managed with far more of a grasp on words than she wanted him to have right now. 'He was the devil of a fellow once upon a time, I wouldn't want you paying too close attention to a rogue like that, even if he is about as tamed and captivated as an ex-rake can be nowadays.'

'Is he now? Somehow I find it difficult to care about your friend and the state of his marriage right now, so be quiet and use your tongue for seducing your wife instead of worrying about someone else's, Gideon Laughraine,' she ordered breathily and, of course, he did exactly as his exacting wife ordered him to, for once.

Chapter Seventeen

'Over that mysterious illness that afflicted you and your wife last night now, are you?' James Winterley greeted Gideon at breakfast the next morning and he felt himself blush like a schoolgirl.

Of course, everyone knew they weren't ill but intimate last night when they stayed closeted in their grand suite of rooms and had their meals sent up to sit in the grand sitting room between her room and his until they weren't so busy. Why he should feel like a secret lover uncovered before he was ready for it when he and Callie had been wed for a decade was beyond him, but under Winterley's cynical gaze he felt like a boy caught stealing sugar plums.

'No,' he responded shortly and helped himself to his breakfast more or less at random. He would never be over that particular ailment and the very thought of waking up next to his wife again at long last made his hand shake and his eyes lose their sharp focus under Winterley's amused gaze. 'You're not my keeper,' he informed him gruffly.

'Thank heavens. I'd have had my hair turned white by some of your exploits these last few years if I was.'

'Tell me,' Callie's voice cut through the much-fresher morning air and how had she managed to creep up on them like that when Gideon thought his every sense was attuned to her nearness?

'Don't,' he argued before he could think sanely about the effect that would have on her curiosity.

'I'm not fool enough to get caught in a lively debate between husband and wife,' Winterley said before Callie could demand more details and Gideon could think of a way of stopping her finding them out.

'Then you'd best hurry up and eat your breakfast and go away,' she said with an unfriendly look, 'because I'm determined to find out what he's been up to somehow or another.'

'If I go away, all you two will find is your way back upstairs and I have business to discuss with this hangdog husband of yours, Lady Laughraine.'

Callie looked as if she was about to ring a fine peal over the man, then met his challenging glance and laughed instead. 'You really are very like your great-aunt, Mr Winterley,' she said and nodded militantly at him when he shook his head and looked slightly revolted at the comparison. 'Yes,' she argued, 'she had the exact same way of looking at me as if she knew all my secrets and couldn't imagine why I was trying to outfox her.'

'I recognise the description, but not the likeness,' he said with almost offended dignity.

'Ah, well, we shall see what we see,' she said in her best schoolmistress manner and Gideon fervently wished he could distract her from Winterley, breakfast and his own dark secrets for a return to the pleasures of being man and wife for the first time in almost an hour.

'What business?' he asked before his mind could completely haze over with the delights of being Callie's husband again.

'I can't think how any of us were ever fooled by that dry-as-dust manner of yours, Laughraine,' James Winterley said on the brink of a boyish grin before he recalled he was a cynical gentleman of fashion in the nick of time. 'I might be in need of a good lawyer soon, although it might be as well if you recovered your wits first.'

'Why so? Do you have a guilty conscience? I won't touch a paternity suit if you've been fishing in the wrong pond.'

'Come now, Laughraine, I might be a dog with a bad name, but I ain't a fool,' he said with an apologetic glance at Callie, who waved her hand and went on with her breakfast as if she hadn't eaten for days, quite untroubled by Winterley's potential sins. 'And I have never yet laid my grubby hands on an innocent, Lady Laughraine,' the man went on as if he actually cared for Callie's good opinion and Gideon wasn't quite sure how he felt about that idea.

'If you don't want a lawyer to defend you against the wrath of a furious parent and his misused daughter, what the devil *do* you want one for?' he barked.

'I'm thinking of buying a house. No, revise that, Master Lawyer, I'm thinking of buying an apology for a house. More of a few standing walls and half a roof than a house.'

'It sounds like the last place a peacock like you should take up residence.'

'It is, but it has some of the best farmland I ever saw going to rack and ruin round it and a fine set of gallops to train racehorses on. The stables aren't as shabby as the house either, so I suppose I'll have to live in them with my groom and the horses for a while, if I'm fool enough to purchase the place.'

'With winter on its way, it is to be hoped you get even the stables neat and watertight before the worst of the weather sets in so we'd best hurry the business along if you're serious. Are you going to tell me where this ruin is, or am I supposed to guess?'

'It's Brackley House—your uncle called it the old Saltash place.'

'No one has lived there for years and it's at the back of beyond. What can a man like you want with it?'

'Peace,' James said with a closed-in expression Gideon recognised. 'I'm weary of James Winterley and his quest to prove he's worse than his despairing family suspect. I want a place where I can be myself, Laughraine, or as close as I can get when I'm not quite sure who I am. Horses don't care about a man's reputation or the state of his conscience. All that matters to them is he treats them well, feeds them and races the fidgets out of them when they're full of oats and have the devil in them.'

'It all sounds so simple put like that, but I

doubt any man's life can be that quiet, even in the middle of nowhere,' Callie put in her four-penny-worth before helping herself to coffee and giving Gideon a look that said she hadn't forgotten he owed her a long explanation of his own sins and evasions.

'Maybe not,' Winterley replied with a nod that held surprising respect for her and her opinions and Gideon had to leash his inner beast all over again. 'But that's why I liked the place and will buy it if I can. Your grandfather is a cunning old gentleman, my lady, and I can't help wondering why he pushed me to look at a place that suits my liking for solitude so perfectly and will keep me out of mischief for years. Could he have a scheme up his sleeve to turn us three into bosom bows, do you think?'

'I don't know, could he?' she asked steadily.

'Since I doubt either of you give your friend-ship because a man likes your company better than your absence, how would I know?' James said with that to-hell-with-you-both look that was beginning to show Gideon here was a man nigh as well defended and poker-backed as he had been himself until recently.

'Perhaps if you're going to be a neighbour, we'd best try to be friends. I certainly wouldn't want you as my enemy, Winterley,' he admitted.

'And I wouldn't want to refuse you if you're going to go on glaring at me like an angry bear, but I promise not to presume on you as a friend or a relative. I do have a certain reputation to preserve as an idle gentleman of fashion, you know?'

'You'll have to get over it if you plan to become a gentleman farmer instead then, won't you, Mr Winterley?' Callie said impatiently and Gideon felt that demand to know what he'd been up to all these years coming dangerously close again.

'Clearly,' James Winterley said with a pained glance at his exquisitely cut summer coat and immaculate linen. 'Unlike your friend Mantaigne I do not enjoy getting dirty. I dare say you two spent most of your time at his noble ruin shovelling out stables and planting potatoes this spring.'

'Something like that,' Gideon admitted with a reminiscent smile as he struggled with the notion this finicky Corinthian felt left out of the adventures he and his half-brother and then Virginia's godson had been wrapped up in during their set time of reluctant self-discovery.

'My great-aunt had a way of making fools out of us all,' Winterley said with an almost affectionate smile. 'I suppose it came from being the most renowned beauty of her age, since she must have learnt the way of winding men round her little finger young and not quite given it up even when she met my great-uncle.'

'She was an astonishing female, wasn't she?' Gideon agreed with an apologetic glance at Callie, who couldn't have known her well and probably had a couple of very forthright exchanges with the lady. 'She made sure I was part of her life, despite having the most potent reason not to want a constant reminder of who I really am around the place.'

'Maybe, although I suspect that's why she wanted to know you in the first place. Virginia adored my great-uncle and any trace of him in you would be a comfort rather than a reminder he'd had a brief affair before they met. He never even looked at another woman once he found her, for all they both had reputations that make me look angelic before they met.'

'I've seen those pictures of her at Farenze Lodge and could have been halfway in love with her myself if I'd met her in her prime. The artist who painted them clearly was.'

'Aye, I often wondered why Virgil permitted him to paint so many, but I expect he pitied the poor fool, she barely knew there was another man in the world when he was by.'

'How I wish I'd known him better. I envy you that much of your gilded youth,' Gideon said with genuine regret. 'My father hated his real father and kept me away from him, although he hardly acknowledged I existed most of the time.'

'Lucky you,' James replied moodily, and Gideon saw Callie cast him a long assessing look and nearly groaned out loud.

If Winterley thought Lady Virginia was the only female he knew who was capable of interfering in his life for his own good he was about to discover his error. Gideon resolved to keep his wife firmly occupied whilst the man worked out his own destiny and let the marvel of that sink in as Winterley agreed to go back and take a quiet look at the wreck he wanted to buy before he committed himself to the place and Gideon began the dance of pretending his client didn't really want the place at all to get it for him at the best price.

Once the man Gideon was almost inclined to look on as a friend as well as a secret relative had gone about his business Callie gave him a wary look. 'We have to look in those boxes now, Gideon,' she said as if expecting him to recoil in shocked revulsion at the very idea.

'I wrote to you and your aunt made sure you

didn't get my letters—what is to be gained from reading my boy's outpourings now, love?' he asked because he felt half embarrassed to think what he might have said in his hurt and desperation when she never once replied to his pleas for any sort of reconciliation.

'And I wrote all my fury and grief and loneliness to you and she did the same to my letters as she did to yours, but I didn't mean that, although sooner or later I think we owe it to who we were then to read them. We have to look to find out what Mrs Bartle did to my parents and tell Mama and my grandfather what they need to know.'

'Isn't it her secret rather than ours, though, Callie love?'

'If he was as callous as she thought, no, I think she would rather not be reminded of their disastrous *affaire*. If that woman played the same trick on her sister as she did on us then it will be her choice what to do about it, but Grandfather needs to know either way. I can only imagine how awful it must be to think your son a villain and pray we never need do so.'

'Imagine it, Callie, a boy of our own,' he said on a long stuttering sigh, then wondered if she could endure to put another in the place of their lost girl. 'Will you hate me if we have another girl, or indeed any child at all in the place of the one we lost?' he asked, suddenly afraid she might not think the idea of either boy or girl in any number she cared to give him waking up Raigne with their chatter and mischief half as wondrous as he did.

'They would never take her place, but I can't imagine anything finer than as many children as we can contrive running about this place and making it into a home instead of a fine museum.'

'Care to start now?' he asked with a tomcat smile to divert her from the idea of those boxes again as best he could.

'No, we have far too much to do to indulge in bed sports right now and you know it, Husband,' she said severely.

'Aye, I suppose we'd best plan our wedding before we worry about christening a baby of either sex,' he said as provocatively as he could manage and they just managed to give the maids enough time to make up their grand bed before they dived back into it and made that remarriage of theirs all the more urgent.

'Ah, here come the blushing bride and groom-to-be for the second time. So glad you could join us for your prenuptial celebrations,' James Winterley said with a mocking glance at Callie and Gideon that said he knew exactly why they were late.

'My lady insisted on being here for some odd reason,' Gideon replied with a grin that admitted he would be very happy to skip the lavish dinner Lord Laughraine had arranged for the night before his granddaughter and almost nephew married for the second time in favour of a simpler and more intimate one in their grand suite upstairs.

'I did,' Callie said lightly, but with a challenge in her glance at James Winterley that forbade him to make mischief to entertain himself tonight. 'Now I've got into the way of hobnobbing with aristocrats, I was hardly likely to pass up such an opportunity to spend an evening with so many of them, now was I?'

'I don't think pretending to be humble will get you anywhere with Gideon's family now, do you?' the rogue answered with a warning for her not to let herself be intimidated by the great and the good in his own gaze that she found rather endearing. How he'd hate anyone to think he was anything of the kind and she wondered why he was so determined to be the black sheep of the family.

'Apparently not,' she said with a glance around the lovely old room ablaze with the soft light of candles and alive with laughter and eager conversations.

Gideon was soon hauled away from her side by the current Lord Farenze's daughter and his wife's niece and Callie wondered what mischief those two enterprising young ladies had in mind for her after they acted as bridesmaids tomorrow. No doubt they would behave impeccably during the service, but she suspected they'd see it as their duty to plan a few surprises for the newly re-wed couple as they began a belated honeymoon.

'At least the Winterley clan and Gideon's friends have woken Raigne up from what my grandfather calls its long slumber,' she said with an assessing glance at the abundance of life and colour they gave this stately old parlour.

The ancient plasterwork and intricately carved wood had been cleaned and polished until it couldn't look any more mellow and magnificent. Her grandfather was enjoying playing host to his guests so much it made Callie realise how lonely he'd been here all the time she was lonely twenty miles away. This wasn't a night for self-recrimination and regrets over choices she had not made and roads she was too stubborn to take, though, so she turned back to the most enigmatic member of his clan.

'You belong to a fine family, Mr Winterley.'

His smile went grim and the spark of laughter seemed to flatten to self-mockery again. Callie knew she had been thoughtless to remind him he was among those closest to him by blood and still felt he must stand apart.

'I am fully aware what an honour it is they still own up to me,' he said shortly.

'I imagine they have very little choice as the resemblance between you and your brother is striking. The Winterley stamp is so distinctive I doubt any of you could escape being known as one if you tried.'

Callie's eyes were back on her husband now, since he bore that stamp as strongly as either of his distant cousins and was unmistakably a Winterley tonight. She forced herself to take her gaze off his dark head and broad shoulders for a second or two and noticed James was too busy watching his brother's daughter by his first marriage to notice Callie was obsessed with the man she was going to marry again in the morning. There was a fine tension about James Winterley tonight she suspected he would rather she didn't know about. She sensed the whisper of even deeper secrets than she'd thought under his mysteries with a superstitious shiver.

'About this quest you were all set by Lady Virginia. It isn't over, is it?' she asked, and at least that made him take his brooding gaze off his niece and watch her warily. 'I managed to work it out, you know. Your elder brother went first, then Lord Mantaigne and now Gideon has met his demons head on,' she persisted with a wry smile at the thought of herself as chief of those. She knew whatever was secret between Lady Farenze and her lawyers yesterday was in this man's possession now. 'So you're next.' She made it an observation rather than a question. He would deny anyone the chance to manipulate his life if he could, even the great-aunt he loved.

'Must I? I doubt it,' he said sombrely as he stood on the sidelines of all the animated family discussions and pretended he wanted no part of it.

'Never mind the love and marriage the tasks outlined in her ladyship's will brought to your half-brother, her ladyship's godson and now

Gideon. You can stand aloof from the rest of the world if you choose with my blessing, but I know you're her fourth knight. Don't shake your head and try to look as if you care for nobody and never have. You loved your greataunt, Mr Winterley. I have learnt how easy it is to fool yourself you can live without love and hope. I really cannot recommend it as a strategy for not being hurt by trying and failing at love, or any other powerful emotions you're struggling with. No, don't argue—I have nine wasted years of mine and Gideon's lives to cite for what happens when you cut yourself off from all the matters to avoid being hurt again. It wasn't happiness I gained by being such a coward—it was numb endurance. So let's be honest with each other this once. You loved Lady Virginia very much, didn't you?' He didn't nod or speak, but it seemed very significant to Callie that he couldn't deny it, either. 'I know you will do whatever she asked you to. You're a man with too many emotions bottled up in his stubborn head instead of too few, Mr James Winterley.'

'How well you do claim to know me, Lady Laughraine, and I wonder what your husband would say about that?'

'He would say he trusts me, although he's never too sure about your motives,' Callie said with such certainty it made her laugh when he tried to look faintly revolted.

'The moment I heard Peters was Virginia's mystery card I thought here was a man far too buttoned up and rational to tumble headfirst into love and marriage like my brother and his unreliable best friend. As it turns out he's the worst of all. He couldn't fall in love this summer because he'd done it ten years ago, when he should have been minding his books and learning to be a much stuffier lawyer and you're not a lot better, my lady. Apparently it's up to me to prove Virginia can't drive four men determined up the aisle in a twelvemonth.'

'At the beginning of that year I wonder if any one of you thought she would succeed with even one,' Callie reminded him cunningly, then chuckled at his revolted expression. 'If she does manage to work her magic on you, I can see you'll be the most reluctant hero who ever stepped, Mr Winterley,' she teased him because really, somebody ought to. His family treated him with a sort of wary caution that threatened to make her heart bleed for him and for some odd reason of his own he seemed to have let her and Gideon a lot further under his guard than was usual for a cautious rogue like him.

'I'm nobody's hero,' was all he said and she knew he was doing his best to put his aloof persona back together again to face whatever ordeal Lady Virginia had left him.

'Lady Virginia was a fine judge of character.'

'You didn't do as she wanted and take my cousin back when she came here and begged you to give him a second chance, though, did you?'

'How did you know about that?' she asked, and realised how clever this rogue was when he raised that one eyebrow and let her know he had been guessing. 'Very clever, Mr Winterley.'

'I am, Lady Laughraine. I've refused to dance to anyone's tune but my own since I was old enough to have a choice and I'm reluctant to do as I'm bid even by Virginia.'

'What a precocious and mule-like little boy you must have been. No wonder Lady Virginia doted on you,' she counter-attacked.

'She wasn't the type of female to dote on any of us,' he said as if he was horrified by the notion and looked restlessly about the room for a reason to leave her to play hostess instead of examining him for emotions he didn't want to know about.

'All of us who consider you an intrinsic part of the family are grateful to her for *not* letting you know you had a special place in her heart. You would have grown up unbearable.'

'For a person who only met my great-aunt once, you claim to know a lot about her.'

'I do, don't I?' Callie said with a smile a little to the one side of her handsome adversary. 'Feminine intuition,' she argued blandly.

'Gideon,' he argued suspiciously. 'Or did one of them tell you they only agreed to do as Virginia bid them because the prospect of succeeding in their quests meant I would inherit a fortune so they could finally be rid of me?'

'One of them?' she echoed mockingly. 'You mean one of your band of brothers?'

'I only have one half-brother and he wishes I'd never been born.'

'Somehow I doubt it, but whatever the facts of your relationships, you four are like as peas in a pod—never mind if you're related or not,' Callie said as she turned to face her own returning hero with all the joy and love she felt in him blatantly on display. 'Come now, Mr Winterley, you're an adventurer, aren't you? When did you ever turn down a challenge, particularly one that will be to your advantage if you get it right?' she chided him absently as Gideon took her hand and everyone else in the room went a little less vivid for her, including James Winterley.

Chapter Eighteen

'You look far too serious,' Gideon teased as he smiled down at her as if he couldn't be solemn about anything tonight, because at last she was his openly declared true love again and he was hers.

'This is a very sober occasion I will have you know. I'm going to marry Lady Virginia's latest hero in the morning.'

'I know, and what a woman she was, wasn't she?' he said with sincere love and admiration in his grey-green eyes. 'I was the cuckoo in her nest and she still managed to love me. Heaven knows what she has in store for you, Winterley. You always were her favourite.'

'Ah, so you have been talking to your wife about me, have you? How flattering to think I feature so highly in your private conversations when you can't seem to string together two rational words between you when I come across you nowadays.'

'Actually you are never foremost in our minds when we're alone together. Sorry to disappoint you, Winterley, but you're some way down our list of favourite topics.'

'How else could Callie have got hold of that ridiculous idea, as well, then?'

'I expect that's because it's true, she is a woman of great perception and sound common sense.'

'Rubbish, you're both as deluded as each other, but so long as you're unhinged together I don't suppose it will bother the rest of the world. I wish you very happy, Sir Gideon and Lady Peters-Winterley-Laughraine, but kindly confine yourselves to your own business in future and stay out of mine,' he said, and spun on the low heel of his elegant evening shoes and walked away.

'I *think* he means well, Callie,' Gideon confided with a shake of his dark head for the conundrum who was his cousin and, yes, his friend.

'So do I. Perhaps Lady Virginia was right about him, after all.'

'How do you know she had a special place for James in her heart, love?' he asked idly as he did his best not to look too hard at her and make them both want each other unbearably again before dinner was announced and their absence from their own celebrations became stark and rude.

'Because she left him until last, of course. She started with Lord Farenze as possibly the least stubborn of the stubborn Winterleys and she worked her way down the list until she came to the hardest nut of all. Did she tell you all his fate depended on you?'

'You really must be a witch to know about that bit of her will. I don't talk in my sleep, do I?'

'Not about James Winterley, I'm very pleased to say,' she teased him with a demure look that threatened him with all sorts of stories about what he really did say in his sleep.

'I should never have wed a lady novelist,' he replied and, oh, but she loved this man so much it almost hurt.

'Now I think you should, only think how much it will liven up our dull lives as lord and lady of the manor one day,' she said with all sorts of likely scenarios hinted at in that almost promise of her wildest imaginings adding even more spice to their marriage. 'No, Gideon, we can't. Grandfather would never forgive us if we're not here to be suitably lionised tonight.'

'Do you think any of them would be shocked?' he asked with a wide gesture at the assembled company of Winterleys, Banburghs and Seabornes, most of them intent on their respective spouses and almost as distracted by them in their evening finery as she was by Gideon in his. 'I don't think any of us will be sitting up late tonight, do you?'

'I very much doubt it, but you were right, Gideon—'

'Of course,' he interrupted her in his best parody of a solemn lawyer.

'I was about to say you were right about your friends and all these secret relatives of yours. I do like them, even more so because they seem deeply in love with their spouses. Even Lady Freya Seaborne seems more interested in the person under the fine clothes than which bed they were born in and I hear her brother is very high in the instep.'

'She is a dear girl and not at all haughty since she managed to tame Richard Seaborne, and she has exquisite taste in gowns,' he said with a hot gaze over the one Lady Freya's favourite modiste had so expertly made up in a glowing shade of rose pink to make the most of Callie's creamy skin, almost-tamed dark hair and velvet-brown eyes. The clever cut and draping managed to accentuate her narrow waist and feminine curves despite the fashion and clearly met with his approval. 'You look very fine indeed, love,' he added, but his heated gaze centred on the famous diamond-and-pearl pendant the Laughraine heir always gave his bride on the eve of their wedding and the blaze in his green-and-grey eyes informed her he would very much like to see her wearing nothing else.

'Stop it, Gideon, I won't be able to stand much longer if you don't behave yourself.'

'I have behaved myself for years, Callie, and look where it got me,' he said with all those years bleak in his gaze for a moment and tears swam in her eyes at the thought of the ordeal she had put them through.

'It got us to here and now,' she offered a little hesitantly, as if not quite sure even this was enough to make up for nine years of tortured self-denial.

'Which makes it was worth every agonising moment,' he said more lightly.

'True, but I think I could be with child again, Gideon,' she blurted out the news she had been trying to make herself share with him for days now and not found a moment when they weren't so busy loving she forgot everything but him. Or, if she was being completely honest with herself, a moment when she felt she wouldn't stutter into haunted memories of last time as soon as she opened her mouth.

'I know,' he said so softly she read it on his lips as much as heard it and of course he did, how could he not?

'You didn't say anything,' she mouthed back at him, the very intimacy of their urgent loving, the relearning of each other's bodies and minds they had done these last weeks and months piling up to remind her she was a fool. 'Of course you would know. We're not a pair of unworldly children now.'

'I felt it,' he said and his clear gaze was serious again now and she knew he didn't only mean the slight sensitivity in her breasts, or even the fact she occasionally had to wait until he was up and about the business of the Raigne estates before she dared get out of bed and cast up her accounts in a chamber pot.

'Do you mind? I suppose we should have been more careful.'

'I couldn't be, Callie,' he admitted hoarsely, as if it was a fault in him that he wanted her so urgently it was as if they had all those years' worth of loving to squeeze into the rest of their lives as soon as possible. 'I only have to look at you and I want you. No, that's not quite right. I want to make love with you until the rest of the world fades away wherever we both happen to be. I don't even need to look. The truth is that I forgot to take care of you once again, my love, and I'm so sorry.'

'I'm not,' she said, a little bit offended that he didn't think she was capable of telling him to at least try and make sure he didn't get her pregnant if she didn't want to be. 'I want this child, Gideon.'

'So do I, but I want you even more,' he admitted and that painful conversation they had the first night they made love again came back to her and made it impossible for her to keep her hands off her handsome husband any longer.

She reached up to cup a hand to his strong jaw. 'I don't care what anyone else says, this time I want you to be with me when my time comes, Gideon. Why should they keep you out when we each had to go through all that agony last time without each other?'

'I'm not sure whoever decrees a man cannot see his much-loved wife give birth to their child will agree to that, love.'

'Then we'll do it without them. I can't think

of anyone I would rather have with me than you. It's our family, I think we both ought to have a say in how it happens.'

'If you don't mind me keeping every doctor and midwife I can lay hands on nearby to soothe my nerves then, yes, my lady, I agree.'

'Well, good, what point is there being destined to be one of the lords of creation if you can't make up your own rules sometimes?'

'None at all, my Calliope,' he said, and reluctantly brought his hand up to remove hers from a wicked exploration of his strongly sculpted jaw in public. 'And don't forget you're named for a goddess, will you?' he asked as he kissed her hand palm upwards to punish her for winding them into a fever of need when there was no time or place to do a thing about it.

'Even better then, maybe I shall decree another faint. Then you would have to carry me upstairs and stay with me to make sure I was all right, wouldn't you, Gideon, my darling?'

'I don't think that would be the reason I left your grandfather to host a wedding-eve celebration without a bride or a groom, do you? Now behave yourself, lover. You may be willing to do that to him, but I don't think I can bring myself to rob him of his triumph a second time.'

'Neither do I, but it's not his triumph—

it's ours,' she said seriously as the lingering thought he might feel he'd been trapped into marriage with her in the first place haunted her for a dark moment.

'I know. I would like to claim it was love at first sight, but you did give me a bloody nose and call me a worm when you were six and I was seven, so we'll have to settle for me learning to love you at the grand old age of seventeen when you were more ladylike and almost as irresistible as you are now.'

'I'm quite content to settle for that, in fact...'

'Mr and Mrs Willoughby and Mr Thomas Willoughby, my lord,' Craddock intoned solemnly from the doorway. Callie had noticed him enter out of the corner of her eye and had absently decided dinner must be ready and maybe they could get it eaten and over with as soon as possible, then find an excuse to retire early and celebrate another new start to their marriage and this longed-for new baby all at the same time.

'My mother?' she gasped now and turned to stare at the three travellers blinking in the light of so many candles, then swung round to eye her husband with suspicion. 'If you knew about this and didn't tell me, I shall indeed banish you from my grand bed tonight, Gideon Laughraine,' she informed him haughtily.

'Just as well I had no more idea your grandfather invited them than you then, isn't it?' he said, enough challenge in his eyes for her to know that distrust hurt him.

'I'm sorry, would you like me to faint now, after all, to make up for my mistake, then?'

'No, love, behave yourself and come and greet your mother like a proper baronet's lady,' he said with a boyish grin as he took her hand and tucked it into the crook of his elbow.

'I'm not going to meekly do as I'm bid without question ever again, Gideon,' she whispered as the guests parted to let them through. 'Look where that got us,' she added even as she braced herself to meet her mother's blue eyes and see no feeling in them for her eldest daughter at all.

'Nine years of peace and quiet?'

'No, an eternity of longing and frustration. Now be quiet and behave yourself, Husband.'

'Nag.'

'Buffoon.'

'Ah, there you are, my dears,' Lord Laughraine greeted them. 'Here is…'

'Your mother,' Mrs Willoughby said defiantly, looking straight at Callie and refusing to let her gaze drop away or skim off to take an interest in a more important being as it always had before.

'Mama?' Callie asked, the form of it not feeling quite right on her lips when she had never felt she had a mother before and wasn't quite sure about it now.

'My dear,' her mother said and, heavens above; were those really tears in her eyes? Could she possibly mean it, was she dear to the woman who birthed her, after all? Given twenty-seven years of making it clear she had one daughter more than she was prepared to admit to, was this really the right time to declare herself mother of the bride?

'I'm not sure about this, Mrs Willoughby,' her husband said with a shake of his grey head and a furtive look at the august company his stepdaughter was keeping.

'Seraphina cannot touch me now the truth is in the open at last, Giles. I refuse to kowtow to her demands I stay out of my own daughter's life for one more day,' his wife overruled him with a firmness Callie would have thought her incapable of if she hadn't heard it with her own ears. 'We have discussed this over and over and I won't be kept away from Calliope's wedding a second time.'

The tall young man with his father's mid-brown hair and aquiline nose stepped out of the shadows and bowed to Callie with a rather endearing grin and a twinkle in the bright blue eyes he'd clearly inherited from their mother.

'You must be my big sister, Lady Laughraine, if you choose to acknowledge me?' he greeted her as if he was quite happy to meet her and tactful enough to divert attention from his parents as they stood stiffly waiting for the sky to fall on their heads.

'I always wanted a little brother,' she replied, finding it unexpectedly easy to return his smile and invitation to find this situation funny, at least the bits that weren't a little unreal and full of pitfalls. That one time she and Gideon were invited to Willoughby Manor he was away at school and Mr Willoughby scurried his youngest daughters out of the back door to stay with their paternal grandmother practically the instant she came in through the front one. It said a lot about her mother's determination and this handsome boy's good nature that he was here tonight doing his best to pretend he was proud of her. 'If only I'd known you when you weren't a foot taller than I am, I might have been able to exploit the advantage of being the eldest a lot more thoroughly than I can now.'

'I, on the other hand, am deeply relieved to

have been spared yet another sister determined to plague the life out of me in my nursery days.'

'I should have been a braver man and taken you into my home along with your mama all those years ago,' Mr Willoughby interrupted gruffly and Callie was still not convinced he meant it. 'Would have made me uncomfortable and scandalised the neighbours, but my wife never quite forgave herself for leaving you behind at King's Raigne Vicarage when we wed. I ought to have told that confounded sister of hers to do her worst and tell the world what she chose to twenty-five years ago.' He ended with as big an olive branch as he could offer her when he would clearly have preferred to let sleeping dogs lie even now.

'I was quite happy with Grandfather Sommers,' she told her mother. Somehow she knew Mr Willoughby would never have taken her fully into his family and raised her as his own, even if Callie had gone with her mother to Willoughby Manor all those years ago. 'And if I had lived with you all those years I might never have met Gideon,' she managed to lie almost convincingly, because she knew perfectly well her grandfathers would have made sure she did, wherever she happened to be living at the time. How could she have encountered the brooding young Adonis he was at eighteen without falling headlong into love with him on the spot? Impossible, she decided as she glanced at him and found him even more handsome and dashing now than she had then, if that was possible.

'Made for each other,' her grandfather put in indulgently. 'I admit I sent copies of Will's letters to Mrs Willoughby along with her own, my dear, when I begged her to allow the truth to come out at last and the Laughraine succession to rest on you two once and for all. I told her about your second wedding to this rogue and sent an invitation for her and her family to attend it, but it is her choice to do so as mother of the bride. I think you a brave woman to agree to do so, ma'am, and a forgiving one to come back here when it must hold some very difficult memories for you.'

'Thank you, my lord,' Mrs Willoughby said with a composure in her voice Callie had never heard before. 'My sister is a cold and bitter woman, but I suppose she was never lucky enough to have children and a good husband to teach her the value of compassion. I wish she had never interfered between me and your son for my daughter's sake, but I don't think we would have rejoiced in the sort of marriage Calliope has or the one Mr Willoughby and I have made somehow between us over the years.'

Her mother was still a beautiful woman and something told Callie when she wed her Mr Willoughby he was more in love with her than she was with him. Mrs Willoughby had achieved something her sister never would and learnt love as she went. If she had not made much effort to find room in her life for the bastard child of the man she had loved with all the intensity of a besotted girl while she was doing so, was it Callie's place to judge her when she had Grandfather Sommers to love and protect her? Mr Willoughby would never have found it in his heart to do any of that for the child of a man he had to be jealous of.

'Luckily for you, Grandfather Laughraine, I agree with you,' Callie told him with what he called her *I'll deal with you later* look.

'And so do I,' Gideon said as he stepped forward and Callie had to hide a chuckle behind a polite little cough as her mother reverted to type and cast her son-in-law a coy smile and almost preened like a turtle dove. 'Thank you for coming, Mrs Willoughby, you are very welcome and I cannot think of any guest I would rather welcome to our wedding than my wife's mother and her family. I'm sure my uncle has ordered bedchambers aired and made ready against your arrival, since he didn't see fit to inform the rest of us that you were coming.'

'Of course I have, my boy, d'you think my wits are out for an airing just because you're getting married to this girl of mine again? I quite understand if you're too fatigued to stay and eat with us tonight, my dear lady, but if you could see your way to sit down to dinner with us I'll have it put back half an hour in order for you to refresh yourselves. We're only sitting down to a little family affair tonight, Willoughby. No need to stand on ceremony,' the Lord of Raigne said with a dismissive gesture at the glittering company of fifty or so of his and his heir's closest friends and some of the most influential people in the land.

'I'd be glad to, my lord,' the squire said, looking a little dazed by the sort of the people his host considered family and friends familiar enough to be casual about. 'What say you, my dear?'

'In all our dirt? That's clearly impossible and you must tell Gresley I need her immediately, Tom, before they let her go upstairs and tell the footmen I shall need the largest of our trunks immediately. Oh, and my jewellery box, of course.'

Mrs Willoughby turned to leave the room as if in charge of her own household, then recalled exactly where she was and blushed slightly and recalled her manners, as well.

'If you will excuse us for a few minutes, of course, Lord Laughraine?' she asked with the languishing air of an established beauty Callie doubted she would ever lose now.

After a solemn assurance her host quite understood the necessity to change for dinner after their journey, Mrs Willoughby swept out of the room in a fine bustle at the thought of getting changed and ready to dine in such an impossibly short period of time.

'That's families for you. Are you sure you want to own up to more of that vexed commodity than you thought you were entitled to, Lady Laughraine?' James Winterley asked satirically from behind them again and Callie thought that for a man who claimed to be so indifferent to his own family he was always close by when he thought one of them might be in need of a barbed comments and his reluctant support.

'Do you know, I think I could get to like it,' she said with an impish smile and walked shamelessly into her husband's arms. Gideon opened them to receive her, as if he refused to ever pretend not to adore her again, whatever unladylike stunts she embarked on. 'Can I faint now, Husband?' she asked wickedly, and he laughed out loud.

'Perhaps later, my love,' he said, and kissed her full on the lips in front of all his family and friends.

* * * * *

**Don't miss Sarah Morgan's
next Puffin Island story**

Some Kind of Wonderful

Brittany Forrest has stayed away from Puffin Island
since her relationship with Zach Flynn went bad.
They were married for ten days and only just
managed not to kill each other by the
end of the honeymoon.

But, when a broken arm means she must return,
Brittany moves back to her Puffin Island home.
Only to discover that Zac is there as well.

Will a summer together help two lovers reunite or
will their stormy relationship crash on to the
rocks of Puffin Island?

Some Kind of Wonderful
COMING JULY 2015
Pre-order your copy today

0315/MB507